AMERICAN ORPHAN

AMERICAN ORPHAN

JIMMY SANTIAGO BACA

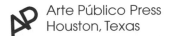

Arte Público Press
Houston, Texas

American Orphan is made possible through a grant from the National Endowment for the Arts. We are grateful for their support.

Recovering the past, creating the future

Arte Público Press
University of Houston
4902 Gulf Fwy, Bldg 19, Rm 100
Houston, Texas 77204-2004

Photograph by John M. Valadez
Cover design by Mora Des!gn

Library of Congress Control Number: 2020951745

21 22 23   4 3 2 1

I owe much to many for their emotional support, inspiration, understanding. I dedicate this book to my wife Stacy, my brilliant kids, professors, teachers, activists, poets and writers all over the world who came before me and set the bar high, who never relinquished the highest literary standards to which I aspired in my work.

To my friends Nora Edelstein and David for your courage and staunch friendship and to the many others who I don't have room to mention. They all offered their life experience and literary expertise by reading and commenting on this work. I am especially grateful to Ronald and his sharp insights, to Dr. Ben D. and to Arturo Sandoval for believing in me.

To the thousands of Chicano kids and grown-ups locked up with whom I worked with, sent books to, conducted writing and reading workshops with, visited. To those suffering addiction. To those abused by religious, civic and correctional authorities, this is your book, a humble compensation for the horrors you've suffered.

Lastly, to my brother who died an addict in an alley because he could not endure the trauma of being abused by priests . . . this novel written in his memory.

1

WHEN I FIRST GOT HERE, I got the name Ghost Boy from the
other kids because I didn't talk for a long time. Nobody knew
anything about me. The state only had details on me, mostly
all wrong, but they looked good on the official papers they
had to fill out to keep me locked up for as long as they did.
They details were turned into numbers that made the statistics look good, the statistics made the counselors and guards
look good job. It was all made up.

My grandma told me once that when someone suffers
something so bad and horrible that the soul cannot endure it,
the soul leaves for a while. That happened to me I think. I
was suffering from *susto*, where a part of the soul is so terrified by a bad event that it leaves you incapable of speaking
or responding in any way. You sort of go into hiding from the
world.

My brother Camilo told me our parents left because they
were addicts. He said they were long gone by the day we were
out playing in grandma's yard in our village and the authorities showed up in a blue government car and took us away.
Camilo didn't explain any more. I think it hurt him to even
think about that day. I don't remember it. He said our older
sister Karina was taken away to live with a *tía* in Albuquerque
to work cleaning people's houses.

1

Bad things happened to the kid I used to be and not to Ghost Boy, so my nickname was also a kind of chance to start over. Bad things still happened the first few years at DYA, the Denver Youth Authority, but at least they could pass right through me because Ghost Boy was a ghost, right? The bad things went right through me and didn't stick in my memory. They emptied into a big black hole in my brain.

Even the CO's started calling me Ghost Boy. Everybody knew I had no family, didn't actually come from anywhere— no past, present or future. I blocked out a lot of stuff when I first arrived. After a year and a half or so though, I started to talk again.

I liked my name. I like being Ghost Boy. It was not only going to be hard to get used to my other name again, but weird. My real name was connected to the outside world— now it was time to take it. I was finishing my seven-year sentence for smuggling weed: locked down at fifteen, released at twenty-two. Seven years in the DYA. I was going to take back my real name because out I had to, because there in the world, that's who I used to be, and still was, I guess.

My strategy for a smooth return to society had as much to do with haphazard reasoning as with my belief that angels were watching over me. Back then, I was not the type given to protecting my welfare. When lapses of sound calculation failed me, my angels came to the rescue.

Leaving my angels aside for the moment, people were curious how I survived, once I was out. I was naïve, sure, as any twenty-two-year old is, especially one with hardly any experience living in society. My reentry into the world was horrific. But I was lucky; I went to live with Camilo, then twenty-three. He could build or fix anything when it came to wood. In his letters he kept telling me not to worry, he had everything set up. *"No te preocupes, carnalito,* I got this shit lined up." The plan was to renovate old houses. He'd teach me the trade. Work was what I needed to overcome the seemingly insurmountable obstacles that sent most juvies back, and I was all about making it. I had spent almost all of my life in institutions, and to be honest, I hated them. No more, I promised myself, a million times. Never again.

∽ ∽ ∽

I was released in August 1980, and I was scared. But like I said, I had big plans, *chingón* plans. After I landed at Albuquerque Airport, I boarded a city bus. From my seat, looking out the window at a place I once knew but which was now unfamiliar, all the way from the airport to my brother's, I got anxious because I knew nothing about being free. I mean, how does one handle freedom when he's never had it? What does one do with it? What even is it? I just assumed, with a cavalier attitude, that getting my life going would be hard, but I could do it. I was nervous. I needed to walk, so I got off the bus and took off across fields.

I got to thinking about the DYA, how I had stressed if I'd ever get out. I was so tired of the broken windows, gashed and grime-spattered walls and floors, visiting room tables graffitied with gang signs, leaky ceilings, electrical outlets with exposed wiring, the main yard phones all ripped out, the perennial stench of pepper spray from staff breaking up fights, the spitting and biting and gang banging, the living with tense situations daily, the violent eruptions of kids who lost it mentally, the assaults on staff and the solitary confinement that followed. . . . Everything carried the signs of our frustration and despair; even the basketball goal post was bent. I was tired.

3

While waiting in my cell for my release, I was assailed by a relentless fear that I might never get out. You know, like those Mexican kids (a lot of them) who came here as refugees or asylum seekers and ended up incarcerated and forgotten. It freaked me out. They were forgotten for years, until one day, being too old for DYA, years after their sentence had expired, they vanished. These guys in Border Patrol uniforms showed up, took them out, dumped them in Mexico, I supposed. Just like that. Gone.

I didn't want that to happen to me. In my cell, I remember pacing, caught in the grip of a grim despair that something had to go wrong and that, yes, the BP would show up and take me out to the desert, and who knew what they might do? Rumors had it that they buried a lot of kids out there. It's the world we live in, you know.

I often skipped dinner. I felt full of dread. I couldn't control my paranoia. My mind kept telling me that I'd waste away in this youth facility. It kept telling me: You're kidding yourself, they'll never let you out, you got nobody on the streets who cares to make them release you, nobody's going to know if you stay. You'll join the rest of the homeless kids who have nowhere to go and no one out there who cares for them. You are one of the forgotten ones, just like them. You are what they call a no-future person. No future. An only-now person. A no-tomorrow person. You only exist now, not tomorrow, not tonight, you have no future, and you don't know what will happen next. A no-future person.

Exhausted one night by hours of heart-wringing worry, I managed to nap a bit. I dreamt I stood in an empty courtroom in front of a black-robed judge sitting high up on his bench. "I sentence you to seven years," he declared, "and like a magician, I pound my gavel and make you imaginary, make you vanish. You're gone, bitch! With the bang of my gavel, you will be like Dorothy in *The Wizard of Oz*. Life as you know it will disappear. No matter how many times you click the heels of your brogans, you will never return to society."

"But I've changed," I heard myself say. Rousing from sleep, rubbing my eyes, I muttered, "I'll be good . . ."

That's when a voice came from beyond the margins of my dream. I looked up, my dream still in my eyes, and saw a guard in shadows, rasping, "Get your crap."

Keys jangled at his waist and a walkie-talkie crackled from his black belt as he shuffled me out with a methodical ordinariness that conveyed nothing special about my release. I was just one more to escort across the yard. I dropped my box at the Property Room, picked up my hundred bucks, a pouch of bus tokens, a YMCA room voucher and an airline ticket to Albuquerque.

When I stepped over the threshold of the giant DYA gate and my foot hit freedom ground, I felt a palpable easing in my throat. I could breathe again without that tightness, that strain in my chest.

On the inside, it had felt like some evil presence had put me on my back, straddled my chest, pinned my arms down with its knees, choking me. As soon as I crossed through that gate, the evil grip went slack. As I walked away, an expectancy of what the world might have to offer me now rushed over me. That's when the invisible monster vanished once and for all. Whatever it was that kept torturing me all those years, hurting me every day, vanished. I could feel myself again. The fear, the panic, the paranoia were gone. And it was all replaced by me.

I would have fought it if I could see it, but I understood in a vague way that it was a system made of rules and regulations upheld by corrupt judges, lawyers and cops to break me, a system I could feel pressing down on me every day, a force as real as my blood and bones. The system turned us against each other because of the color of our skin or ethnicity or the gangs we belonged to in order to make us wage war against each other. The system broke us down day by day.

I would have taken the barber shears and stabbed it. During the time when all the kids were moving in lines, during the work detail call, I would have hit it over the head with a baseball bat. But you couldn't reach out and touch it, couldn't speak to it, couldn't reason with it. It was a faceless system,everywhere and nowhere, present but never visible. Its mission was to destroy us, criminalizing us in ways we could never recover from, teaching us to hate each other; blacks against whites, Chicanos and Indians against whites and blacks, turning us into racists—greedy and manipulative, when we never were before.

It depressed us. It disgraced us. It made us hate ourselves until we were no longer like regular kids but fit only to join the military service, where we wouldn't have to think, just carry out orders when commanded to kill men and women and kids. I really thought we were being trained for that, until the second I walked over the threshold of that gate and inhaled fragrant desert air, sweet dirt, pebbles and dew. I saw stars and a horizon without bars or wires or walls obstructing the view for the first time in years, all sync'd up to a God plan. I tapped my chest with my fist and kissed two fingers to my lips in thanks to God that I made it out.

The only other time I had ever felt such joyous freedom was in the orphanage, when we went to pick apples in Corrales. I was an orphan boy of twelve years after the day of the blue government car. Even today I still can't believe I was there from age five to seventeen. But there were plenty of good times too, and one of them was going out to pick apples and then coming back, riding in the truck bed on top of a huge mountain of them. I stood up and waved at motorists and pedestrians and felt like a king.

And now, leaving DYA, I embraced that joy again, lifted my face to the moon, thinking, *Ahhh, no more eyeing you between guard towers or with razor wire running across you, no more peering at you through a scratch in the painted window.*

I thought as I stepped toward the waiting van, *One small step for the criminal kind, one giant step for Orlando Lucero!*

From there to here, the feeling still stays with me, even now, hours later, on my way to my brother's. It's night. I walk in the dark. Everything is still except for barking; the headlights of someone leaving for work, a few porch lights. Darkness all around, but not menacing, not the kind one feels when crossing hostile neighborhoods. It's an affectionate darkness that one sees in gorilla eyes, a dark stillness that wraps everything in its knowing, making plants, trees and earth into magical creatures that know you. The morning light is just as startling in its beauty as it illuminates the new world. A seam of light along the horizon slowly unrolls tapestries of light all over the barrio.

It feels strange to be moving past furrowed fields that reminded me of those I once hoed and raked and pruned all day. They were fields owned by private corporations (GEO Group, Inc., CoreCivic) and ranchers and leased to DYA and its endless supply of free, teenage labor. I was one of the hundreds who worked eight-hour days for years.

The fields knew: leafy, rooted greens knew the injustice mulched into the dirt. The roots absorbed our blood, sweat, tears and despair. The harvest was shipped to a public dulled with the pleasure of apathy. Slave work smashed my heart so hard it felt like a swollen eye after a beating. I couldn't see or feel anything but bitterness toward the system and the mostly white male flunkies who managed it.

As I walk to my brother's it suddenly strikes me that not a single person waited to meet me when I crossed the gate into freedom. Not one person in the whole world came to see my release. If you're an orphan, then a prisoner, you get used to those things. No matter. I took pleasure in the feeling that the eye of my heart opened for the first time with a smile, and not a grimace as if it had been punched.

∾ ∾ ∾

I double-check the address my brother gave me and walk down Isleta Street. The possibility for a better life over-whelms me now. I arrive at the address, step into the drive-way alongside the landlord's yellow and white frame house and follow the gravel path to the back yard, where a cin-derblock rental squats in a corner with an old, red pick-up next to it. Inside the cab, torn apart carbs, fuel pump pieces, rubber gaskets, radiator hoses, beer cans, whiskey bottles, cigarette butts, hamburger wrappers, fast food cartons. I check the address on my scrap of paper again, thinking maybe I wrote it down wrong.

I walk to the front house, knock on the back door. I ask an old Chicano man still in his pajamas about Camilo, if it's his place back there.

"*Sí*," he answers.

"*¿Y no sabes ónde está?*"

He shakes his head no. I nod. "*Bueno.*"

I figure the truck must be someone's junker, walk back to the rental and knock. No answer. I go around the *casita*, call-ing, "Camilo, Camilo, *pues abre la puerta, pinche vato.*" Open the door. Open the door.

He must be working, I think. I decide to sit on the stoop and wait. After ten minutes, I get up and start walking away, thinking I'll check out the barrio, maybe grab a burrito or taco somewhere. But I hear a sound come from behind me in the brick house. I pound on the front window, back door, bathroom window, until the front door creaks.

I squint my eyes to adjust to the murky interior, make out an old face, a scrawny body knuckled with jutting bones in boxer shorts. He's gaunt. I look past him to see an after-meal of chicken bones littering the room.

"Excuse me. I'm Orlando, Camilo's brother. Do you know where he is?"

I go in, eyes blinking to the dark. I follow the silhouette shuffling to the kitchen sink, where it cups a glass meth pipe off the counter and turns toward the bathroom.

"Cam . . . ilo?"

I can't believe it's him. The healthy, robust bother of mine, of my memories, turns, and I see the manic look of someone who's ceased to struggle to free himself, who's let the meth carry him in its jaws until his will to fight was reduced to a mere wish. I'd seen it in many kids inside, who when they came in were raped or beaten so badly they surrendered their souls to the devil.

"Be right out," he says and locks the bathroom door.

I sit on the couch and wait. So much for his letters, I think, where he wrote me all was well and that he had everything set up.

Brakes grind and tires skid on gravel outside. I peek through the blinds at a dirty, multi-colored panel van. It idles, smoke curling out of the muffler. I see the driver pour powder on the dashboard, cut three lines, one for him, one for the two others.

Camilo hollers through the door. "Almost . . . there."

I try to flick on a lamp. No bulb. I draw the gnarled blinds. Sunlight spreads over the wrecked interior. Dust floats on the air. I search through the filthy dishes on the counter, find a steak knife, slide it into my waistband.

I'll be ready.

Camilo comes out. "Let's go."

I hesitate.

"Come on. Come on, *vato!*" he snaps. "In the plans . . ."

∽ ∽ ∽

I'm in the back of the van next to a guy I don't know, eyes on my brother up front, sitting shotgun. I don't detect anything for a while, but I feel it. Then I see the first sign of trouble: the driver's hand slides across and drops a pistol into my brother's lap.

I just got out! a scream in my head goes off.

He turns to me. His eyes warn, *Stay calm, little brother, I know how you are, don't be jumping crazy, be cool. I got this.*

We pull into a 7-11, and the guy next to me slides the van door open. All three strut into the convenience store. My mind goes blank, my body numbs as I watch my brother hold a pistol eye-level at the cashier and demand money. The other two scramble through the aisles. One at the coolers grabs six-packs of beer. The other one dumps whiskey bottles into a grocery sack.

Then we're speeding off. They're talking about drugs and brindle pitbulls and what they're going to buy their girlfriends. We get back to Camilo's. I'm too paralyzed to move when Camilo tells me to get out, but when I manage to move. I drill my eyes into the others with a promise that if I ever see them again, I'll mess them up.

We go inside, Camilo grabs the truck keys and tells me, it's time to celebrate. He holds the door so he can lock it behind me. I follow him out the back to a fence. We climb over, walk into the field, stop at a thicket of weeds.

"See? . . ." He parts the weeds.

I stare at a pile of salvaged 2x6s and tangled fencing and broken fixtures and rubbish.

"I been taking material off job sites so you and I can start our remodel business. And here . . ." He steps a few paces to the left, tosses off old rotten plywood, broken benches and tables, and pulls off shredded blankets and carpets. "Yours." He smiles, indicating a desk with three legs and a chair with a cracked seat. "I'm going to fix them up, varnish them for you."

That moment splinters me. Do I show my gratitude with a false smile that our lives are good and we have a future, or with the fatal acceptance that our lives are fucked up?

I mean, he meant well. I tried to act happy. For the first time since I left DYA, I saw my chances of making it going down. Was it even possible for me to make a new life out here, in a place where I feel as out of place as any human being ever felt? An anchor drags across my heart, digging deep with the answer, *There's no way you can do this reentry thing.*

I don't know what to say. I'm sad, confused. Afraid. I walk around in the weeds looking at the ground where someone dumped a bunch of trash. Old *Rolling Stone* magazines. Headlines: Nixon resigned; Vietnam War ending; Jimmy Carter; *Roe v. Wade;* Jim Jones; 900 people in Guyana die in a mass suicide; Iranian militant students seize the US embassy in Tehran; César Chávez; Brown Berets; Black Panthers; Patty Hearst and black revolutionaries. George Wallace is shot; Elvis dies. What I read makes me feel like I'm waking up from a decade-long coma. At that moment, I realize while I was in the devil's daycare, time had left me behind.

∾ ∾ ∾

We drive to the foothills in silence. It's August, early afternoon, and the sun warms the Tijeras Canyon. At a steakhouse, we drink a few tequilas. Camilo is wired from meth. We recall the old times.

"The keggers after the games, *vato*, and all the chicks . . . man . . . you had a sweet jumper."

"You remember . . . what's her name? María?"

"You kidding? I had the biggest crush on her, but she only loved you."

"Yeah! She takes me on the ditch bank in the trees to make out, and I caught you spying on us." He laughs.

"Man, was I *soooo* embarrassed," I say, feeling great that we're bonding. "I remember when you were at the Cactus Motel, all you talked about was meeting Evel Knievel."

"Yeah. . . . Remember we souped up that Karmann Ghia, we cruised Louey's hamburger joint for chicks?"

Camilo nods, cheeks and forehead blushing. As we toast our third shot, his eyes glaze. A second later, he threatens to kick my ass. His words hit me like a wrecking ball that comes out of nowhere, crashing between us, shattering me.

Fears surge up in me at his threat. I want to warn him that I'm different. In DYA, another part of me was born out of survival, a necessary evil. Ghost Boy. When *he* takes over, he doesn't care about anything. I don't know where Ghost Boy came from, how to reason with him. All I know is that he is the angry part of me. The one with no memory, uncontrollable when he surfaces. He emerges when I'm threatened. I want to tell Camilo to pull back, chill, he can't threaten me. He doesn't know that if he touches me, Ghost Boy will bare his claws and lunge.

I wanted to say, "We change, Camilo," but I don't.

12

He is not the brother he was a minute ago. He raises his hand to slap me. I catch it midair, stare, gritting my teeth.

"Please," I say, ". . . some . . . thing happen-ed-to-me."

I can't breathe. I hold my palm to my mouth, like I'm about to weep or puke, to motion him stop. I feel heat all inside me, rushing from my heart to my veins all over my body. My hands shake from the burning, my head and neck tremble, and Camilo swings and hits me with his free hand.

A dark force whirls inside me, suffocates me. I cough. I choke on the bitter bile in my mouth, in my nostrils. My mind goes into a white-out. The whiteness spreads to my knees, and I can't, I can't take it. I leap out of my chair, grab Camilo and shove him outside.

"Quit hitting me!" I yell, tears in my eyes. "Man. Some. Thing. Happened. To Meeee!"

The whole world beyond the steakhouse collapses, fills with those who have betrayed me since I was born: parents, teachers . . . I see me roaming the streets, scared, scared of women and men, boys who bullied me, frightened of shadows and strangers and being unprotected, a homeless boy, exposed and at the mercy of rapists, murderers, brutal police, drug dealers and gangbangers. Alone and hated by white society, stigmatized by every glare and every cruel word etching its condemnation onto my heart, telling me that I am worthless.

I strike Camilo. I knock him down on the asphalt. I swing at the malicious violations against me, at all the guilty perpetrators who scoffed at me as Camilo's grin does, as my own grin used to sneer at enemies beating on me. His smile says to me, *Beat me, little brother, break me into pieces that can never be put back together,* and I want to wipe it off his face, because the pendulum blade swings back to a time when I too grinned at all the pain and sorrow as if it didn't hurt or matter. It did, it did. It hurt bad, but I never let anyone know.

His eyes mock me like mine once mocked the world, saying, *You're doing right, little brother. We came into this world through a drug addict's vagina, skittering like rats in the trash. Hit me!* Every drop of his blood I spill on the pavement affirms my worthlessness, that I do not belong except on the ground with the world beating me, with me leering, my don't- care grin—until I am gone, until I return to the nothingness from where I came.

Just then, he gets up and starts beating me. He picks up a board and hits me. I don't fight back. I find love for him in my helplessness, solace in my surrender, because it is the only way I have of showing him I love him.

He says with his smirk, *Yes, little brother, I'll beat you until you can finally sigh with relief that you are no more, that this world can no longer hurt you. Like you, I crawled into this life owned by others to beat and starve, not allowed to speak, with no right to feelings, no right to my face or hands or feet or sleep or dreams. I am a mistake to erase from the page of the living. Make my blood wash over me and make me forget, force me to fade away, to drift into the unknown where men like you and me, unknown men, arrive unknown and live unknown and are removed as if they never existed. Remove me, little brother, please, like I remove you.*

I want him to stop, but he keeps on until Ghost Boy whispers, *Never go down.* I want to scream to drown out Ghost Boy's voice, but it comes: *Don't let life do this to you, fight back with every breath!*

I attack. I try to wipe away the look in Camilo's eyes that keeps saying in the language of the oppressed and hopeless: *Hit me, make me vanish.*

"Defend yourself!" I scream, and I beat and beat him until I can't swing anymore.

When I stop, I don't recognize where I am, except that this region of hell is unnamable. I back away in remorse and shock. I move but feel immobile, pant but can't breathe, really frightened but fearless, in the world but out of it, looking in at me standing bloody-fisted over my brother.

I trudge back to town like a sleepwalker. A sad scene, me walking down that mountain road, embracing myself with my arms, head down, all the sorrow in the world rising to my eyes as I hold my tears back and refuse to cry.

Soon, I worry about him. So I return to the restaurant and find my brother has left. A cop car is in the parking lot, the cop questions me, handcuffs me, puts me in the back seat. On the way to jail I have the feeling my whole life is a crime scene, and I am a crime that corrupts everything I touch.

They take me to a hospital and X-ray me to check if anything is broken. The clinician comes out from behind the curtains to ask if I am wearing anything metal, a medal or chain, and I say no. She shows me the X-ray, dozens of scattered beads radiate light over the black plastic. I tell the clinician I was shot once, they're bird-shot pellets. Thirty-two of them. I think the X-ray looks like a night sky with stars—Orlando's night sky.

They let me go. I check in at the downtown Y and sit down in my room on the floor, feeling the floorboards shake with the industrial washer and dryer downstairs cycling the Y's bedding. Late morning, I walk down 4th Street to a coffee house.

Caló, my people's secret dialect, fills the air—*voces de la plebe, mi gente, la raza*, from Chicanos and barrio *vatos y locos* to *abuelitos,* city workers, college students, *profes*, tattooed *pintos*, political gangsters, muralists and Chicanas as beautiful as they are powerful thinkers and radicals. Their voices sooth my soul with the Chicano slang I grew up with:

¿Pos qué, chingao?
A la verga, bro.
¿Cómo estás, abuelita?
¡Quiúbole, carnalito!
Fue un pinche desmadre.
¡Rascuache, mamón!
¡Paga la cuenta, baboso!
Te amo con todo, preem.
¿Qué onda?
¡Aliviánate, pelao!

I order *pozole* with cubed steak, garlic, red onion, lime wedge, potatoes, *chile con cilantro*. While I wait for my food, I eavesdrop on conversations.

"*Quiúbole, ese*, wanna get buzzed? I'm talkin' lit up, all neon, Sunset Boulevard, shit. . . . I got some good *coca!*"

"*¡Qué papote! Vato, ¿qué chingao tienes?* . . . You're always going to be a fiend, *pinche ese*."

"Not today," his friend says with conviction and smiles.

A guy rolls up, slaps another guy on the shoulder: "Come on, *vato*, kick the *chanclas* and get your toes in the sand. What you doing?"

"You still a *loco*."

"Always."

"Whatever, Za-Pa-Ta, dial me up when you want, *ese,* and we'll get down with some *rucas*." He struts off, bumping his fist to his chest to mean, *We're down for the brown.*

It's our *onda*, our way, *güey*.

After I finish eating I sit and think, then pull out the envelope I've been carrying since my release. I place it on the table and study the airline ticket Lila included in her letter.

I use the café payphone, call collect and tell Lila I'm coming. We can do what we wrote in our letters. I'll move there.

We can make crazy love all night and day. Making love in every possible way we can imagine is almost all we ever wrote about. After being locked up as long as I have, my imagination has really gone wild. Now, after talking to her, I can't wait to see her.

I take another way on my walk back to the Y, past the zoo, where I hear caged elephants moaning, lions roaring, bird cries raking across the hot sky. I sit down on a concrete bench and listen.

Across the street I can see a couple under a steel canopy in the park. I get up and walk toward them. I slow down on the sidewalk. I hear her reading him her poem. Or a letter maybe. I kneel to tie my shoe, which doesn't need tying, and listen. It's about them being in a forest, blanket on the ground or on a boulder next to a creek, enjoying cheese and wine and crackers while birds swoop in and out of branches, shaking sunrays from the leaves that light their faces with love.

2

I SETTLE IN A SEAT in the rear of the plane, look out as it taxis and soars. I look out the port window, see the South Valley barrio below, where Camilo lives. I recite a prayer asking God to bless him. He has lost his way and he doesn't know how to get back. I can see the orphanage where the officials dropped us off that long-ago night. If I learned to adapt to orphanage life, I think, I know I can deal with this reentry. It just takes time and a couple of good breaks.

As I soar above the clouds, memories come flying back to me. I remember my aunt sometimes came on weekends and would drive us east through Tijeras Canyon, across the *llano* and past Estancia. She would drop us off at Uncle Max's in Willard. I didn't like him very much; his pretending to be John Wayne or some other swaggering hero, always wearing a big cowboy hat, clomping around in manure-stinking boots, making me clean his damn school bus. It was the longest model the dealership offered. After I had spent all day brushing and oiling its leather seats and scrubbing rubber-mat floors, the miser would give me a quarter. Even an orphan who never handled money knew that was a lower-than-scrooge move. I also knew if I didn't clean it, I'd get beat and busted up. That's how John Wayne treated Mexicans in the movies, that's how Max treated me.

I didn't mind the treatment much because I knew that my four cousins would be there in the old board and tar-paper shack on the only one on the prairie. All four were beautiful, in their late teens, skin sweet as peyote petals, laughter fertile as an apricot tree in August. They were long-haired beauties in tight jeans, cowgirl boots, western shirts, muscled and tough enough to wrestle pig or man down for dinner.

They could plow fields dawn to dusk, cut a cord of cedar with an ax and fill the kitchen with the musky fragrance of sweat, their young bodies ripening into rare fruit. They were sensuous, defiant as a herd of wild, cliff-edge rearing mustangs. When it came to talk about boyfriends, they were boisterous, clamoring like a village marching band. After breakfast they would go off to work as truck-stop waitress, barmaid and junkyard dismantler.

I loved being around their voluptuous bodies, their carefree, husky way of talking about their secrets—how he wants to do it, but she wouldn't yet—all said in innuendo and code. Even at that young age, six or seven, I sensed what they were talking about.

Now here I am, on a plane heading to see this woman. Every amorous yearning in my twenty-two-year-old body yowls in me, churning buttery honey between my loins, raising the dough-batter of my heart, making it a flame-toasted tortilla.

I've never had a woman. Due to circumstances, I've pretty much led a life of abstinence. But now, I can feel every nerve on fire, desperately seeking out a woman's touch. When we talked about having sex in our letters, my imagination got the best of me. I told her how I needed minty, churned-earth, hardcore, skin-slapping, arm-wrestling, arms-and-legs-knotted-up-and-turning-in-physical-bites-and-buttslaps-and-lunges kind of loving. That's what I thought love was. And she came right back at me with passages even more fierce and physical.

~ ~ ~

For the moment, I reclined and sighed a breath of relief. It felt good to be me, at this place, this time, this day.

I fall asleep easy, but am awakened like jumper cables hitting the battery posts, sparks and smoke, as the plane's tires thump hard on the runway, jolt my paperweight heart, make it crack and release the butterfly inside to flutter above the heads of passengers in the cabin.

Once inside the terminal, I follow the signs to retrieve my cardboard box from the baggage claim carousel. Then I set out to meet the woman of my dreams, more nervous and intimidated than I've ever been. I freeze, too many people zigzagging everywhere. In the terminal I take the nearest seat. I spot the water fountain. I am thirsty but I dare not move. Next to me, a rangy kid plays on the floor with his dad's shoelaces. Two chairs over, a man spits chewing tobacco into a Folger's coffee can. Talk hums. Smug mothers and tired boyfriends clutch bouquets of flowers. Some people stand to greet sun-tanned students in school uniforms at an arrival gate. For a moment, it's all too much—I am afraid. I want to leave, find the nearest interstate and hitchhike back to New Mexico. Maybe this ain't a good idea. Maybe I've messed up again. I'm stunned with indecision.

My sister Karina's voice comes back to me, at the moment when I told her I was leaving: "Don't run away and give up." Nodding her head, thin lips pursed with contempt, she said, "You don't know what you're doing. Listen to me, Orlando. You can't make a living reading books or whatever the hell you do. Work. Be a laborer, dishwasher or janitor. Be a *man* for once. Look at me. I dropped out of school at nine, married at fourteen—not for love, just to get out on my own and away from that bitch of an aunt. And look, I have a nice house and husband and money and kids—I'm doing good. You don't need no school. Work."

Steadying myself, I decide on this burning day in August 1980, my game plan is to plan nothing. To let benevolent coincidence lead me into the stewing maelstrom like a mountain ram rubbing its curved horns against a boulder, ready for battle.

I'm getting a chance to make a life and I'm going to take it. I gather as much courage as I can at that moment. I have an opportunity to change my life for the better, and all I can do is dig my heels in and make it happen. I feel like I'm on an important mission, although I don't fully understand the mission's purpose. I mean, yes, I'm following what we wrote to each other in our letters. Yes, the love letters I wrote Lila, promising everything under the moon, made me wonder how many boys are mad enough to lift the words off a page and live them. The kind of kid like me who has been stripped of any protections, with no life to protect . . . It makes it possible to throw myself wholeheartedly into her kindness, because there's nothing else for me beyond her. Here and now, she's all I've got.

I know without a doubt that I'm a special kind of emotionally deprived boy, that the trauma of abandonment and imprisonment and never having a girlfriend are beyond any fixing. Yet, none of this seemed to bother her. She never mocked my being an orphan or my inexperience with women.

Naturally, I have mixed feelings about what I wrote, but I trust her. Am I trying to excuse my sexual appetites, ashamed even, thinking I went too far with the sex stuff? But surely she understood they were only letters, not some bibli-

cal prophecy I had to abide by. After all, you can write anything in a letter when you're sitting in a cell.

Our correspondence explored everything heretofore illicit
in my life, opened our secrets to each other. I urged her to go
even deeper, tread on more dangerous ground, use our letters
to write really nasty stuff and to expose her deepest secrets.

And here I am, hungrier not only for her but for food as
I watch people eating fried chicken, mash potatoes, corn, grits
and barbecue, forking up apple pie. These folks have a lot of
money to spend on food. The criminal part of my brain kicks
in: *Okay, when the cook turns the other way, reach in, grab
a bunch of those blood sausages in the stainless-steel con-
tainer under the heat lamp.* Then the other part of my brain
responds: *No, don't do that. Remember you've gotta go
straight.* It urges me to control my impulses. This is not the
DYA chow-hall line, fool.

Then it strikes me: this whole thing is a joke. For a fleet-
ing moment, my mind is in awe of my hilarious and absurd
coupling: Lila and me; two completely different human beings, she's a white woman ten years older than me and I'm
just a Chicano who has never traveled east of the Rio Grande.
We're okra and fried greens meets chili and tamales, surrendering to the ambivalent abyss of fate, free-falling into our
ambitious cravings to attend our cosmic dinner. *Holy crap,
what am I getting myself into?!*

The airport lobby is lined with display cases of Civil War
soldier uniforms, muskets and old rifles, crusty Confederate
journals, ammo belts, photos of battlefields, blood-spattered
pants and hats. There are pictures of hog farms with what
seem to be millions of hogs, pictures of docks with boats
heaped with fish and boiled clams and crawfish, chafed-
cheeked men with nets, steaming shrimp in kettles with the
water behind them gleaming. Then, pictures of tobacco

farms, acres of tobacco plants as far as the horizon in every direction. And slaves. Lots of slave pictures that for a moment make me sick and angry. Statues of Confederate generals. Military men with swords on horses. I fight off a desire to spit at the pictures.

I tell myself if I'm going to make it, I have to get rid of my temper, my pride. I can't flail against the current—*flow, baby, flow. Dale gas, compa, déjate caer la greña. You can do it, vato*, I tell myself. No self-righteous chest beating. I've got to listen to the voice in my head that often warned me in the past, but that I failed to listen to, distracted by more important things, like drugs and partying. *Learn, you idiot,* I tell myself, *learn to be accountable for your mistakes. Be responsible. Ignore that troublesome urge in your heart to mess this up.*

I walk down a long hallway clogged with travelers to the baggage claim. It's a county fair: food carts with Dixie flags and cast-iron statuary depicting bird dogs and more Civil War heroes, fat cattlemen with manure-caked rubber boots, hickory-hard young men wearing patched overalls smelling of farm stalls. These are the descendants of slave owners, white men whose grandfathers bought slaves and worked, whipped, chained, starved and raped them to make their wealth and establish their power. Here I was, about to bed down one of their own, a crime that in the past would have warranted a lynching.

The terminal is no bigger than a high school football field with fake white pillars, scuffed linoleum floors and quaint knick-knack shops. Many of the faces are weathered, as if time was a laundry line and they've been on it a long time, in harsh weather.

Grandmas piddle out crumpled dollar bills from coin purses pinned to the inside of their bras to buy a snowcone or cotton candy from the cart. Husky boys chomp buttered corn-cobs. Sportsmen shoulder at the bar with frosty beer mugs foaming over and half-eaten pork chops on their plates, shouting at the TV showing a football game.

I take a deep breath, wind my way through the people to the luggage area, grab my box and head outside, where the humidity makes my clothes sticky.

In the orphanage on Friday night we used to watch Paul Newman, Gregory Peck and Steve McQueen movies. There this sort of humidity made swamp women unsnap their jeans and bras and drawl love down by the sultry magnolias. A slavering old escapee chased by slop-drooling mastiffs sniff-ing, shaking water off, as the prisoner waited for his bog-mis-tress to leash him up in her succulent sex—all us kids yelling and clapping and squealing.

I stand still. I wait. I hope.

The instant I see her driving up, all life condenses to the bulge at my crotch. A dragon that hunkered for years, grinds its fiery maw against my jeans, tired of biding its time, ready to dive between Lila's beautiful, fairyland thighs and into the mythic island where many a Chicano kid has sunk his ship laden with enchiladas, *tequila, mota, sopapillas, ristras y po-zole* and lost his soul.

For the second time in less than an hour, my paperweight heart cracks, startled wings shatter the crystal and fly translu-cent above people's heads, each flutter of the wings sounding the word dreamtime, dreamtime . . .

I step off the sidewalk into the street, all ready for the BIG MEETING, and . . . and she drives right past me. The butterfly falls to the wet tarmac, gets run over by the muddy tires of a farm truck.

Standing there embarrassed, I immediately want to strike out at someone because of the disappointment. Men at the curb smirk at me. With my pride wounded, I feel ashamed, awkward, and step back onto the sidewalk.

Swarms of insects nibble on me. They think I'm some sort of free lunch wagon. They swarm, every kind of vermin that breeds in moist climates stings me. I slap at the air trying to wave away the flies and mosquitoes, but they attack with renewed ferocity, in my nostrils, mouth, ears. Sweat drips down my back, soaks the waistline of my boxers, and I'm standing there the whole time thinking: *She's changed her mind.*

I glance at the bull-necked, wagon-shouldered crackers, look down at the pavement, conjuring a "Deliverance" movie scene. I'm kidnapped out to some dank, backwoods shack after being raped by cadaver-eating hicks. I'm skewered and marinated in white-lightning in a skillet and served up to hogs in an occult ritual these boys have been known to practice on Mexicans.

Ghost Boy wants to mad-dog back, but a voice in my head advises, *Give it up, give it up.*

Seconds later, as I'm watching her recede in the distance, I see the rear lights go bright red as she slams the brakes, stops, shifts in reverse and backs up. *¡Órale!*

Sweet as an eight ball in the pocket break. *Yeah!*

3

I THINK BACK to that young man searching for a life, heart wide open, exploring, searching every option so that one day he might have a life like others; family, friends, respect. And I do have a family. Back then, I was a long way from New Mexico, but I knew one thing: my survival instincts were my real home. And my pride was based on how much danger I could carelessly subject myself to or how much self-denigration and neglect I could endure.

I learned to control my fear, ignore it in the heat of a challenge, swallow when I felt like I might throw up; swagger and glare someone down to signal my dangerous intent for violence, give mad-dog stares to convey my disregard for consequences, tilt my face back, push my chin out and nod, *Y qué, puto, what ya gonna do, huh?* I learned to move in a way that warned predators without words that my courage was dominant, my response blind, no matter the size or age or color. My don't-mess-with-me attitude was the only place I felt safe; my getting it on on the spot if you mess with me was my calling card, my defiant silence my security.

All that changed with time. I learned new ways of dealing with people. I kissed Ghost Boy goodbye. If I was going to make it, I had to and did learn to take crap, put my head down, walk away. I didn't confront bullies trying to incite me. I backed away, even if it meant I looked like a coward. It seemed the only way to make it out here.

That was back then. It's now April 2018, and in a few days I plan on heading up to my cabin to write, hike, read, do some irrigation work, search the woods for flagstone and latillas to bring back, at my wife's insistence, for our fence here in Albuquerque. (Our Italian Mastiff keeps chewing them to splinters, so I have to replace them frequently.)

I believe I got my love of nature as early as three or four years old through scent: I knew my whole world by smell. I remember when Mom left us in the care of Grandma Weaver in Santa Fe; lilac and sage intoxicated my sensibility—there, beyond the open windows with tattered curtains, the ripped screen door, paradise lay in the tumultuous vegetation and flowers.

It must have also been when I was allowed to visit my paternal grandma, Petra. I inhaled a different type of fragrance, that of the high prairie desert, of things ancient and eternal: the dirt, the stones, the prairie winds, the chilled pines, snowmelt carried on the breeze that swept across our small village, mixed with horse manure, sheep, desert grass, old corrals, windmills, rusting cars, smoke from wood stoves and freshly made tortillas. The sunlight was overpowering. It touched all things, made them surrender their fragrance. Saddles, harnesses, field tools, all things exuded their souls in the arid heat. They offered their distinct, rich odor to the air, which I couldn't help but inhale, since I was always outside. When I came in to the kitchen, drawn by the scent of fresh-made tortillas, beans and red chili, Grandma would scold me for always smelling like a goat.

Later, in the orphanage, its circular front drive trimmed with roses of all colors flavored the air with floral scents like no other heady perfume I have ever inhaled. It made me want to leap, take four steps at a time down the staircase, dash through the hallways, slam classroom doors and yelp like a young colt testing his legs, galloping for the first time.

It could have been all of that.

Or the times on certain holidays, when the nuns bussed us to Doc's Long Picnic Area in the Sandias east of Albu-querque, or to the Jemez Mountains to Camp Shaver, where I offered in homage my soul to the towering pines, to the mesquite trees, to the creeks and to the bull-shouldered cliffs. My heart pounded for release, hammering my rib cage with urgency to leave my body, lose itself in the forest and in the ancient legacy of all things wild.

I went from one extreme to the other, from Nature in all her abundant living to being a hostage in urban environments, a captive of concrete and glass, school rooms, dorms. I took what meager joy I could on Sundays, when the nuns allowed us to watch "Bonanza," "The Rifleman," "Gun Smoke" and some Disney fairytales.

∾ ∾ ∾

In the 1990s I find myself in an Albuquerque apartment not doing so well. I'm out of touch with time—days, weeks, months, even the year is a blur. I'm partying way too much, hardly writing because in my half-baked brain I've decided to give it up.

As a last resort to keep my sanity in these, my early for-ties, I find myself rising in the dark before sunrise to jog on a trail winding through the Rio Grande Bosque. I do it to clear my head and heart, to keep hope alive, to remind myself that I still can achieve the kind of life I want and the kind of so-briety I dream of.

I see mallards in the ditches, roadrunners, coyotes, Canadian geese overhead, blue herons stilting in the shallows, and the ever beautiful water of the Rio Grande flowing with the tranquility of a cooing mother's hand on her infant's cheek.

I find myself wishing many times to be more the river than myself. *Be the river.* I want to be like Geppetto's Pinocchio: unscrew my legs from my hips and drop them, reach in, pull my lungs out, toss them away to hang like deflated vines in the treetops, cut whatever strings are binding me and holding me up and finally fling my bones into the river grass where decaying twigs and fallen bark welcome them. Then, I dash low and high, beneath low-hanging branches and bounding above fallen logs—in spirit form, flashing along the running path.

Be the river.

Sometimes, I'll drive to West Mesa, where no one is around. I run the rattlesnake-infested desert path, head for the distant, dormant volcanoes. I inhale the fragrant dryness of the dust and rocks, the utterly tough ropes of nopal cacti. I jog around illegal dumping sites, where real estate signs and refrigerators, political placards, washing machines, tires, twisted bicycle frames, blood-stained mattresses, box springs, glimmering piles of beer bottles that snarl at me. No matter. I run on, get whatever's in me out, purge this skin, this face, this life and merge with the ugliest scenes the desert presents—which is still far better than the best I have in any moment of any city day.

∽ ∽ ∽

Then it's 2004, my friend Ben, our family doctor for many years, calls to tell me he wants to show me something. A day later I ride with him two hours north of Albuquerque, to his cabin in the most beautiful setting I have ever seen; breathtaking cliffs, gorgeous green pastures, springs that run from rocks everywhere, threading their way into the main creek that feeds into Abiquiu Lake, the source of water for Santa Fe and Albuquerque and all the towns down south.

Ancient Anasazi pueblos top the mesa. Black bear, mountain lion, elk and white tail deer are spotted almost daily. The dirt road is festooned with green vines, is bordered by hefty, flowered fields. We bump and jolt down a dirt path that winds into hidden meadows. There are rock crevices as big as an auditoriums. We see eagles, turkey vultures, red-tailed hawks, turkeys, owls and hummingbirds. I'm blown away. I ask if he might know anyone I can rent a cabin from, so I can come up and write. He does.

A year later I buy ten acres and build a two-story cabin, completely off the grid, without applying for permits or using a blueprint. As soon as I can, I bring the lady (Stacy) of my life up, and my two kids (I have four) still living at home. We begin to live the happiest days of my life for the next three years. Unfortunately, we have to move back to the city for the kids' education because the schools are terrible up there, the closest one is a three-hour bus ride down treacherous mountains roads.

It was heaven while it lasted. My whole soul was aroused with exhilarating hunger to hike a new trail every morning, and every trail conjured a delightful hypnosis, every bird call conjuring a soulful remedy in my bones.

Since then, I have rarely lived such meaningful days of being absorbed into the heart of the nature that nurtured me so greatly. I grew new mes, infinite mes, glorious and happy mes in that piece of wilderness.

I grew in strength, character, dreams, love. . . . I'm sure that nature has instilled in my cells a harmonious longevity borne of those field flowers and four-foot snow swells and sunshine, and the most delicate rain showers. In my blood still flow the daily-live particles of tribal peoples who lived on mesas and peaks I climbed. Flashing like fish scales are the microscopic life forms of creeks I fished and trails I hiked, breathing it all in as if it were my very sustenance, circulating now in my metabolism, as I write this.

With the exception of family, I went months without seeing another human being. It truly was the paradise I had dreamed of since childhood, packed with brilliant days as it was. There is only one other time that even remotely compares to this in joy and fulfillment and achievement: when I arrived in North Carolina to live with Lila and drive through the countryside to her house, my new home.

~ ~ ~

She is wearing a short blue skirt with a green blouse. Her hair is the color of a faded rose and her green eyes peer from behind large oval glasses, giving off the impression that she reads a lot. She is thirty-two, ten years older than me, her body voluptuous and lithe. Every aspect of her is beautiful. She is a white version of Celia Cruz.

"You're here! Thank God, the waiting is over." She hugs me.

At that moment, there is no one on earth luckier than me. I feel a pig-belly-deep-in-mud lucky feeling.

Still thawing out from DYA and unsure of how to be in the company of a woman, I am speechless, so nervous that I need to say something.

"Made it!" I blurt out, and I feel stupid the instant I announce it.

She laughs at my awkwardness. "You're here. Yay, Orlando!"

She opens the door, shoves my box in the back seat and we drive off.

We pass dented roadside mailboxes, withering barns, wind-slapped houses and huge trees. Warehouses. Chicken farms. Pig farms.

I sneak a look at her breasts and her lips. Lust courses through every cell of my body as abundantly as the kudzu overflowing into the road shoulders. The breeze dances in thick tobacco leaves, taps a hoeing slave song and the late afternoon hums a sweet, succulent harmony that makes my mouth water.

She smiles, her hand trembling as she lights another Benson & Hedges cigarette. The air, the space, the sky, all of it a dream come true. Lila downshifts, speeds up past red-brick-and-clapboard flour mills and brick houses set in quiet clearings.

I lean my head back, glad to be free, healthy and young. I stand up on the seat, raise my arms to the wind the way I've seen kids do in movies full of red-appled joy. As I am now, with Cat Stevens on the radio, we speed by meadows, Guernseys grazing, silos, strawberry, wheat and tobacco fields and clay-packed farm roads. She brakes, accelerates up and down through the Piedmont foothills, fingers clutching the steering wheel, racing down a long road bordered with pines.

The world is freshly created.

She makes a sharp turn at a grocery store called Green Mill, then we race down a blacktop through churned dirt fields. In the shade of plank barns warped from having been too long in hot and cold seasons, barn dogs snooze or scratch their ears. Harness-scarred mules mosey one step at a time and stop, then, after a bit, step again.

Finally, we slow, turn into a fenceless yard, where a small, red-brick house sits. A pump house stands next to it. She parks, turns off the ignition.

"Welcome."

She kisses me, beveling her tongue inside my mouth. She sweeps it back down my throat, on the sides of my tongue, inside my cheeks, licking. Then sucks my bottom lip. The greatest kiss ever.

Her small red-brick house with its unkempt yard gives way to fields spreading out to the forest on three sides. It makes me think of The Ponderosa.

Once inside, I lift her Siamese cat from an armchair and set it on the floor. I sit down. It leaps up on my lap and bites me so quick I doubt it happened. Blood beads in neat rows of two up my left arm, wrist to elbow. Lila doesn't see it—she's at the table in the back of the big common room. I shoo the cat off, pretending nothing happened. But I'm a little freaked, composing myself, when her father putters in.

"I'll be right back," Lila says to me. Then, on her way out the door, "Hi Daddy, here he is, love of loves."

Mr. Chambers, late-seventies or so—hard to tell—is goat-lean. Lila has written me about how he was born with backwards feet, how the doctor twisted them around. He wears (and by the looks of it has always worn) an oily fedora, khaki pants with suspenders, red Converse high-tops and a frayed casual sport jacket pinned with quilt patches. He's missing buttons, zippers. He falls into the chair at the table, blows his nose, folds his handkerchief and pockets it. Then he pulls out a pint of cheap Peach wine.

He gazes out the big window spanning the back kitchen wall, at the churned-up fields. It looks as if vegetable planting and picking have textured him like a barn or barbed-wire fence, year to year, until he has acquired a gnarly grit in his speech and mannerisms. His gray eyes shine like minerals.

"You a poet fella, uh?"

His words are small but something makes them wide and deep, resembling something that's been growing a long time, like a tree or canyon.

"Orlando Lucero, sir."

"Welcome . . . welcome."

He turns to glance at the field with the slightest hint of a smile. Gratitude, maybe. And in that moment I recognize the outcome of a life of give, of compromise with weather. I see time spent toddling gingerly about his house and riding on his tractor, he and his dog moseying out to check furrows.

We sit in silence until the door opens and Lila comes in, but not by herself. Her two sisters, Nancy and Kimberly, step in behind her.

"I'm taking you with me to Longfield Federal prison," Nancy says, "where I volunteer as an art teacher. Not right away. Give you a little time to relax, might even make clay mugs or something. I made Lila a cup for her pens."

"Oh," Kimberly says, "and afterwards you get to sit at her house on the porch in the evening and smoke Columbian bud."

"It helps my cataracts," Nancy says.

"I'm sure. Just eases the pain, don't it, sis?" Kimberly teases and turns to me. "Honey, I'm a receptionist at the sheriff's department. If you need a driver's license without having to show any paperwork or prove identity, come on down, I'll take care of you."

After they leave, I go out to get my box from the car. Her brother Brandon drives up; twenty-six years old, pole man for a surveying company, woodsy, beer-drinking type, sunburned with skin flaking his red nose, leather worn off the toes of his steel-tipped boots, patched plaid shirt with suspenders clipped to the waistline of his Dickies.

"Welcome to Green Mill," he says, getting out and pushing his smudged eyeglasses up the sunburned bridge of his nose.

I shake his hand, dried dirt crumbles from his palm.

"I'm right across the road if you need anything."

On his way out, he turns. "Fish all the ponds you want, but there's one you can't catch: The General. He's mine. We got this *thing* between us."

I learn he means the bigmouth bass in the pond behind his daddy's house. I hardly ever see Brandon after that. Early mornings, still dark, he pulls out of the yard in his beat-up Ford Ranger with the mud-spattered surveying company logo on the door and doesn't return until late.

My first week there, I meet others. Big Foot, a giant of a Black sharecropper, gentle and loving, walks everywhere barefooted. They took his license away for drinking. I learn he went from truck to tractor to lawnmower to feet—snow, mud, blistering-hot black-top, gravel, asphalt—no matter. When he wants a drink, he crosses forest creeks, wades ponds, his sense of smell finding white lightning better than any hound around.

His wife Fanny Bell is a large black woman as beautiful and muscled and healthy as a field of okra and eggplant. They have a daughter, Opal, toasty and warm as a buckwheat biscuit. She works as a housekeeper for Lila's parents across the road.

"Look here." Lila points to the fridge. "Recognize?"

I run my index finger along the paper taped to the door and read what I wrote her:

woman whose touch flames the thing you've touched
and buried hurts rise in my breast,
you pluck them from my winding arteries
and throw them into the fire
I am shy of you, but also, I am wild for you.
Like a child, I put my hand into your fire.

∾ ∾ ∾

On Saturday, Lila wakes up excited about a surprise she has for me. I walk into the kitchen, pour a cup of coffee and put some toast in the toaster. The toast pops up, and I butter it. It's the first time I've ever done that.

Lila is effusive. She beams a wholesomeness and suggests a drive into Chapel Hill and Raleigh to meet her friends—other poets and writers—and hear them read. I'm excited to do that.

So, we launch off on our adventure. As we're driving, her older son Bruce gives me a stare. I've known petulant boys in my time in institutions and thought of them as needing bibs and pacifiers. It wasn't my job to clean the applesauce from their chins or change their diapers. Let Bruce stew.

Black birds fly up from the red fields bordering the road. Insects cloud around ponds, frogs croak and hop; it seems to be lunch time in the forest. Forest greenery snarls at the neatly mowed, organized lawns as if to say, *Watch out, we're coming.*

Lila says, "He's fine. Teenagers have problems with everyone. One minute to the next, you never know what they're thinking." She gives me a grin to remind me I am not as old, physically or emotionally, as I sometimes act.

We arrive at this beautiful old red-brick mansion, so old the edges of the brick are rounded from wear. It's surrounded by sprawling grassy hills and tall evergreen trees. Brown pine needles cover the rooftops and sidewalks, pinecones are scattered in the grass. People casually roam the grounds. Groups, couples, talking intimately with each other. They wear loose, comfortable cotton clothing, nothing formal, but they are refined in their manners.

Lila and I walk into a theater filled with people, all listening to this one man on stage reading poetry from a book. This is the first formal poetry reading I ever attend. It is wonderful and gives me renewed enthusiasm for books. I vow to read more.

Outside, we stroll the park-like grounds. I feel as if I have been part of a prayer session. God talked to me in that theater and told me I, too, will one day walk along the sidewalks and sit at one of the many garden benches, discussing literature with others.

Lila has more surprises.

We drive over to a house in Chapel Hill, and I can't quite put my finger on the mystery of the place. I'm sure I feel good vibrations in the air. There is a long dirt driveway crowded in on both sides with bushes and trees. At the end of the driveway is a large, two-story clapboard house with so many coats of peeling paint it's hard to determine its original color. The whole place has a weathered, ancient look, something like an animal lair. There's not much detail to it, but lots of a lived-in, eaten-in, slept-in and isolated look to it.

We go around back, the land expands into a huge field with large circus cages everywhere, holding tigers, leopards, lions, jaguars—all sorts of other big cats I don't know the name of. I feel excitement rise up in me. A man comes flying out of the back of the house behind us. He wears a white laboratory coat, looks like a scientist who still hasn't thrown off his hippy days. He has long salt-and-pepper hair, a scruffy beard and the kind of gentle, welcoming smile that comes when you're high on good bud or have found karmic peace with yourself in your heart.

He apparently knows Lila well enough to give her a hug that includes rubbing up against her large breasts. I like him. He exudes a serenity that comes from doing what you love. There's a grounded tranquility there. I like him, and besides, anybody who raises big cats has my admiration. My ancestors—the Mayans, Aztecs, Incas, Mechicas—held big cats in the highest reverence.

He gives us a tour of the cages, points out at least a dozen different types of cats I've never heard of. He claims that this one particular snow leopard has suction-cup paws and can walk on ceilings. I don't know if that's true or not, but I believe him.

"We were able to rescue these beautiful felines. They were brought to me by plane when they were cubs, and we nursed them until they could be returned to the jungle they came from. But these here could never return, they'd been so severely maimed as cubs, they couldn't survive in the wild."

Then he says, "Hold on a minute," and he goes back into his house and returns soon with a jaguar cub.

I'm instantly in love with the kitten. After hugging, kissing and caressing her, I hand her back.

He totally shocks me when he says, "No, no, she's yours to take home, but I have to give you instructions on how to care for her. When she gets big enough to fend for herself in the jungles of Oaxaca, bring her back, we'll return her. Her parents were murdered by poachers."

"Give them to Lila," I say, barely able to contain my joy.

I turn and walk away. Looking down into my new friend's eyes, I gasp, "You're ours!" I keep kissing her, scratching her behind her ears, kneading her beautiful paws, feeling her claws . . . I smell her until I inhale her whole being into my heart.

She is me in a jaguar body.

On the drive back, she sleeps curled on my lap. My first poetry reading, my first jaguar—it's been an incredible day. We name her Griselda, lay down a thick blanket, a dish of water and say goodnight. Then we slide the door closed.

The best day of my life.

∾ ∾ ∾

Friday morning, the third week in August, the heat is oppressive, pushing everything down under its sumo weight. I grab my fishing pole and tackle box in one hand, a lunch and water bottle in the other and head out to the forest behind Chamber's house.

I don't know which I enjoy more, catching a nice largemouth bass and filleting it or just tramping through the woods, wondering what new pond I might run into next. I put all my stuff down at the side of a pond busy with bass puckering the surface for insects. I roam. I encounter my first cottonmouth nestled in a cool root pit. I see herons, massive bullfrogs and a fox.

I get home in the early evening as a thick net of gnats, flies, wasps and other insects cover the air just before dark. Waves of heat mirror up from the blacktop in wavering shimmers, making a distant stranger walking toward me seem like a dark mirage.

I throw myself on the floor and fall asleep. Later, I wake up with Lila on the floor next to me, wrapping her arms around my waist and nodding at my letter excerpt taped to the fridge door.

"Xeroxed our letters and gave them to a friend to read, and she cut out some of her favorites passages," she informs me. "She had over two hundred."

"You worked late," I say.

"I did. Wrote two columns, one on southern poets and the other on the benefits of marijuana."

Lila gets up and swirls to the cabinet above the sink. "This calls for drinks."

She brings over two glasses and a bottle of vodka and places them on the floor.

I look out the big window. The full moon lights the night. Hawks circle the broad field and forest behind the house. Lila packs a pipe with weed and smokes. After our second glass of gin, my worries and inhibitions vanish.

The night grows. We remain sitting on the floor, talking, kissing. Her eyes linger on me, then she lunges at me, making me laugh and spill some of my vodka.

"Come, my lost little lamb. There's a surprise I've been saving for you. Bring the bottle."

I follow her to the car. She's soon driving like a maniac down the long blacktop road. She doesn't talk. Her mood is intense, almost somber, but more than that, a giant pulsing possesses her, her body a heartbeat emanating energy. I feel it, feel the energy radiating off her flesh, rippling, changing her.

In that moment I feel lost, drifting in the space where darkness meets the margin of light, where light blurs and loses its illumination to the overwhelming night, at the boundary where we don't understand the meaning of ourselves and become afraid because, there, we lose the ability to see with reason and rely on hope. Something like that happens to me, something in the ten-minute ride has changed everything.

We drive, the country road heavy with tobacco plants on both sides. We turn at the bottom of a mountain with a lake shimmering silvery under the moon. We continue around it, up a dirt road until we come to a cabin. We get out, and I look around: stars, the lake below, and tiny lights from other cabins twinkling in the dark. There are a few moored small boats. The humid evening fills with the sounds of frogs belching and crickets twittering like chopsticks.

"This is Frog King's cabin. I wrote you about him, the southern Dixie mafia godfather. He has others in Georgia, Florida, Virginia—lots of them—for gambling in the mountains."

I don't pay attention. I'm blown away looking up at the stars. How clear they are, so many.

"There ain't nothing poor about them," Lila says as she pulls the door open and we go inside.

The place is rustic, modestly furnished, big round table in the large room. Bookshelves line the wall. There are two bedrooms, a kitchen, a TV, big soft chairs and lots of liquor to drink, weed to smoke.

Lila comes around the table and puts her face next to mine. "Time to cure your shyness." She leans in and licks my cheek. "And," she says, pushing me onto a chair and straddling me, "tell me how much you love me and missed me and how you want to be mine . . . forever. . . ." She unbuckles my jeans and unbuttons her blouse. ". . . How you wanted to take me driving back from the airport. Tell me. I saw you looking at my legs while I was driving."

"Guilty on all counts."

"Well, I've been a bad girl thinking bad thoughts about you, what I want you to do to me."

"I'm ready."

"I am the judge. . . ."

She jumps back and laughs, pours another vodka, sits down sideways on my lap and kisses my neck. She stands up, then leads me into the bedroom, pushes me against the wall.

"I have something special for you. Remember our letters? I asked how far you were willing to go?"

"I said—"

". . . All the way. You did. Did you know what you were getting yourself into?"

"What?"

"I'll show you."

She leads me back into the living room. We drink white lightning the Frog King has stored under the kitchen sink in a plastic milk jug. We smoke weed, and she tells me to go wait in the main open area. She closes the bedroom door behind her.

I sit down in a huge, leather La-Z-Boy, sipping white lightning. I browse the spines of paperbacks lined on a wall shelf next to me. Then I go into the kitchen to check the fridge, the cupboards. I open the front door, step outside, look at the stars. Bullfrogs in the pond below plop and splash in the dark, clouds of insects circle the porch light. This is freedom. It is wonderful Griselda my little Jaguar, fishing, exploring the woods and a beautiful woman that loves me.

I watch a man paddle out to the middle of the lake to fish. A café's neon light announces half-priced bait. I realize the area is a resort. There are cabins with their lights on and expensive boats down on the other side of the lake. I see a car coming up the steep, winding lake road. It brings to mind the security guards that circled the perimeter of DYA at night, me inside a dorm, watching them through the bars.

~ ~ ~

I wish words stayed on the page. I wish words had no meaning. I wish sometimes I didn't understand how to write. Or how to speak.

But I do, knowing how I handle anything in life. I push, provoke to see how far I'll go. I let the words do their work. No matter what I say before I think, I carry a simple but deep faith that the outcome will be positive. Even as I test the unknown, dismissing consequences, disregarding danger, the thrill to experience the impact words have attracts me, how words can incite, deceive, pacify. The challenge is always to see what happens when it happens.

It happens when Lila calls my name. I walk into the bedroom, close the door behind me. She is naked on the bed, legs spread, one arm splayed, tied with leather to the four-poster. She's wearing a neck chain. There are three small whips on the dresser.

"I wrote you about the master and slave game. Tie this."

I lean over her, tie her free hand, then pick up the smallest whip and gently lash her over her thighs and breasts. I feel excited but feel fear too, feel out of place. A wave of nausea sweeps through me. I can't back away. I whip her harder. She murmurs, "Master . . ."

I know we wrote about doing this, but it doesn't feel right. She calls me master, I whip harder, hurtling into the vortex of some primordial pleasure, loathing, mystery of a new unnameable power.

When I tantalized her in my letters—saying I wanted to be her master—she believed me, offered up my fantasy on a dream platter, ushering me through the door to my illicit desires. But now that I am whipping her harder and harder, it feels like what I am doing is a crime, a sin. By turns, it shocks me, arouses me. I keep going. I whip to show her how much I like her, whip to show her our irreversible collusion. No matter how much I want to stop, I can't. I have to do it, especially after I wrote how ready and willing I was for any and all sexual indulgence.

I couldn't disappoint her. I gave her permission. She came on a search-and-rescue mission, burning the brush of my Catholic upbringing, until my sexual impulses leaped out of the grass like escaped fugitives hidden too long, who fell helplessly on her because she offered me total freedom to avail myself in my descent of the soul, searching for meaning.

I pick up a longer whip and continue.

I wrote: "Help free me of past restraints, let my nature develop freely."

She said she'd be my prayer, my juju, my salvation. I relied on her to understand and direct me, to accommodate my deprivation with her body cuddling me in her nest of charms; but this is a whole other reality, no longer a twenty-two-year-old in DYA sitting at his library typewriter knocking out a passionate letter. No, now it feels dangerous.

My whipping gets harder. A dark impulse drives my hand, inflicting pain beyond what she expects. I am losing control. I don't know how far I will go. Welts flower on her breasts, red stripes leaf over her white thighs, purple feathers quiver over her skin.

I press my lips against her sides until I feel her ribs with my teeth. I kiss her hip bone, rub my cheek against her inner thighs, lick and moan.

I wrote: "I want to feel like I have just fallen and landed in an overpowering and strange place."

I whip her more

She winces. "Master, my love . . . you will give me anything, that's what you wrote."

"Yes," I murmur.

She gasps as I reach out, stroke her with the leather along her sex, then I lick her, soothing her burning flesh.

She cries, "Yesssuuuhh!"

I wrote, "I am burning up with the need for sexual fore-play, and beyond that. My words take on a life of their own, buoyant and tossed freely on the enchanted elixir of my power over you, my blood mushrooms with a fierce desire to consume you, signal my departure from all confinement."

I don't need saving anymore. I am fine.

Then I feel him take over. Ghost Boy grips my forearm and walks me through the ritual, wills me on. I watch from outside of myself as Ghost Boy blinds me with a violent hunger, relishing her submission. I trust him to protect me. I follow him deeper into what decency prohibits. Our dark longing and willingness imply that Lila and I will be together forever.

Ghost Boy fixates on her flesh, with his unwavering au-thority. I plunge my fingers between her legs, wanting to for-ever ingrain myself in her soul, inscribe my love on her heart, wrest it open to make a place to bury my innocence, replace it with Ghost Boy's lust.

Until I can't, until it's too much for me, until I'm scared of what I'm doing, until I want to flee because I am going to get in trouble—because people are going to find out what kind of evil boy I am, they will find out what the priest does, until the devil owns my soul and makes me his, until, whip in hand, breathless, I sense a dark covenant of forbidden trust born between us. Ghost Boy, who protects me, takes me with him, we exit the real world, lose ourselves in this quandary of illicit, formidable perversions, where all else seeks shelter in the trenches of the written word.

I don't remember what happened, didn't want to, or how I ended up sitting at the lake on a park bench, staring at the dark waters, the moon bobbing on the surface. My arms are trembling. I can't stop my hands shaking. My teeth are chattering, but it's not cold. I am consumed with panic, I look back at the cabin and see no lights. I keep thinking I encouraged her, boasted I wanted her to give me all of it. I told her I could handle anything. I expected her to prove her loyalty, and she did. I was the disappointment.

4

MY FIRST EXCURSION into the world was riddled with doubt, failure and confusion. Time has not diminished the wonder I still feel when looking back at my Green Mill days. I'm amazed that I somehow was able to walk away from that experience.

Today it's June 3rd, 2019. The days here in northern New Mexico are turning hotter than usual with climate change clawing the land. It's not that bad, though. It's still good weather for hiking. Way up here in the towering heights of the Santa Fe forest, I rest on a boulder and drink spring water pouring from a boulder crevice. I think about Lila, how kind and generous she was with her time and affection.

The incident made me question everything I knew about what a man was. It was clear my ideas back in the early 1980s about what made a man a man were wrong. Those ideas were grown and harvested out of the smoky ruins of warfare and hostile landscapes of reformatories, orphanages and youth facilities. They came out of the jagged land strewn with missing parents and abandoned kids, uneducated fools, deceptive predators, drug addicts and trusted adults sexually abusing children.

It was hard to trust kindness, especially when it hurt you, lied to you, exploited you. But I did accept it from others because it was part of living. I practiced some kindness myself toward others. It was one of the most difficult exercises in my reentry. I repeatedly failed to perform it as I had wished.

Out of insecurity and fear, I was enamored with being a *tough guy,* a man who didn't cry or admit to feeling pain. Being a bad boy. Acting like I didn't care about my socialization enough to be civil toward strangers. I immediately assumed their intent toward me was malevolent.

Grown-up people in power, the authorities, were resentful—maybe because they hated themselves or their lives, maybe they were hurt or had lost hope—they took it out me. They targeted me with labels that suited their needs, to raise more money, to build more facilities, to feel better about themselves, to get more power, to feel in control . . . who knows? Because of my background they assumed I was violent, an addict, a drunk. It might have been as true as it is for anyone for a time. But it didn't remain so, even though their labels stuck to me and branded me as such.

I would not be like them. I remained hopeful, full of brash love for life. I dismissed those sticky, warted tongues pandering for insectual-approval from the industry (literary, financial, educational, etc.), ensuring those bigots would reap rewards for their subsidized subservience—plaques, money, positions. . . . I witnessed them fall prey to the cultural auctioneers who bought and sold authenticity and unique family legacy and ethnic pride and replaced it with their skin-shed cures to make us appear white, demeaning us in order to make themselves feel superior. I would not bend, I would never become a company-bought and industry-molded idiot who'd commit any indiscretion to get ahead.

Never.

Lila wasn't one of them. She had three bilingual books of published poems, but to see her you wouldn't think so. She was down-home, country-modest. Lila's strength of character exuded love, even though that word, abused, faded to lusterless shreds by most, had no meaning for me. The way I used the word love with Lila meant strength. She was the strong one, I was weak. She stood by her words. I didn't. She was sincere, I was opportunistic.

I was a superficial kid, full of myself.

In the beginning of our correspondence, language foamed over the page margins freely from my sweltering imagination. Her friendship made me feel part of something special, made me feel smart. Important. I mattered, and that meant I had something other kids in DYA didn't: purpose.

She had published poetry, was a scholar of pre-Colombian literature, a translator of Nahuatl poetry. For being only thirty-two, she kicked butt. No matter what side you looked at, she was impressive. I wrote her about the barbarian life in Gladiator School, our exchanges lathered into flowering gardens of abundant romantic confessions and sexual fantasies. They were instigated and prodded on by me.

I knew I needed fixing, that there was something missing in me—seven years in the orphanage, two in juvey, one in Gladiator School and seven in DYA would jack any kid up. Those years did something to me. There were invisible but virulent vestiges in my every step and gesture. They made it difficult to talk to women; when I talked about love, it always had to be sexual, sex-sex-sex, lacking tenderness or affection. I just thought that was normal. I was a twenty-two-year-old with a six-year-old's emotional make-up.

I guess it was the six-year-old grieving his mother's absence, the six-year-old angry over her abandonment, the six-year-old not knowing anything about affection, not trusting it, afraid . . . saying all the words and making all the promises. And it was the six-year-old also believing in super-human heroes performing amazing feats, all according to the words he had written in letters to her, believing in the most outrageous and extraterrestrial powers he thought he had. I thought if I willed it, it would happen. I mean, I really thought she could hear me thinking and feeling, like words spoken aloud in her presence.

Still, writing was new to me. I was amazed at how one word followed another to invoke an unexpected image, how they were arranged on paper and called sentences. They made me embrace a whole new world of possible meanings. They could carry one's feelings, hopes or dreams, be sent off, received on the other end and start a full, new life unguessed, unimagined.

That's how it was for me. Once I started writing Lila, our correspondence taught me how to talk to a woman, trust her enough to divulge my deepest erotic fantasies, even create wildly pornographic scenes to quench years of deprivation and curiosity.

It was heaven for me, got me through some dark times.

One letter every two weeks turned into three a week. Soon I was counting the days by the arrival of her letters: so many letters made a month, months became a year. Somewhere in the middle of those letters I was writing her love-me-forever letters. Besides the obvious, the exercise improved my writing, helped me express my feelings, broaden and deepen my vocabulary.

Her words were enchanting music. I was so easily affected by them, going from deep, tumultuous agony, rising to ecstatic soaring so liberating that for hours I was not even conscious I was confined.

Even as I tested the virginal shores of my imagination, even while realizing with an infant's delight that I was writing something verging on the occult and it was wrong, I still

wanted to be bad. I was defiant being bad. My words sum-
moned nuns in my head screaming at me that I was a hea-
then, bound to burn in hell. I smiled as I wrote even more
disgraceful sentences.

I wrote on, sometimes recoiled at the metaphors of sex
marathons, writing what I had been taught by pious, hypo-
critical people; priests, devout Christians—even my paternal
grandma and grandpa, reading the Bible every day. They all
scolded me in my head that what I was writing was evil. But
I soldiered on, breaking through my fears, recklessly flailing
my Chicano magic wand of a pencil putting it all down on
paper: the most loving and precious scenes my imagination
could summon, filled with promises and violent, erotic dom-
ination, imagining sadistic and cruel sex scenes . . . which she
welcomed.

She kept asking in her letters: *Are you sure you want to go
this way, are you positive you want me to open up your fantasy world, trust me with your darkest fantasies, pour your
soul into my hands? It can be dangerous, there's no turning
back, are you sure you want to go this way? Please, think
about it.*

I was not thinking. Here was an opportunity to know
women, to revel in and understand how they thought, what
made them love a man, how far they would go . . . could you
possess them, was coupling eternal, was there even such a
thing as love, or only lust. . . . ?

In her letters she asked that I tread carefully, consider
where I was taking our correspondence, not to make light of
it and be sure about the promises I was making, because she
was changing her life around them.

I ignored every warning for the joy of unmitigated intox-
ication in what was taboo. Every day for a year, two people
who had never met wrote each other ten-page letters. Enve-

lope-freighters moved, brimming with the passionate cargo of our dreams to be together forever, criss-crossing America between North Carolina and Denver, drifting over cities and rivers, over the heads of millions entangled in their lives, dying or living, in sorrow or joy. Like clouds, our letters came and went, oblivious to the real world over which they sailed.

She put it to me in no uncertain way, and when I insisted, in one of her letters, she whipped out the hack saw, cut the bars of my sheltered innocence and wrote: *Then tell me what the hell you really want to know, and I'll lay it out for you on the table like gorgeous, gleaming knives you can cut your wrists with and kill this adolescent bullshit fantasy you carry called a woman in your screwed-up, institutionalized head.*

Zero tolerance for the bullshit.

She had been Frog King's mistress for years, now she was breaking it off to be only mine. That's how loyal she was, how committed, how serious she was taking my words.

It didn't even occur to me then, being locked up, starving for affection, that I would have to deliver on those promises. I realized too late and I paid the consequences for my naivety. I set aside all her misgivings, ignored the gravity of my words as something that would take care of itself in time. All was well. Even when she commented that if I followed the tip of my soul down to its thick and massive root system, it would be rooted in the poisoned soil of abandonment and drug-crazed parents—the toxins of my self-hatred, the hurt, the fear my mother caused in me when she left.

Did I dismiss Lila's warning? Did I survive years of being alone in a hostile place, fending for myself in dangerous situations? I did. I assumed that Lila's precautions on woman-power, with my sincere interest at heart, were less to be feared and easily handled, at least easier than facing gangs intent on raping you or being swept away in the middle of the night from your home at five-years-old and delivered to strangers dressed in dark gowns on a rainy night.

After writing her not to worry, I'd lay down on my bunk, mind depleted and on the edge of disintegration, waiting until lights were out. Then I'd conjure her image, masturbating with the thoughts of us having sex in a dozen ways until I was exhausted.

When I banged her in my fantasies, I was not in DYA. In the dark under the covers, I invented myself into a man with means who knew the world, and her into a woman in my mind, just the way I wanted her, doing and saying and behaving as I wished. I was with her in a field or in bed every way possible until I lay gasping with an erection under my blanket, sweating, my arms and hands cramped from stroking myself so long.

The written word opened a new world. It revealed such pleasures as never imagined.

I urged her to go that way, use our letters to break down sexual taboos, and she was only too happy to free me from the throes of my own parochial misgivings. Yes, at times I felt vaguely uneasy, told her so, but she swept aside my doubts, reminding me, *You've committed yourself, no turning back, no regrets, no second thoughts. Follow through with the promises of eternal loyalty and love you've made. You are my master and I am yours to do whatever you want to do with me.*

Those last words terrified me as much as they pleased me. I didn't know their meaning, what they required of me. What was a master's job? What did the work and responsibility of a master entailed? They also got me excited. A powerful, erotic force exuded from those words, strong enough to lead me on, straight into a matrix. So I went with it. Mine is not a cautionary tale, but a story about a fool's mindless excursion into the lethal hinterlands of a woman's most secret desires. I replied, *I will be.*

And so I was: vulnerable, willing to say anything to lessen the frustration of being so isolated, craving attention. I unleashed reams of sentimental infatuations I thought were God-inspired, earth-shattering truths, because as I did, I felt like I was flying high in the sky above the world as I knew it—so far up I could almost kiss God's cheek, in some way creating, controlling my destiny, building a determined life. I wanted to believe everything I wrote her, that I could do it all. I believed it all, even up to the very moment when I heard Lila call my name and I entered the bedroom.

~ ~ ~

I knew nothing about love when I got released from DYA. I found myself in a van with a bunch of other young gangsters. I hopped into the van idling in the parking lot, breathed with relief that I was finally leaving.

There are only two things I'm afraid in this world. One is the court system, especially as a Chicano. They railroad you every time, they strip you of every right, you have no control over your destiny; you know that all the lawyers, judges and counselors are in the game for themselves They don't care about you. They waste you every time, as sure as if they're executing you before a firing squad. I tremble even at the mention of the words court, legal paper or official appointment with one of the legal ghouls. The second is being forgotten in the correctional system, like some of the immigrant kids. They're ripped from their parents and hurled into the dark, oblivious pit of No-Return. They stay confined long after they're supposed to leave, no one cares about them. I don't want to be forgotten.

I sent my sister Karina two cardboard boxes of note-books—mostly graffiti lettering, tattoo sketches, some cartoon drawings, some poems—books, letters. I kept one box. While waiting for my release escort, I checked the box a hundred times. A couple of paperbacks, a journal, letters, two changes of underwear, jeans, T-shirts, pairs of socks, toothpaste and brush. I folded the flaps, set it on the cot, minutes later, checked it again. To calm my nerves, I read one of the letters Lila had sent me saying she'd be waiting.

∽ ∽ ∽

Finally out and riding away, we pass telephone poles, houses, wrecks on bricks being worked on in yards, office buildings, closed bars and gas stations. The exhaust pipe sputters, on the radio Willie Nelson croons "On the Road Again" and the guard puffs his discount cigarette from the rez.

Three other kids from a different part of the complex are released with me. We hunch in silence. I know them. Locked down in segregation for disobeying orders, they hate authority as much as I do. They're the same kind of kids I'd known at the orphanage, except older than their years.

The black brother, Gary, nineteen years old, wipes condensation from the glass and says, "Man, ain't shit out there 'cept them fields and lights on the golf course and pool at Sanford place where they keep them Watergate criminals."

"Country club for whites—no black allowed." Sickle, eighteen, an Aryan, comments. "Shoulda been a politician, Gary. What'd you expect, a welcome committee by the Queen of Sheba?"

Gary grumbles, spits sunflower seed shells into his palm.

"Much time as the State took, Queen of Sheba'd be a good start. I'm hungry for some fried chicken," he says.

The Chicano seated next to me, Chuy, seventeen, says, "And mariachis, buttered popcorn, cocaine and a big mamacita with huge boobies and *nalgas*."

"Calvinists believed punishment was a deterrent for your inherent evil," the guard adds. "Ain't none of you going to say anything? I'm giving you my best sermon, kind of a 'Hey, you're free, suckers, you're saved.'"

"Let's have fun on our way to hell," Sickle says.

"I'm going to community college" the guard says. "And in my philosophy class, I read that Calvinists believe that if you're born into poverty, you are the sinful, the wicked who can never change—criminals by your DNA. Ha, that's right!"

The motor and tires hum until the guard scoffs, "Reason no one's here to greet you, they all dead from drugs, doing time or deported."

"Punk-ass," Chuy retorts.

The fat, white guard chuckles, reaches for a donut in the box on the passenger seat.

Chuy asks, "What's Watergate, *ese*?"

"I don't know," I say. "Gary?"

"Republicans got busted burglarizing Democratic offices. Sentenced to Sanford across the street. . . ."

". . . Playground for the rich," Sickle breaks in. "Talk about sermons. Mom wanted me to follow 'em, gave 'em donations to get me Christian. Guy called Colson scammed all them believes with a faith-based hustle to rake in the bucks. Took my mama's money."

"People'll do anything to believe God is on their side," I say.

"Evangelicals," Gary snorts. "Swill more charity money than hogs at a trough from people who still think America should only be run by whites. That means you, Sickle."

"Hell, yeah," he laughs. "Master race, mother."

"What about that chick you writing?" Chuy asks. "You goin' with her?"

"Never turn down a chance," Sickle grins.

"I don't know, probably work for my brother first, make some money," I say.

"Whatcha got on freedom?" I ask Gary, who can rap.

My request brings a big smile to his face. "Tell you something about freedom, my brother. I spit some dark shit out: Pray Satan to appear wielding a fiery trident commanding legions of armed angels to descend and destroy all these urban-heathens, seething to avenge my maimed heart on all unlucky to be present when I blow . . ."

"Oh hell . . ." Sickle says. "Shit ya . . ."

From the dark roadside a dog dashes out, we all hear a yelp, bone and body thuds turning over under the van. We're all disgusted by the meanness of it and swell with anger.

Dogs are sacred: you fart and it don't bother them. No matter what, they're always happy to see you. We stare out the chilled windows as our hands tighten into fists, violent images of hurting the guard whirl in our imaginations.

"Not what Martin Luther King would preach," Gary says.

"Or César Chávez," Chuy adds.

"But nice," Sickle growls.

Gary recites more: "Business as usual in America, happening every morning where youth holding facilities support the town's economy; refugees like us, American kids, broken into criminalized brutes, who waited a long time for the hour to fall to purge our rage for the unjust torture inflicted on us."

"¡Simón, vato!" Chuy exclaims.

"Where'd you get that from? That's good, bro," I say.

"Photographic memory," Gary replies. "While you guys were busy declaring war on every kid that looked at you sideways, I was reading."

"I got a photo-whatever power too," Chuy says. "Naked ladies in my head, I'm making love to all of them."

". . . purge our rage . . ." Sickle repeats.

"We ain't no rehabilitated knights on a medieval quest for the Holy Grail," Gary says.

Gary laughs, mimics Barry White with a baritone chuckle. "We America's children, criminalized into thieves, addicts and dealers."

"Now you got it," I say.

Sickle's reflection gleams in the frosted window, his tremor voice utters in a trance, "And I'm going to blow, I'm gonna blow, baby!"

His breath mists the pane and his index finger traces the word RAGE on the glass. Four years from this morning, he'll be high on meth. I'll hear on the TV news that Sickle went into a school in Alexandria, Louisiana, with a semi-automatic rifle and killed four people: two kids, two adults.

Eventually we glide under the neon-lit, corrugated airport terminal and the guard announces, "Here's where daddy leaves his girls." He swings to the curb and opens the doors. We get out, he locks the van doors and off he goes, pulling out as quickly as possible, leaving us stranded like plucked ducks at a busy intersection.

Told what to do for so long, we wait for an order on which way to walk. I watch as the last vestige of DYA drives away, returning to that massive earth-ship of iron and concrete, that hulking empire of the doomed, moving into the dark horizon without me, collecting debris of more broken lives.

I am a product of institutions. Without somebody guarding me, telling me what to do, I get scared. I want to yell, "Stop! Hey! You can't leave me!"

A sickening feeling of dread sours my stomach as I stand there remembering the night long ago when the State official dropped my brother and me off at the orphanage. Four nuns in dark, hooded cassocks stood on the steps to receive us. I'd never seen a nun, especially none dressed in cowls and robes. They looked like alien, like dark angels about to take me into hell. I was terrified.

When the official took us to the orphanage, I turned and yelled, "Don't leave me, please!" The nuns grabbed my arms and dragged me into the building. I screamed, "I want my mom, my father! Please don't take me, please come back!" I watched the official's car leave just like I watch the van leave.

"A drink 'fore I slap you suckers," Gary says.

Sickle follows Chuy, I take up the rear. We go into the lounge. I sit down on an end stool at the counter, in case shit breaks out. I order a ginger ale, Sickle, a Jack and Coke, Chuy a tequila and Gary vodka.

The bartender gives us a once over. "Just got out, eh? See it all over your faces . . . and also that you're not old enough to drink. But from what I hear about DYA, you deserve one."

We stare in the mirror, and Chuy says, "We with each other for years and released at the same time. Will I ever shake yous?" He grins with a hint of camaraderie as he downs his drink and shoots two fingers at the bartender.

"Unusual punishment." Sickle cocks his head, slugs his whiskey. "Here-here!" He pushes his shotglass down the counter. "Deuce it."

"Been a long time." Gary licks the last grain of salt off his glass rim, smacks his lips and gazes in the mirror, pleased with the feeling the vodka gives him. He motions for another. "I'll take it how they give it: seconds, minutes, hours, days or years. All the freedom they wanna give, daddy mac's here to take."

"Had a million reasons to mess you up, but out here . . . can't scratch up one," Sickle says.

We stare at our reflections in the mirror, turn from our own eyes. I know what they're thinking, what we're all thinking: TIME has broken us, taken so much from us, so much life has slipped past already. We're damaged goods, the wreckage irreversible. None of us know when or how it happened, but we feel it in our souls.

Rather than stew in our misery as failures, we each opt for the lie that DYA life is the real life, that hitting the streets is like Spring Break with a serrated edge. Get jacked, party, do all kinds of insane shit, commit crimes, take drugs in any amount, chase the moment's pleasure, screw until you can't and then back to the real world, real life of DYA . . . eventually prison.

As if Sickle can hear my thoughts, he says, "Detention doesn't scare anyone. It messes your head up though . . . pretty fucking good."

Chuy says, "It give me a kind of honor, part of *la vida loca.*"

"Never saw it as a deterrent, I'll tell you that," Gary says. "It was something to look forward to."

We sound like soldiers coming back from war. We had our innocence taken by force, we suffered a lot of injustices. Our faces mirror that back to us as if confirming the loss. Our eyes measure the incalculable damage years in Gladiator School inflicted, not one of us able or willing to say aloud or wanting to notice what could have been and never was. Our response to the gnawing pain that numbed our hearts is to order more liquor.

The airport intercom announces my flight. Chuy hugs me. "If you ever draw the short straw, *carnal,* here, take this rabbit foot."

I wrote their information on a napkin: a pool hall in Dallas, a video arcade in Detroit, a laundromat in Portland. Riding the escalator up to my boarding gate, a passenger, hurrying to the baggage claim tosses a paperback in the trash. I reach in, clean it off and put it in my pocket. Books are my best friends, I'm not leaving this one behind.

∾ ∾ ∾

That's who I was. Freedom, books, friends but definitely not a love king, despite all those letters attesting to my amorous mastery. I don't remember exactly what happened in the cabin that night, I blocked it out, all I know is, you don't mess with a thirty-two-year-old woman. I thought I was on top of my game, she showed me I was just a kid with a horny cock, big mouth, big fantasies, a very lively but distorted notion of who women were. Most importantly, I had been deprived of any relationship with a woman, ever. I knew nothing about what I was telling her to do.

She showed me what I was made of: fear, shame, hypocrisy. I mean, I told her I wanted to do all those sexual things in letters, but when she called me on it, I freaked. There was something deeper at work there, but I couldn't put my finger on exactly what it was. I hardly ever had recoiled like that, in any situation. I was always able to regain my composure or limit my shock, but not that night. Not with her. It was like something had come out of the sky, slammed me unconscious, leveled me, trampled me to the ground and buried me a thousand feet down in some weird trap-hole I couldn't claw myself up out of.

It wasn't the first time my boldface bravado had caught me up in shit. Ever since I was a kid I was like that, always jumping to prove I was one of the boys. Later when the consequence came down, I'd shake like a frightened rabbit. In the end, I always failed and was ashamed. I lived with the guilt that I would never be as good as any other kid, that I was a coward and there was no redemption. I felt that something was wrong with me that could never be fixed.

The threat of any kind of punishment always held the specter of the world ending, that if I got caught, everything would fall apart, I would die a torturous death. I'd be lost again in the dark, be nothing, turn into nothing and disappear.

I guess I was trying to overcome this posing in me with Lila, when I thought I was stronger but wasn't. Instead of wrecking everything, commanding me to leave and never return, she was kind enough to trust me and forgive me.

No one has ever shown that understanding to me. She accepted my lies, embraced my fragility and insecurity. She accepted my bullshit without coming back with acrimony and revenge. She taught me a lifetime lesson: When it comes to saying something on paper, you better mean it.

As I mentioned, to be honest, I don't remember much of that night, as far as what happened afterward. I think I took the whips down to the bullfrog pond and threw them in, and I must have taken off in the night, running for my life, probably thinking the whole world had gone mad and the end was near. That's how crazy the whip thing affected me; turning over her ass, me slapping it, sucking her nipples, licking her thighs, whipping harder, seeing the stinging pain in her pinched features and smiling for more.

All I know is I found myself sitting down at the lake shore. My heart thundered, my soul screamed. I wanted out of there, to pretend it never happened. I wanted God to save me from myself, from what I promised her, from my lies; what I said I could do, as if I was really a badass and experienced and shit.

I wasn't.

Shortly after that night, it came back to me in a nightmare. I dropped the whips, flew from the room and sprinted down the hill in the moonlit dark until I reached the lake. I sat down in the lakeshore grass and hugged my knees to my chest, too scared to even cry. I felt a lifetime of rejection all at once, because I had once again thought more of myself than what was really there. I had nothing again. I was no one again.

I plunged my hand in the water and doused my face, hair, neck. It cooled the burning inside. I lay down, listened to the night's heartbeat in the mountain silence. A few inches from my cheek, a black snake slithered through the grass and into the water. Frogs croaked. I watched crickets, grasshoppers, water spiders. Rings rippled from puckering fish.

Freedom was too crazy, it messed me up.

If I would have known my reentry was going to be like this, I would have stayed in. I would have done something to get more time. I wanted to go back to a time when I didn't have words. They are dangerous and can screw you up. Life is more than words in a letter, a lot more.

～ ～ ～

It's a warm day in late August. I stand before Lila's library reading the book spines. I pull a Graham Greene novel and a Walt Whitman book of poems, carry them in one hand, balancing my coffee in the other. I walk into the bedroom, set my coffee on the side table, lie down and read. I resolve to escape into the safety of books. Later I go fishing, hike, take long walks in the forest. Then I read more.

The August days slowly lose their humidity and heat. Soon it's early September and the weather turns cool. Geese migrate, deer appear in the fields nibbling at sparse grass.

One morning I'm in bed reading, after a while I move to the kitchen table, compare same-theme poems by William Carlos Williams and Seamus Heaney and scribble a few lines of my own on the same theme. It's just some notes, mess around with the lines of a poem I feel forming in my mind. I pause, look around the room listening to the sound of engines. By their sound, I count several vehicles pulling into the yard. There's a knock at the screen door. I holler, "Come in!"

He doesn't introduce himself, from the descriptions in Lila's letter I know it's Frog King, the southern Dixie mafia Godfather himself. He smells outdoorsy, root- and green-smelling, a tobacco field breeze that blows into my living room and looms before me. All six-foot-seven inches, four hundred pounds of him—along with two of his strong-arm guys. Frog King, around fifty or so, wears weathered denim overalls, a cocked baseball cap with a feed store emblem, a plaid cotton shirt, massive lace-up boots warped from hard use. Their leather tongues lolling out on the side.

He bellows, "How the hell are ya?" and, without waiting for an answer, tosses a brown paper lunch bag on the table and roars, "There's a goddamn truck with a camper in the yard with the keys in it. I want you to get the hell out. Take it, it's yours."

I peek into the paper bag at a neat stack of hundred-dollar bills tied with a rubber band.

"There's five thousand. Don't come back."

I lob the sack back. "If I leave, no one's telling me when."

The moment requires every bit of character I can conjure. I feel I'm about to fall to the floor and faint. Another instance of someone commanding me to do something—court-figure, judge-in-robes, shit—I'm not going to obey, even though every single nerve in my body burns hot with fear.

Memories of me at the orphanage spring up; there I am, waiting at the gate for my mother every Sunday. She never comes. I wait every Sunday for a year, watching car after car pull up, praying with every last vestige of hope in me that it's her. I sneak up to the Blue Room, the visiting room, and watch other boys visit with their grandmas and aunts, thinking one might invite me to sit in on his visit, pretend for a minute she is my grandma or aunt too.

I run away to go find my mom. I'm ordered to stop, spanked harder each time I'm caught. A dozen times I'm brought back. Under the paddle, my flesh goes numb for disobeying their rules, but some heart sickness in me takes over, and the beatings don't matter. With every whack on my bare buttocks, I turn my head down and brood. I will not listen to a single threat or word they scream at me. Something in me braces, tightens to steel. I am not going to obey, no matter the punishment.

This is the same thing. I am not going to do anything someone says to me in an authoritarian way.

What I say to Frog King makes him convulse. I swear, I've never heard anyone laugh so hard as he does. His whole body shakes, an avalanche of flesh, moving with such earthquake force that the velocity and depth of his laughter makes the floorboards tremor. Even the table rattles.

"I'll be goddamned, boy! Sonofabitch!"

He laughs again, an apple-wood cracking laughter, his facial features crumpling in on themselves, flesh folding over flesh, his shoulders shaking until finally the earthquake subsides into a mean hound's glare

He growls, "I ever see another bruise on her, you hurt her in any way, I'll kill you."

I say, "I won't . . . never with love . . . people get hurt sometimes. That's what love is. . . ." I don't know what else to say, feeling ashamed I did something really bad like it was my fault. I have a hard time admitting it.

Again it comes, this bouldering, crackle-lightning, raucous, laughing thunder that takes all the oxygen out of a ten-mile radius. Then he turns, and leaves with the two guys. I understand why they call him Frog King: that down-home laughter borne of cayenne gumbo, cinnamon-sprinkled sweet potatoes, black-eyed peas, bacon grease. If the moon could howl, it would sound like Frog King; if it could eat, it would devour a bowl of Frog King gumbo.

I don't know much about him, except what Lila hinted at in her letters and told me the other night. To my mind, he seems like a country hoodlum redneck. A southern hog bum-farmer on the government's welfare roster or a plain and simple roadkill scavenger. Without his family's fortune, he'd be a hyena-like vagrant. I don't waste a second on his threat. I've lived my whole life with bullies; my strategy is always to stay out of their way. When that's not possible, I always overreact, pick up the nearest weapon—a rock, a board, dirt, wire—out of fear, I defend myself. If nothing is available, I let them hit me, I show no reaction to the blows. Crazy attracts crazy.

∾ ∾ ∾

As September leaves turn golden, mornings become so cold the wall heater bellows burning through propane. I sit at the big table in the main room by the large window, study the frost-covered fields and forest, try to come up with a plan to get my life started.

Should I sign up for school? A GED program? How do I do that? Who do I talk to? Where do I go? These half-hearted ruminations always end in anxiety. To alleviate the stress of boredom, just do something, I jog down the long blacktop road bordered on each side by tall, fat tobacco plants. I run hard, feel free for about an hour or two until I get back to face my empty life again.

After a good run, I normally throw myself on the hard-wood floor, stretch out, stare at the ceiling and listen to the silence. But this time when I close my eyes, I hear Lila's voice. A kid's head appears at the screen.

"I'll introduce you, Peter . . . patience, honey."

A sandy-haired, seven- or eight-year-old boy stands on the step, gives me a mile-wide grin. "Something wrong with you, mister?"

"Nope." I kneel up, stand.

"Honey, let's see about getting you settled in at Daddy's."

Peter leaps, dashes about the room with a prong-horned giddiness—bandy-legged excitement a kid in the country develops, having run free most of his life.

He stops, his cheeks flushed, and pants. "You that man . . . from prison . . . huh? Mom loves you." He spins on his heels, laughs.

"Peter. Peter, hold on for second. Good to meet you," I say.

He smells like sweet grass along a forest creek.

"I know where the fish are," Peter declares. His eyes are green moss. In the sun rays they turn soft blue.

"I've never fished," I tell him, "but I'd love to. It's always been a dream. Will you take me, show me those ponds your mother wrote me about?"

"Good!" Peter claps his hands as if to announce something, helicopters around. On each pass, he confides in me with whispers, "I know . . . where Confederate . . . ghosts are too. . . . Seen 'em walking in the woods through the trees. Bet you never seen that!"

Peter's older brother, Bruce, about ten or eleven, comes in then. Without a word, he goes into his bedroom and comes out carrying a laundry basket of his belongings. He pauses long enough to glare at me and tells Peter, "Let's go." The tenor of his voice festers with resentment at my presence.

"Well," Lila says, "I got errands." She kisses her boys. "I've got to pick up Mom's medicine, get wine and cigs. Be right back. Come on, boys, get a-moving."

I stand at the screen door, watching them cross the road. Peter and Bruce make several trips hauling their belongings. Emotion wells up in me while I force myself to fight back the tears, thinking how I'd been at their age. I ran away, lived on the streets, moved room to room in dozens of scary boarding houses. I was wary, beyond the reach of lawyers, bankers, politicians or businessmen roaming the premises at night, trawling for kids to indulge their sexual debauchery.

∾ ∾ ∾

Hawks circle the fields for rodents, deer come out of the forest to grub on shoots. The autumn landscape is ragged like leftover greens on the cutting board.

I worry about getting a job, try to concentrate on what it is that I need to do to get going with my reentry. I have no training in this kind of stuff, the stuff called free-living—getting up, working, talking to people, doing what people do. I don't know how to move with them in crowds, in classes, in socializing groups. I have no experience of any kind being normal. The days are coming and going in uneventful succession. I sit still, reading, thinking, worrying, doing nothing. Time moves fast in freedom; if you aren't up on your game, it leaves you behind.

It's the middle of September, and life seems to be idle. You can see the colors changing, but all else stands by. Wednesday morning, I carry my toast and coffee into my office, a cubbyhole to the right of the front door. It has a small window looking out on the pump house, beyond that black-top country road and woods. There's a spindle-backed chair, a desk with knob-handled drawers, a Royal typewriter, an ashtray, a stack of typing paper, a screen cylinder basket with pencils, white-out, an eraser, typewriter ribbons, envelopes, stamps. There's a four-drawer steel filing cabinet to the left, a plank and brick bookshelf to the right lined with Irish and Mexican poetry books.

There is this poet Denise I met while I was inside. She writes me from time to time, tells me that reading can help with my reentry, socialize me. I can use it as an important key to open doors that in the past I didn't understand how to open. So I try to read with the hope that it might help me order my thoughts, make my thinking clearer.

I make a baloney sandwich and notice Lila has taped a new excerpt from our letters on the fridge:

My love grows in ferocious growls for you
I fend for no one but a wound in me, a wound
so great it's taken on a being of itself
breathing and speaking in my blood
my hands clench your hair, the fangs of my fingers
want to tear you apart, I have so much hunger for you.

I should be proud that she thinks enough of my poem to post it on the fridge, but there is a wariness, a mistrust of this act. In the furthest reaches of my heart, I know whatever I do is somehow contaminated. A suspicion arises in me that she might be trying to tell me something. It's just a feeling one

69

gets when something doesn't seem right. Maybe it's nothing, maybe she just likes it, is proud of me.

I make another sandwich, another cup of instant coffee and return to reading hoping Peter to come flying in, gusting about the main room, sweet-headed, human butterfly wanting to take off fishing. Eventually he does come in, but I'm wrapped up in work ideas. He keeps himself busy on the floor of the main room.

In my office, I write down a list of jobs I should apply for on a yellow legal pad: dishwasher, car wash attendant, etc.

In the middle of figuring out my strategy for filling out employment applications, UPS drops off the boxes I sent to my sister from DYA. Peter and I go through them; nothing special, really: notebooks with tattoo sketches, poems, letters. *Cheap scribbles.*

I peer into one box, full of stacks of love letters between Lila and me. There are some from Denise too. Two very decent women whose affection placed me at the right hand of God, the brother of Aztec kings. Because of them I'm standing toe to toe with Mayan gladiators.

∾ ∾ ∾

Denise sent me books. Welsh mother, Russian-Jewish father, she was a no-mess-around person. She didn't hesitate to share her disdain for the Israeli occupation/oppression of Palestine. Until we wrote each other, I had never heard of Palestine nor Israelis killing Palestinian civilians, nor Nazi concentration camps, nor politics in general. I'd send Denise a few things I wrote—not even poems really—just half pages of a diary or a journal, excerpts or pieces of a letter I was writing. She'd direct me to a book to read, historical figures, slave writing, white supremacy killers . . . stuff I needed to know in order to think and understand the sources of the issues I faced in DYA.

Unlike with Lila, Denise and I never once trekked into erotic territory. Our correspondence was all about books, learning and plans to get my GED. I was amazed by the way she wrote, making her spirit rise from between the words, making a sentence kind of levitate off the page. Reading her words, I could feel her very close to me.

The words she wrote me also had wings and hands. Often I was down on one knee in an attitude of surrender: to give up my attempt at the straight life, instead live the criminal life, be done with trying to better myself. I was fooling myself. I didn't have the self-esteem or courage to become a better man. But no, her words took me by my arms, raised me up on my feet, shook the dust off my clothing and pointed to the road ahead. She pushed me forward, writing in that special way of hers: "The journey's just begun, Orlando. You must continue." With each of her letters and postcards, I felt my life get clearer in meaning, in possibilities.

Denise spent half her time in Mexico, in Oaxaca. The cold was getting to be too much for her to bear in Somerville, Massachusetts. She felt restless, doubled her anti-war efforts: writing, giving speeches, marching against Johnson, Nixon, eventually the Reagan administration. She shifted her poetry from pastoral lyricism to defiant politics. Once she read in Central Park, her eloquence of opposition tolling like a bell at dawn, drawing millions of converts to the religion of activism. The example of how she lived her life and the poems she wrote resurrected me. I was a Chicano Lazarus got up, strutting down the road.

Her poems brought back memories, painted vivid pictures, transforming my cell into a burial site in El Salvador she had visited or a lavish palace where billionaire Saudis bought young girls for their pleasure. I found myself trying to mimic her, writing free-verse protest poems—they honestly were not very good.

Her envelopes bulged with images of farmers, peasants massacred by soldiers. She made me lean toward taking a civic role, that of witness, of resistance. I found myself breaking up fights, telling kids not to talk about "Blacks and Mexicans" in a racist way, urging my homies to read books, get their GEDs. My heart felt like every atom had been split. No longer could I just dream about making money or partying, no longer could I simply observe life or trust the appearance of things. I learned to question authority. Every alphabet carried the presence of God. I was no longer the child sounding my vowels in a classroom with a nun at the orphanage. Now, the words attached themselves to a woman's tears, a child's hunger, a white man raping a brown woman (my sister and cousins).

Somehow, she understood the prisoner's plight. How she was able to go from her reality, her world—dining with world-renowned poets, speaking at the United Nations on behalf of oppressed peoples—into my world with such compassion was beyond me. Somehow, that dark-haired, brown-eyed, Essex-born Welsh poet, teaching a yearly semester at Stanford, recognized in me a common heart capable of appreciating the suffering of others and expressing it.

She inspired me to be fierce. My letters became my lyrical storm surges. I could feel my voice, with pride, a renewed sense of solitary purpose, soaring above the indifferent, complacent kids and guards all around me. While others skedaddled from the fight to the sidelines, never standing up for human rights or protesting a wrongfully accused kid, she rushed out to engage the enemy. But still, because so many had promised to do things for me before, I did not believe her when she wrote me promising to be there for me when I was released.

~ ~ ~

It's a blustery, cold Autumn afternoon. I'm in my cranny office, reading aloud to Peter about how to make fishing flies. The red wall-phone with the long extension cord rings in the other room. Lila answers it. Peter and I get ready and take off. By day's end, we've caught six bigmouth bass, each around twelve to fifteen inches.

As we walk back, I tell Peter, "Hey, I started some ideas about a poem I'm writing for you."

"Really?"

"It's still in my head."

"Yessss! Let me hear one line. Please!"

"Okay, here goes. This is only the beginning, but here: 'There was a little boy named Peter, who, when it came to fish, was a real eater. But when it came to beans, he was a real farter!'"

Peter laughs, repeats it until he memorizes it to tell his friends at school.

"Come by tomorrow, we'll look for a new pond," I say.

"Okay."

As he heads for his grandpa's house, I carry our fish to the pump house, where I scale and fillet them for cooking later. I have to admit that despite my lack of employment and my general unease with doing nothing but depending on Lila for everything, I am enjoying a blissful succession of days.

When she comes home from her job at the Durham newspaper, where she's a columnist and editor, I take her on long walks. That's followed by an a hour or so in bed reading to her. Sometimes, when it's warm out, she takes the day off and we picnic in a forest clearing where spring waters trickle over stones and fern. On weekends, we pack a bottle of wine and fried chicken and drive to artist colonies. Wild-haired men and supple-bodied women work clay and teach me how to make yogurt. We go to movies, museums and bookstores, linger on the back steps in silence, gazing at the dusk until the stars come out.

Our affection has taken a soft turn, gradually moved from slam-dunk sex to soup-spoon sips: smoky cuddles, wispy caresses, sucking, nibbling, fingertips touching, earlobe nipping and napping to classical music in the late afternoon.

One night when we're in bed reading, she places her book open on her breasts and says, "You love me less, don't you?"

"I don't think so. Just watching you walk around the house in your panties gets the juices running in me."

"But why don't you make love to me? You know, the way you used to? Is it that night, the whips?"

"I don't know . . . I mean, not really . . . but it gave me a spin. Did you know your panties smell like buttered toast and cinnamon? I smelled them. . . ." I blush.

"Orlando, you smell my panties?"

"I'm not a pervert."

"No, there's nothing wrong with that. You can smell my panties anytime you want. When you're sleeping," she goes on, "I sniff your arms, your chest, your face. You have a wild, smoky scent. It reaches down into my soul and I want to go wild on you."

"Why did you choose me, a guy ten years younger? I mean, you could have anyone. It wasn't mercy or pity, was it, or some kind of weird thing with bad boys?"

"Well, I do have a soft spot for bad boys . . . but I don't care about the age difference. It's stupid. If you like someone, what the hell does age have to do with it?"

"So what was it?"

"I didn't know our letters would go the way they did. It was something you needed. You kept toying with the idea, hinting that you loved me . . . wanting to talk dirty. I helped you admit it when you were too scared to. Anyway, I got your name and address from an art newsletter that said incarcerated kids needed pen pals, so they gave me yours . . . and here we are."

"But why did you go for me?"

"Actually, I wanted to encourage you to believe in yourself, to know that there are kind people out here. I was willing to help you, but you turned that desire of mine into a desire, for me to tell you how much I wanted you, sexually. You, my sweet man, sexualized our friendship. That's okay . . . you needed it. But it was, is your innocence, your imagination that really attracted me, turned me on. In fact. . . . Your letters were beautiful . . . made me believe in love again. Healed my heart."

"I don't know what got a hold of me. I went crazy with sex, masturbating every night after I read your letters, imagining us messing around in every position . . . never had a woman that let me do that, you know, talk about it open like that . . . and it just went . . ."

"I was amused when you first moved in. It was chilly outside, but you wouldn't adjust the thermostat. If a window was left open, you left it open . . . or during the day when a light was left on, dishes in the sink, you didn't close the window or turn off the light or wash a dish. You left everything like it was, almost as if you didn't know how to do things. It was very odd. Then I realized you were not used to making decisions . . . that was done for you for years."

∾ ∾ ∾

My outdoors routine gets better after Lila buys me a fishing vest, tackle box with all kinds of cool fishing bait and a rod. I get up and read, write letters to my brother and sister or to a couple of friends in DYA, then make a Spam sandwich, read, nap and fish the rest of the day. I especially enjoy exploring the forest, going for miles through thick brush to discover a beautiful hidden pond. I stand there all day tossing out my bait, looking at the water. Sometimes until the moon comes out.

Doing this heals something in me. It is a good time. I drift emotionally into a zone where all my worries are set aside. Then one day, my fear of impending violence returns, grips me in its bitter throes. Just after I return from a run, I find a community newspaper on the doorstep. A note is attached:

> We don't take to Mexicans mixing with
> our white women—KKK.

I ask Lila what these White nationalists are capable of, but she dismisses them as ignorant meth heads.

"But are they violent? Will they come in the middle of the night, to burn us out? I've seen that kind of stuff in those movies with Sidney Poitier."

"If they try, they're dead. Frog King's reputation is fierce enough to keep them from acting stupid. If they had their way, they'd ban you from sharing the air they think they own, much less just living with me and walking the country they walk."

"So . . . don't worry?"

"They've gotta do better than throwing that rag on the doorstep to make us break up."

"DYA had skinheads, but we kept them in line . . . they never caused problems, except among themselves. They were crazy, had no code, no honor, did anything for money or drugs . . . killed their own brothers.

"My friend Sickle was cool, though. He acted like he hated us Chicanos. I asked him why one day, and he said that his White people were going extinct, they needed to strike back at us, take back what was theirs. We all laughed at him in his funky Star Wars psycho, but he wasn't as paranoid as some of the others."

A couple days later, on a warm sunny morning, I pick up the grocery list and money Lila has left on the table and jog down to Green Mill grocery store. When I pull up in front panting, resting hands on my knees to catch my breath, there's a bunch of guys in plaid jackets, feed-store caps and hillbilly overalls. Two of them are on their knees, one leaning his weight on the back of a turtle, hands firmly planted on its shell. The other guy has a pair of vise grips on the turtle's beak and he leans back pulling as hard as he can to stretch the turtle's neck out. Another man above him swings a hand ax down; it can't cut through the turtle's neck. It keeps bouncing off, and they continue to struggle, holding the turtle in place while the man with the ax continues to swing.

I do all I can not to intervene, which will lead to getting my ass kicked or going back inside. I just watch, wanting to tell them to leave the turtle alone. I now put a face to the type of man who would throw a KKK rag on my doorstep—just this type. I imagine grabbing one of them, showing him how it feels to have someone swing an ax on his neck. Instead I stand with growing contempt.

One of the men turns, gestures at me with his hand holding a beer. "What you looking at, wetback? You got a problem?"

"No," I say. My hands shake with nervous fear.

I'm scared, but I feel a twinge of pride as I walk inside the store for controlling my temper, not spitting back in his face, "Yeah, I got a problem with you."

For once, I do the right thing.

I think it over as I go down the aisles picking up toilet paper and toothpaste. It's a blessing and a miracle that I'm even standing here and witnessing this country store. I have no illusion of ever being free enough of my pride not to react and leap into a fight with these guys or any others. I'm conditioned, used to fighting as the course of action. But I've learned, after reading books, that most people don't react that way. So I'm proud to hold my ground.

My friend Denise would be pleased to see how I handle this, buying groceries and walking home instead of ending up in jail for fighting turtle killers. However, to counter the pleasure I feel in avoiding a conflict, I won't lie and tell you I'm brave, because I'm not. As I stood there with them staring down at me with hateful glares, a frightening expectation of violence overwhelmed me. I envisioned my own demise. It had always been the dread that filled the space between me and my opponents. It wasn't so much the beating in store for me, but that the violent history of my past weighed heavy in the space between them and me. The history of my father's car driving up late at night and me in the bed with my brother and sister, all of us terrified at my father's drunken footsteps as they approached the front of door. Then there was the noise of broken lamps and bodies hitting the floor, screams and growls, me hiding under the covers clutching my sister and brother, waiting in the dark for the moment when the door opened. A slant of light cutting into the darkness, my drunken dad lifting me up, carrying me out like a suitcase into the car . . . or he beating my mother or my mother yelling at him . . .

or so many other dreadful moments that lay like hot coals burning me, scorching me before I even dared think of owning up to my wrongs. I was terrified, filled with the dread of things to come, of the impending end of life, the end of Orlando.

∾ ∾ ∾

It's an incredible morning. I never have heard so many birds chirping madly in the forest behind BJ's house. Blissful September. I am so happy with the gray cast of days, the smell of greens on the air, the scent of toast, coffee. And me? I'm in the first new pajamas I've ever worn. I walk outside, smoke a cigarette, look around with no guard to yell at me. There are no steel cell doors clanging, no intercoms screeching out numbers or work details. Orders for us to shower or eat or sleep or turn lights off don't exist.

I try cooking my first burgers. I end up burning them as I watch crows glean the fields. I make my first salad, take my first bath, plant my first pine tree next to the door, take walks in the morning at my own speed; I don't have to roll out of my bunk at any particular time, can sleep as long as I want. I sit at the table for the first time, eat with Lila to enjoy the green chili soup and fried potatoes I've made. I open the windows to let in the chill September morning scented with the smell of burnt cinnamon from the forest leaf mulch, the aroma of warm dirt giving off its stored resins to the brisk dawn chill.

Cloudy mornings make me feel like writing. I try a poem about the conquistadores coming north, fighting with the Indians, the pueblos in New Mexico, but I end up laughing at my poem because the Indians and conquistadores were making love and trading and living with each other in peace.

There is so much I never knew that there is no way to feel but sorry that I can never catch up. I just resign myself to the fact that I don't know much. I bury myself in books about the Europeans slaughtering the natives, raping women, throwing infants off pyramids, burning entire cities, enslaving millions. . . . I consume enough violence in the pages of Lila's history books to last me a lifetime.

While reading, sometimes I lift my eyes and gaze at the space in front of me. Sometimes a few tears run down my cheeks. Sometimes I bite my lip trying not to cry from gratitude. I am a great pretender, appearing tough on the outside and really vulnerable inside. You have to know this is the way it has to be, otherwise in the aggressive environments I grew up in, I would have been squashed under cruel heels like a cockroach. My cockiness was my defense, and there was no such thing as a supportive environment, essential as it seems for a growing kid. I held my own with a brazen exterior. Also, my resistance to adults who were kind was based on resentment—I could not trust anyone. My defiant thinking showed its fear of kindness. I could not believe people who had not gone through what I had; they were undeserving of my approval or acceptance. I considered them beneath me. I dismissed teachers and counselors offering me constructive feedback, people who wanted to believe in me. I didn't need them, because when I really did, they were never around: after work they went home, had money, food, clothes, went shopping at malls.

I was their paycheck. I paid for their lawns and swimming pools and birthday parties and their kids living in nice dorms or apartments. I was only their work-place kid, their part-time problem. Arrogant, outlaw-cool, I told myself I'd rather get the respect of a thug or someone who beat on me than of a fair-weather stranger only around to collect a check for what he claims is the work he does "helping me."

Despite all of this distancing of myself from those who sought to aid me in my times of distress, to be honest, as much of a risk-taker as I was, I knew I was the luckiest Come Back Kid of all time . . . whether you want to call it God or the Creator, I felt it, felt this thing stirring in me. I was saved by this mysterious uplift in my spirit that always came on when I needed it. I don't know how to explain it, but it was a kindling of growing light in my spirit that filled my thinking with an adamant passion that, if I only had one break in life, I would take the journey to freedom and see what was out there for myself my way.

∾ ∾ ∾

I sit on the doorstep looking up at the stars. Between the stars, I see my brother's face. He's standing on the other side of the fence the night we planned to run away together to grandma's. I knew it wasn't just a fence that separated us.

Back in the early sixties when we were in the orphanage, I never thought about. Nor at Green Mill. It didn't come to me until now, as I write this in 2019. That fence where my brother and I stood that evening, when I begged him to come with me, to climb over and follow me, was much more than a fence. It separated our worlds. I can see his face now before me, his brown eyes filled with fear. I knew he'd be behind that fence forever, that he was gentle and sensitive and caring and loving and that when four older boys raped him, when they beat him up, something that made him a loving child in the world had been taken and burned to ash. I knew for a fact he would always live behind a fence. I understood, looking into his face, that we had to go our own ways in life, that'd he stand there forever behind the mother-fence, his fear fence, behind the drug-fence, always behind a fence afraid to come over into a universe brimming with freedom. See his small, gentle hands clutching the wire with the barbs piercing deep into his palms like a young Christ, the metal thorns digging deeper and deeper as he gripped them with ever more fierce desperation, until they punctured his heart and stabbed at the last hope, bits of his flesh left on the fence like some animal's fur that had tried to escape but failed. His failure was fatal, and he'd do his best to hide from the pain or numb it with drugs. He'd live as a slave to it, always roaming along fence lines, looking over into freedom, under the illusion he was safe, that the adults ordering his day would give him true freedom, would come with wire cutters and send him on; he'd wait forever not knowing it would never come. Still, he believed that things would turn okay if only he obeyed the adults. Instead, I would have the unknown universe to explore, the freedom I dreamed of, the same freedom the crawdads, praying mantis, grasshoppers, deer and rabbits have. Me climbing over that fence that night meant we would live with two different hearts, in two separate countries—one of hope and the other of despair—and that I would be led on by the stars and moon in my life, stars I found I could never get enough of. Many evenings I'd find myself sitting on Lila's stoop, wondering how it could be that all those stars and planets went on forever.

The word forever got me. I couldn't think of something as forever, especially since my whole life up to that point was always broken up into bureaucratic or religious blocks, schedules: wake up, march to Mass every morning at six am; move me here, take me there, move me to the next dorm, the next cell, the next housing unit. . . . Nothing was forever except my imprisonment, my abandonment. When it came to the world and me in it, I lived in the context of waiting: waiting for my mom to come back, waiting for chowtime, waiting for rec field, waiting for my time to get done, waiting for Jesus to step in and save me, waiting for my hurt to go away, waiting for prayers to work their power, waiting, waiting, waiting. . . . Time and how it worked was always in the hands of my overseers. I never controlled it, never had it in my dominion to shape and form and plan a goal at the end of such-and-such a time. *They* decided my life, *they* decided my day, every hour, every minute . . . except when I broke the perimeters and took Time back.

It was one night in 1964. I was six. I stood at the fence boundary of the orphanage. Earlier in the week, I pleaded with my brother to come with me. He agreed, and we planned our escape . . . to our happiness. We'd find our parents. I told him they were being held hostage behind locked doors. He agreed. "Let's save Mom." When the lights were off in the dorm, the nun turned in, closed her door and we snuck out from our separate dorms and met under the apple tree. We walked to the fence; I climbed over, creeped low in the irrigation ditch. All I could think was that the stars would guide us to our parents—that's how it worked in Disney movies, how it worked with baby Jesus being born and the Three Kings. I picked a star that was going to take us to her. I felt like a star, glowing with light in Heaven because I was at last free like them. I rose, leapt out of the ditch, jumped through the fields, panting as I turned to tell my brother, We did it! We did it! But he was not there.

I searched the dark, dashed back, turning along the ditch to the fence to find Camilo standing on the other side.

"What happened?"

"I'm not going, Orlando."

"What do you mean? I know the way, you don't have to worry. It'll be okay. We follow the stars. They'll take us. I talked to God already, and he says it's okay, he'll make sure we're okay."

"You don't even know where Mom is, stupid. She's gone."

I grabbed the fence and yanked it, angrily replying, "No she isn't! She wants us to come save her!"

"Oh yeah, where is she?"

"That's why we're going to see Grandma and Grandpa. They'll help us—they know. And besides, all we have to do is follow the stars. She told me in my dream, I talk to her there."

"You don't even know the way. You're going to be in bad trouble, get the beating of your life or get lost and killed."

"No. Just follow the moon over there. See it, she's waiting on us to go now, so we better."

Camilo lowered his head. He vanished in the dark, headed back to the dorms. I ran fast as I could in the direction I thought Grandpa lived. I looked up at the sky and stars and said, "I'm coming, just don't leave me. I'm right behind you."

I can still do it. Sometimes the stars disappear behind trees or behind hills or buildings, but they always come back up, and I am right behind them.

I felt alive, full of adventure, looked forward to what was coming: the embrace from Grandma, the food, the love, kisses, tears. "Let's run away. Let's run, let's run," I kept saying to myself aloud. And I answered, "Yes, okay, I am doing it."

After hours and miles, the sun rose on the horizon, I found a place under a bridge to fall asleep. I awoke later to someone picking me up. A policeman.

They took me back. Camilo was right: I was beaten with paddles by four nuns taking turns. But I vowed to try again. After I could walk, shower and my welts went down and turned from black to purple to red, I could run. I would.

Many times after that, many paddles later, I ran away, all the way into my seventh year. I ran, kept running, but never found my mom.

∾ ∾ ∾

As the memories recede, I'm back in Green Mill. I haven't changed much. It's mid-September, pines shake with the breeze at dawn, crows swoop and herons glide in and perch on logs in ponds. I'm having the time of my life here, still guided by the stars. I'm out in the wild; on one side the coastal plain, on the other the Appalachian mountains and me in the Piedmont foothills. That's me sitting on a doorstep at night in Green Mill, the same stars burning all over the world as they did on my runaway nights . . . cattails and saw grass, bullfrogs.

I tried it their way—that is, the way of the nuns when they told me prayer had the power to do miracles. I needed those miracles as much as I needed air to breathe. I tried kneeling at the altar, God knows, for days, weeks, months, saying hundreds of Our Fathers and Hail Marys that Father Gallagher gave me for penance. I knew there were some things I could not even talk to God about, like the same Father Gallagher who propped us on his lap, fondled our butts, stuck his fingers in our anuses, played with our penises and sodomized the older boys (my brother included). I had to keep that secret, or God would burn me to a crisp, even if I whispered it.

I knelt on the marble ledge of the side altar knowing all this, certain God had a plan, that it was okay, that were supposed to let Father do nasty stuff; otherwise he might tell God not to bring our parents back. Because he was God's emissary, his servant, God's power came through him to us. So really, I thought, God was fine with him doing that.

I looked up at the life-sized holy ones—St. Anthony, Baby Jesus, Our Virgin Mary—studied their creamy faces with the softest brown eyes, their beautiful, long, slender fingers extended in such a way that I knew they were blessing me. I knelt until I grew calluses on my kneecaps, crossed myself with Holy Water a thousand times, stood erect in the choir loft and sang the loudest any kid ever sang—sang more sincerely, more passionately than *anyone* ever did, thinking the louder I was, the more likely He could hear me and listen.

I studied hard for my first Communion, sunlight stabbing my eyes blind where I stood on the steps in the front of the big building where visitors entered. This was the driveway where the official had dropped us off one night. This was where I then wore a white shirt and black tie and polished black shoes and smiled, squinting my eyes, at the camera. I held a tulip in my right hand, a Bible and black rosary in my left.

Even now, I blame the sun for my tears as I wondered if my mom would show up. It was a special day, almost every kid's family was there: grandmas, grandpas, aunts, uncles, cousins, brothers, sisters—they all came that day. Lines of cars pulled around the oval-shaped, gravel driveway.

She never did. Nights after that, I knelt at my cot, clasped my tiny hands and prayed for the Lord to fix things. I promised to obey Him, even become a priest, obey the nuns and even take on all kinds of extra chores. I'd collect the sheets on the third floor of the main building, where the older boys slept, roll them into huge bundles, tie them and pull the huge bundles down the long fire-escape tube-slide attached to the side of the 3-story building that went all the way down onto the courtyard. From there, I'd lug them to the laundryroom across the courtyard, help wash them, alongside the nuns dressed in white smocks, white veils and white aprons. We'd sweat together in the midst of the big ironing machines, in the billowing steam and acrid detergents. From there, I'd go up to the classrooms, dust-mop hallways to a gleam, then varnish the classroom desks, sweep the three floors of stairs and head to the kitchen to work the massive iron vats for oatmeal, toast dozens of loaves of bread, make cheese sandwiches and push the hot food carts down long corridors to the dining room. Afterwards I'd clean the washroom and pick up the toys in the playroom. Mom never showed up.

One winter day, wrapped in sweater and cap, I buffed the chapel tiles, paused, approached the saints, I begged for love. I wanted for them to show me they were with me, but they did not appear or give me anything. I stared at their placid features smiling down on me. I sat in a pew and wept. I believed I was the worst boy ever born. I must have been, for even saints did not love me. I had made my mother run off. There was nothing left for me to do but run, as fast as I could, into the darkness beyond the fence line; to see what I could find.

∽ ∽ ∽

Now in Green Mill, decades later, I find myself preferring this altar, this benign penance of bookstores and the books within. Books are places without fences. No false Gods. Just human beings working out their problems, some worse than mine, as best they can. There are human beings with terrible flaws, who did wrong to their loved ones, betrayed them, left them, even murdered them. Humans and their wars, people who shocked me by the horror they were capable of, who cried, stole and ran away from their worst fears. They lied, cheated and were all alone in the world.

Lila and I now spend more time together. The days are chilly but refreshing. She arranged her work schedule to work more from home. I like that, I need her around, find the days more pleasant with a woman close to me. I find these to be the best days of my life.

We go into Chapel Hill to visit her friends. I buy my first books: Levertov, Tranströmer, Levine, Alarcón, Baraka, Coleman, Strand, Maggie Estep. We go with her sister Nancy to Ocracoke Island on the Outer Banks, where I fish for Atlantic blues. I visit the home of Thomas Wolfe in Asheville, drive to Raleigh to hear poets read.

Often I am out with Nancy and her family going to the coast, or with her oldest sister Kimberly at Longfield Federal prison facility, where I read poetry to the inmates or with Lila and a poetry publisher in Chapel Hill. Also the neighbor Peter Chambers, his dog Hitman and I tramp around the forest and fish the ponds so brimming with bigmouth bass that we throw many back.

As far back as I can remember, I long to be in Nature. I find myself learning a new dialect, uttered by the wild blackberry bush: new green consonants, bush-bud vowels, mimicking the alliterative chattering of birds in magnolia leaves. The plumage of birds endows me with an ancestral sense of flight. I am privy to the mystery of first-species speech, part of a linguistic habitat babbling all around me: frogs, bass, herons, hummingbirds and mules. The flora and fauna around me form a language in their appearance I understand, and when I am out, I say good morning to them.

I read Lila's mythology books, gain a vague sense of my heritage: Aztec, Mayan . . . Quetzalcoatl, the flying serpent in Aztec mythology, is my God. Quetzalcoatl, heralded as the

God of Dawn or Light, the Plumed Serpent is prophesied to return one day from the East. I believe this: every morning I jog, repeat a prayer to Quetzalcoatl. I don't know why, but I feel Queztalcoatl's presence in the woods, his eyes on me, protecting me from harm. I pray to Him with every mile.

∾ ∾ ∾

Toward the end of September, the bone-crunching cold on the wind numbs my cheeks, sharpens my smell as I inhale distant wood stove smoke. The ground is hard and crusty. From nowhere a darkness falls over the land. Lila suffers a peculiar melancholy with such intensity and rancor it turns her complexion pasty, shrouds the house in a malevolent energy. I don't know what it is. At first, I think I did something wrong, that she's mad at me. I worry even though she tells me it's nothing. She has these recurring fits of depression, they come and go, she says, ignore her if she starts yelling or cursing bad things at me.

I don't understand what she means, but I don't consider her mood swings to be critical. I mean, we all go through stages of sadness and happiness. After the third day, though, it comes to be much more, what I later learn from her sisters is a bipolar episode. I just think she is going crazy—it scares me. She looks at me with murder in her eyes. I sense a spiritual repellent emanating from her. At night I lay in bed feeling its malevolent presence on the floor or creeping up the walls, winding along the ceiling. Heavy stuff.

One night when I go in to sleep, I see a snake on the window screen, crawling up. Another time I find the biggest pack of Japanese hornets I've ever seen under the porch light, each one big as my thumb. I feel sure that, if one stings me, I'll die. Evil things surround me.

The days creep by like crawdads, an emotional chill blows us in opposite directions. Our distance grows. I read a book on the couch, Lila in a chair next to me. I wonder what I'm doing here with this stranger. Once the intensity of our sexual ardor has expired, there isn't really much between us. She hasn't said a single word to me besides cursing under her breath. Her brooding spirals into bizarre looks in my direction. Her angry features reflect an interior conflict. She wrestles with a dark inner force. I wake up at night to find her pacing outside. She's quit reading, won't work on her columns. There's no translating, she won't bathe or shower. She chain-smokes joint after joint, goes through a half carton of Benson & Hedges in three days, locks our bedroom door, isolating herself, stretching on the floor, twisting up, groaning as if in anguish, trying to get something out.

One afternoon, her daddy comes over, talks about these *spells,* warns me with his stone-gray eyes.

"It'll pass, don't meddle none."

"I'm worried," I say.

"They come in no particular way or time. They sort of take over a bit, then the spell lifts and she's fine. This one was due."

I feel the same stomach sickness I felt at the cabin that night. Something is happening out of our control, a malevolent power beyond us, with menacing intentions.

"Oh, she goes crazier than a three-legged hen doing the two-penny jig with a swamp-step frog. You've just sampled the honey . . . the vinegar's a-comin' now."

I see us in the cabin, her tied down on the bed and me whipping her. I feel like some devil was rising around us, taking over our souls. I say nothing.

I think we have love, but it isn't love, not back at the cabin or now. There are stronger, meaner forces at work here, appearing in her eye, in all the crumpled pieces of paper scattered over her office floor, in the empty gin bottles, empty cigarette packs, in her late-night pacing. I sense a demon about. Sometimes she walks around naked as if I'm not even present, patches of skin raw from fresh scratching. The presence takes over everything, every inch of air, ground and flesh. . . .

"Son, do what you're doing. Keep feeling your freedom, and there's plenty to feel, see and do, plenty to write about in that journal of yours. With the *spell,* use that growing you did in that facility—you'll handle it by instinct. Don't hurt her, she's sweet on you and don't mean no harm. It's a chemical thing they say, and you just gotta wait it out. I imagine your patience has been tested more than once on that."

Her mood swings throw me back to DYA, where boys changed from one day to the next. Nice ones became predators, silent ones screamed in horror at night, cowards became gladiators, hard ones fell knees to the ground weeping for mercy and timid ones suddenly grabbed a fork in the kitchen and stabbed the boy seated next to them. The craziness had that bipolar thing in it, like a hair trigger on a pistol that fired unexpectedly, anytime anywhere. Some invisible finger pressed, called, and that bipolar bullet started taking kids out, making them do things you would have never imagined within the realm of possibilities.

It scared me. I often found myself praying under my breath for an angel to watch over me, so I wouldn't be taken too by that bad thing stalking the dorms at night. The whole place filled with a kind of paranoid silence, a yellow pollution from a distant fire that set over a city, threatening at any moment to spread and flare into a huge flame that turns and swallows you up.

That's how it is with Lila. She keeps her silence, and I'm on edge. Then one evening, days later, sunshine throws a blanket of warmth over the land. I come in from a long walk. She is in her bathrobe, smoking a joint. She isn't wearing anything under her robe; it's open but she doesn't seem to notice. Or doesn't care. She lingers at the window with her eyes on the fields that spread from the house to the forest line. She pours us wine, we sit down in the living room, on the sofa against the wall. Her look is sad. She pulls out a letter, reads about some guy's love for his wife.

I say, "That's nice," not knowing where this is going.

She stares at me, then smirks, "You wrote it."

She points to the excerpts on the fridge and says, "You commit yourself to me for life, but it seems like another person had surfaced in the old person's place, trying in attitude and tone to be genuine." She gives me a long look that ends with: "You're playing with me aren't you?"

I tell her what one writes in a cell is different from what one might write on the outside. My letters should be taken in context.

Her glare is bladed with paranoia, drips with the blood of every one of my written promises. They are no longer alive in her heart, but lynched on the tree branches in her daddy's yard.

"You didn't mean it, why'd you write it?"

"I lost control. Any twenty-two-year-old kid would. I just start saying stuff. Nothing more thrilling than writing about sex . . . except doing it. Sorry I hurt you. I didn't mean to. All I can say is I'm sorry."

"You go on about how much you love me, how much you promise to be with me forever, say nothing can change that. I changed my life based on your words, words you vowed were honorable, truthful. I even said goodbye to a man I loved, had been with for fifteen years. I told him I couldn't love him anymore in a sexual way. I believed every word you wrote, Orlando, every . . . word."

"Didn't mean to hurt you. I got caught up. My imagination got away from me, you know . . . language, writing, you new to me—the whole world changed when I started reading and . . ."

"You used this . . . this correspondence . . . as a weapon!"

"No . . . I didn't," I shoot back. "When you've been institutionalized, grow up in the culture of violence, everything, anything is first thought of as a weapon. How can I use this to defend myself? That is the question to every single possession: toothbrush, shirt, shoes, cup, *books*. . . ."

"And why not language? Fill it with lies until you kill love? Is that what you intended? Because that's what it did."

"It was different. I meant what I wrote when I wrote it. "

"Oh, you use your words to fend off predators, but it wasn't your intention to use them against me, these letters to prey on my heart by exploiting me with words I wanted to hear. Yes, your words were a lethal weapon . . . to get inside, execute me with your promises: 'We found each other finally, soul mates . . .' all the other garbage you spewed out."

"If I could take them back . . . if I could go back and undo it all, I would. A lot of the kids write like that, you know. We need someone out here—"

"You used that one already. And I quote, 'to forge them on the anvil of my heart into a Samurai sword and turn it against myself.' I was so gullible. I guess I needed you to say that, to say you loved me when I dreamed of a love like that."

She is crying.

"I realize how you abused me." She wipes tears from her cheeks. "All your words that sounded so sweet and colorful were unintentional lies."

"I didn't mean to . . ."

"Ahhh," she mocks. "And you want me to believe that you thought we'd never quarrel over what you wrote or meant, that I'd be okay with us living together in blissful nirvana with never a cross word between us? After all the lies?"

And then I say the stupidest thing ever. Hearing my words come out of my mouth, I am in disbelief even as I utter them: "To be honest, yes. It never entered my mind at the time that we would ever disagree on anything. There was no way I could imagine us not getting along. Once out, I thought living with you in the country would be paradise, there would never be a problem we couldn't solve."

"Pathetic, Orlando . . . believing that I'd never be in a mad mood, never tired, always ready to pleasure you . . . just be accommodating and happy, cooking, doing laundry."

"Kinda . . ."

"You really are only ten years old, emotionally," she says.

She is right, and right about me being a liar also. I feel helpless. I want to tell her that I am not that kind of person, but she doesn't have any more patience for my good intentions. Her anger lands me smack dab in the middle of the real world, but I keep going, my long-practiced defense system up, ready to spar.

"Listen, it's not that I am not absolutely sincere in what I write you. It's just impossible to anticipate what impact freedom will have. This is a whole new world, I have a new life, and given that newness, I over-reached in my promises. But it doesn't mean I'm not here for you. It's more complicated, not as simple as writing it."

"Words, Orlando. They mean something!"

"The heart thinks bigger than reality is," I say, "it's going to have its way no matter what. I can't explain it."

"You're so full of shit. Did you learn that from Denise?"

"What?"

"Is there something going on between you and her?"

"Just friendship."

"Oh, yeah, I bet! More lies."

"How?"

"How? You've dishonored your words. Do our letters mean anything to you? Oh, forget it . . ."

She gets up and sobs again. Before going into the bedroom slamming the door, she turns. "Orlando, it's you, you're not who you said you were. I want this to work so much. You are *supposed* to come out, go to school, try to be a writer, supposed to . . . you're such a disappointment; you haven't done anything you said you were going to, including love me."

∾ ∾ ∾

The days drag on. Late September mist blankets the forest and fields. A snowstorm follows with a grizzly, ice-raid of sounds of trees cracking that make our misery more cumbersome. Lila deals with this iciness by consuming a lot of weed and gin.

One morning as we sit at the table for the first time in a week, she notes my uneasiness, tells me not to worry about her moodiness, that nice weather is the best therapy. She chalks up her personality change to the evildoings of THE SPELL. We'll work out our problems, she says, I'll learn how to co-exist in a situation not altogether understood by me.

I still can't bring myself to trust her. The change is too sudden. At any moment I expect her to return to the hoary Netherlands in her mind, mining the occult mysteries, she staring at me like a hunted animal fearful of daylight, afraid of going outside.

But no, a couple of days go by and our relationship is replenished. We're friendly again.

But I sink into a sullen space. Under so much recent emotional duress, I can't read. I spend a lot of time outdoors and walk, walk, walk, stumbling in the forest's knee-high snow, among the extraordinarily sculpted icefalls shimmering down in cascades from tree branches. I'm slipping, freezing and admiring the frozen landscape. I track wild turkeys by their prints, wonder, *If I do find them, how can I catch one?*

One day, sitting next to a pond, I start a campfire. I sit there all bundled up, wanting to walk out into the middle of the pond to see if I can do so without falling in. I sit there munching on a tuna and rye sandwich, wondering what the hell is wrong with me.

The guys in DYA would love this. We used to talk about what we'd do when we got out. Lots of them dreamed of being out in the mountains with nature. It was great, but we didn't include life in our daydreams—that is, life with life's problems—while trying to get our reentry going.

Up and down, up and down. Last night another fight. Too many quarrels turn my penitential self-pity to anger, and I begin to feel there is redemption, because I haven't done anything wrong. I am so used to being wrong about everything that a part of me now is trying to figure out how to correct what I don't know I've done or am guilty of. Recently, it seems everything I do is wrong. A part of me is besieged by the feeling that nothing matters. I should just walk away, screw it all, none of it makes sense. Maybe I did intend to hurt her, I don't know. I'm confused.

One thing bothers me above all else: the phrase "You're a disappointment." I know of no words worse than these to mark my heart with a big black X. Say or do anything to me, it won't hurt as much as these words. They seem to sum up my life, describe in the bitterest detail, most piercing pain my very being, the essence of my plagued existence in this world. Christ had the cross, Ceasar the blade; me, these three words.

I have to prove to her I'm not worthless, that I am not a disappointment. She'll see, I'll do something to make her believe in me again.

∽ ∽ ∽

The first week in October brings dark skies, the quietness of coming winter. When you're about to get sentenced to do time in the Youth Authority, you get this feeling that something deep inside you goes to sleep. You say goodbye to the awake part of yourself, *adiós* to another life you dream of living. It's the same feeling I have now.

I carry it for days. I don't talk. Or can't. I call her sisters; they drop by with fried chicken, insist that this moody spell will pass. They tell me to give Lila space, time. Her brother stops by on another morning, offers to take me for a drink after work, but I decline.

Lila and I decode each other's secret intentions by the little changes happening between us: my silences, her silences; me in the room turning away from her before she can hug me; her eyes questioning my cold apathy; then her going into her office, weeping on the floor in the dark.

A tension builds in me as I start to formulate a plan for changing things. I am going to prove to her that I am somebody. As I keep thinking about how to implement the plan, I deflect the disgust that I feel for myself onto her.

I find myself at night in the bed staring into the dark. She knows I am awake, but we don't talk. She asks what is bothering me, and I snap at her. I am angry at myself for allowing myself to get into this mess where she makes all the rules because it's her place, her car, her money.

Several nights a week I grab the car keys and go for a drive. My disdainful demeanor dares her to object. I find myself trolling for a fight, ready to leap at any provocation to accuse, insult or demean her. To avoid arguments, I go on walks or sit on the front step or do something like change the oil, hose the car down, clean or vacuum the interior. Other times, I drive off, park under trees at the back of a field or in a clearing in the forest and listen to the radio, chain-smoke, slap the steering wheel, berate myself for being stupid for getting myself trapped in this affair.

I often go to the pond behind BJ's house, watch the water, listen to the wind in the leaves, marvel at how dragonflies and water spiders live. I count the fish pucker rings breaking the surface, and as I look at the moon, I see what I have to do.

∾ ∾ ∾

October 9th, 1980. Lila feels distraught over the news that John Lennon was shot. It confirms her suspicions that we live in the end of times. Therefore, she needs more weed. I have no feeling either way, since I know so little about the Beatles, except an old memory from back in the orphanage. The nuns took us to a dentist. After we got our teeth cleaned, the dentist gave us all Beatle wigs. I wore mine on the bus back to the orphanage, and people on the sidewalk pointed and smiled as we went by. I remember feeling odd wearing that Beatle wig, thinking it was weird that people liked black beetles, the kind I would pluck from the dirt and play with during recess.

We drive down to Frog King's.

Lila says, "All his cabins have a pond with bullfrogs." She lights another cigarette, exhales. "Why he's called Frog King. He lives in a cinderblock bunker next to his aging, wheel-chair-bound mother, who rarely leaves her mansion. You listening?"

"I've been having the weirdest feeling lately," I say, looking across the fields. "A mild case of pointless paranoia . . . I don't know. I feel it breathing next to me, just beyond arm's reach, I feel it stronger now."

Ten minutes later, we park in a gravel driveway. To the right, a white-columned mansion with a water fountain of a statue of some civil-war military man riding a horse. To the left, a dreary, cinderblock bungalow. In front of us, a row of big sheds where expensive tractors, grime-caked 4x4 trucks and dusty ATVs are parked, along with smaller single-dog pens, open-air lean-tos and field implements. Behind his place, fields stretch out ready to be plowed, seeded.

A dense, industrial grayness hangs over everything. An afternoon breeze clinks the fence-line signs warning "Trespassers Will Be Shot." They are studded with bullet holes. There's a criminal character to it: a stopover where outlaws chug white lightning from plastic milk jugs, recent parolees drop in in the middle of the night to unload crates of stolen rifles, boxes of funny-money printed in a federal prison in Atlanta.

Lila swings the steel door open. I follow her in.

Frog King sits in a corner to my left in a large brown-leather La-Z-Boy recliner. Our eyes meet with the acknowledgment of our previous introduction, when he barged into my house, threatened me, demanded I leave. We say nothing. We understand that remains between us as men. But the second I enter, I know we share something more: the awareness that poverty, anxiety can bend a person's most adamant principles, how flexible the human spirit is when offered a way out of suffering. He knows the dark underbelly of what people are capable of, given the right temptations, enticements. He could find a way to get someone to agree to any crime.

There he sits, all four hundred pounds of him, holding the newspaper open before him. Then he starts laughing, a husky, scalawag chuckle. "Nancy Reagan and John Denver . . . 'Just Say No' is about the stupidest damn nonsense!"

I wonder if the day might come when he leans back too far in his chair, shatters the antique grandfather clock behind him.

As I described earlier, Frog King has the bulk of a bullfrog, is just as predatory in patiently waiting to snatch his victim. Sitting in wait, human weakness buzzes around him, his long tongue unfurls twenty feet beyond his mouth, plucks the unsuspecting man's weakness. His bloated torso, hunched shoulders, brawny neck, redwood thighs make it difficult to get up from his La-Z-Boy to greet us. He throws the paper aside, comments how dry things get around here during Halloween.

"Hell, normally, we get all the weed we want from Florida, tons of Columbian gold bud, but never fails: around October, dry as a eunuch's scrotum," he says. "Can't find it anywhere."

That's when the word comes out of my mouth, the plan I knew was coming into effect, the plan that I had intuited at the pond the other day, the plan that would force my world to flip and boomerang.

He shrewdly dangles the bait. It glimmers midair. He asks if I know where to get weed. My resistance has been worn down by the daily frustration of living in constant need.

I reply, "Maybe," knowing my consent plants enough in my mind that I can't back out, that to him, it's an unwavering yes.

I am aware that an impulsive slip of that one word will dramatically change my life. I'm okay with it.

That one word, *maybe*, makes my mind, my heart amp hot with adrenaline, detaches me from myself, sweeps aside all past promises and moral obstacles. In that split second, my mind's uncertainty learns that self-preservation has two faces—a proud face, a self-loathing one—and he takes note.

In that instant, his malted laughter cements him as a man who finds a person's flaws and uses them to his advantage. He finds mine. He satisfies his wants, he knows the worth of a stranger's conditioning by how he presents himself. He knows we are both part of something dark–call it criminal.

After my implied compliance, to my profound surprise, I begrudgingly find myself in a risk-it-all frame of mind—my heart springing for the first time like a powerful boxer, emboldened by the clarity of my possibilities.

He and Lila talk but I am miles away. I see their mouths move but I am deaf to their voices. They laugh. He shares a story about someone they know. She shows surprise. I notice a book of Lila's poems on the coffee table, wonder when Lila gave it to him.

He notices my look, says, "How the hell do you get those word pictures? Hell of a trick, how you make those pictures out of words. Sit down, sit down. Mind you, there's a cottonmouth loose somewhere around here . . . won't hurt you, more scared of you than you of it."

He offers a glass of moonshine. Lila takes out a plastic milk jug from under the sink and pours a glass for each of us. I drink, making sure not to squint from the burn. I take it down like soda pop laced with blowtorches.

∾ ∾ ∾

Looking back now, seeing myself sitting there on his couch, I know that an hour before entering his bungalow, I would have scoffed at the assertion that I might act against myself out of an instinct more powerful than my own dogged logic.

Looking back now from my house and kids and wife in 2019, I see a divided self. My heart is making the decisions, my heart has always gotten me in trouble, especially when people say I am a disappointment. Shame begs me onto the edge, dares me to jump, and I do. I take the dare rather than stand and face the shame of my being no one.

I remember, ostensibly, in those days I was all about knowing myself. I mean, after all the isolation, condemnation I'd gone through, I thought I knew myself pretty well. Then somehow, the truth was that being a nothing in life was far worse than all the suffering and sorrow I endured.

My mind keeps asking, Why didn't I just say no and keep going with the promise to myself that I could make a good life out here without entering into a criminal hustle?

Looking back, I could have said without reserve, "Not interested." But I didn't. Someone in me, from life-long conditioning, deals the cards, and I stack the chips. That's it. Done. I'm in the game again.

I am over the fence again.

Baffled by how I offered my services so easily, I feel shock that I blindly believed there was no way I'd ever go back to crime.

I marvel at how inconsequential my principles were. While I thought I was operating on and guided by a system of integrity, deep down in my unconscious brain a whole new clandestine engagement was functioning and thriving. Apparently, it stewed there until ready to be ladled out to my hungry criminal heart, willing to sit at the table, make an offer.

There in front of Frog King, the whys, whats, wheres, whens of my journey into a forthright life fracture. I am disappointed to find myself so unpredictable. If there was ever a young man with two glaringly obvious, disproportionate states of character, it is me, laired up in my loathsome stench of cowardice.

I suppose I want to acquire meaning by any means necessary.

On my reentry, I thought I could willfully impose a path of action, garner the gumption to follow it, adhere to my ethical determination. But as it turns out . . . in the bones, in the muscles, in the eyes, hands, feet, tendons, nerves, in the blood, in the imagination's kaleidoscopic circuitry, I am a criminal—as society claims, as all those counselors, teachers, police opined—nothing more than a prairie bramble, thorn-bred hustler with the bastard-virus of an avenging despair in my criminal heart. I see as the one-eyed owl does because the other one has been shot out by the justice system.

Inside Frog King's place, sitting on his cheap couch, I feel I am a make-believe man, decomposed into instant gratification, with no fortitude, no foundation. Here I am talking to a man who has millions, and every single penny came by way of criminal activity. Because he has lawyers and accountants willing to corrupt the law, because he's White, connected to the good ol' slave-working White Boy network, has a brother who is a senator—a real shining knight to the born-again Christians and Evangelicals who kneel, kiss the rings on his fingers—he acts with impunity.

I don't complain? In fact, I want to indulge in the bounty. There is no ethical substance in me that I can claim. What distresses me at that moment, though, is that I realize everything is up for sale. This sentiment repels my heart because I have always wanted to be known as a man *con corazón*, with heart. I value honor.

I want, despite everything, to be true to myself, unchanging, known for my good word. I hate this trait of weakness in me that allows me to dissolve my promises, throw all my day-to-day discipline and the belief in myself out the window. In that moment of loss of self, I go from no one to someone. I have a role in the world now.

It would have been so easy to keep my life simple, focused on school, dedicated to getting employment. Yet, in that moment, it seems so easy to ignore my promise not to get back into the game because it alleviates the day-to-day tensions, confusions of enduring Lila's mood changes.

∽ ∽ ∽

The illusory promise of our old letters declares their sanctity a bad joke. The words explode like landmines triggered by each new day. The words drop from the sky like dead finches. The words melt like a thousand red candles with their wax dripping like blood on the paper. The bleeding between us continues to illuminate our dark resentment, nothing can salvage the cindered remains of our promised love.

I reconcile myself to the war of attrition, forget how I want things to be, accept how they are. Move the hell on, even if it is into the dark regions of the criminal world.

No one warns you about the That's Life principal, working so heartily, intricately in all manner of interaction upon release and reentry. I never heard it from anyone. All I ever heard was that my reentry was going to be hard, but you can do it, you can go to school, get a job that you like, make good money, make new friends.

All of that . . . *puro pinche pedo*.

Instead, they should have warned me about the reality of reentry: when you apply for a job and don't get it 'cuz you got a record. That's life. What about school grants? Can't because you're a delinquent. That's life. People don't trust you 'cuz you wear this invisible veneer that says you're contaminated, you carry the virus of having been locked up, you're not to be trusted. That's life. Or that you want to learn to love this woman but don't know how, never was socialized to trust, never had a healthy relationship. That's life. Every door gets slammed in your face, you can't pay your bills or rent, you have to rely on a woman to support you. That's life.

What are you taught through lived experience? Sometimes the only thing that'll give you a brief respite from the misery is a line of cocaine and a shot of good whiskey. They help you fend off your fear that everything you wanted to achieve you won't, that it will never happen. . . . That's Life.

Real life is Frog King giving Lila a half-filled grocery bag of weed. She and I drive back with it. I look out the window, even thinking about Frog King, I feel his eyes on my back.

We pass black folks gathering in a yard, I watch with envy, know I just forfeited that life. Dogs bark after our car. Black laughter fills the air. Freshly barbered, in colorful blues, greens, two-tone shoes, black high-heels, they lean on their polished used Caddies, wave. I wave back.

I gaze at the forest meadows and reflect with brutal pragmatism that as much as I want to live a crime-free life, as much as I want my reentry to society to work out, I don't have the moral wherewithal. Perhaps the truth is, I have no business in the straight world.

The ruthless reality is I'm living off Lila's kindness. Why? I still can't make it. So why prolong the torture? My life at this moment, even from the perspective of later decades, seems so abstract, profoundly ungrounded, that the only real, intelligent course of action is to get some money, throw some cash down on a fixer-upper shack and start a business with Camilo.

And get away from Lila and Frog King.

Go home.

5

I'M RESTING IN MY LEATHER CHAIR in my sunroom, May, 14, 2019. Most of the day I worked with the crew I hired to install a new sprinkler system, because my twelve-year-old daughter wants one. Her dream is to run through the sprinklers, then lay on the grass under an umbrella with her school friends, listen to songs on the radio and scroll through her Instagram.

Since I found that picture of me at DYA, dressed out in institutional denims with a lonely look on my face as if the whole world were out to get me, I've rummaged through boxes in storage to find more pics. I find one of me, younger, before my mother left, maybe I'm four or five. There I am, standing in front of her, leaning back against her legs, tall as her knees, leaning back into her as if I am holding her back, as if I sensed she would leave soon. My fists clutch her dress tightly, the blue cotton knots up in my tiny fingers, as if saying, "You're not going, you're staying."

My brown eyes are huge, like cups of liquid moon shining in the dark, as if they can fit the whole universe into them. I'm looking up at the camera, telling it she's mine, she's mine, I keep her to myself. My eyebrows lift a little, my eyes keep looking at the camera: "No, you can't have her."

She has her hands on each of my small shoulders. She smiles a forced smile, as if aware of a menace beyond the picture. Her blue eyes have a healing in them, an inner blue bruise on the mend. And that look of mine, innocent and soft, asking for the world to leave us alone, to let us be, that look of supplication becomes a lament over the years, sensually imbuing my days with an emotional plea to the world for mercy, for understanding, for a kindness that never comes. Over time, that look morphs into a cold stare of accusation that the world has betrayed me. Anyone looking at the next picture of me in DYA in denims would want to keep me locked up forever.

I emanate a brazen defiance, my hair combed back pachuco-style. Like the actors in *West Side Story*, my rebellious, haughty posture says to the camera, "*Soy Chicano.* You think I care?" Nobody serves up a cold-hearted snack of I-don't-care like me. My eyes say, "Nothing to live for."

But you do, Orlando. You longed for a life with someone to love you. And now? Now you decide to go back into the game, even if it goes against all you ever dreamed of doing with your life. Why? All Lila ever really wanted was for you to abide by your written words, to get a job, go to school, settle into the routine of daily living. But you were too afraid to look for a job because you didn't know how to answer questions, how to fill out applications, how to enter an office, sit before a stranger, ask for a job. You thought you could only wash dishes or dig a ditch. You were too afraid to sit in a classroom because you were never taught to sit in a classroom. You would have loved it, but you were too afraid the kids would laugh at you, mock you as being stupid, jeer that you were crazy. You rationalized their rejection of you by telling yourself you were too far behind to ever catch up. Besides, you were not like other kids, so you went back to what you knew because you're so afraid of the world, you couldn't bring yourself to share that with anyone.

What happened to all your day dreams, your looking out of your cell window, vowing to yourself that this time it would be different? This time you wouldn't be a disappointment. Remember how every night between the hours of six and eight you'd stand at the bars of your cell, feel as if the hell you were in would never end, you prayed, begged, beseeched the Lord to help you make it out. Once out, you'd change. Now this?

Your life was a sideshow, and you lived in that sideshow purgatory, always behind the curtains, watching the event of life at center stage go on without you, you peeking through the curtains at the people living life.

How you feared that world, the people in it, how you ached to get as far away from it as possible. That you might actually do something else. That you might learn how to live without being a criminal. That you might save your life by creating a better one. You hoped so badly for that salvation. That you might abide by what you wrote in the letters expressing your desire for a good life, that people might be proud of you, that you might raise your arms to heaven like a convert, changing everything about your life, recovering the truth in yourself, feeling wonder for the day again, making that wonder a common feature of your day-to-day life. How you would serve your community, how people would be happy to see you, be next to you. You'd find yourself growing deeper, more meaningful, appreciating yourself, feeling centered, grounded, swaying to the rhythms of the stars and releasing your jealousy, resentments, anger—embracing your loving self, ceasing to do what others expected, following your own heart, so you could leave behind your disguise as a hardened youth, a tough thug, become a beautiful, amazing you.

∾ ∾ ∾

The question of how to bring up a load of marijuana festers in my mind. I rehearse each proposition, decline it and think of another plan, test it, question it, think of alternatives. I know that if I can only get one load up here, I'll have enough money to set things straight, buy a used truck, help out Lila, maybe even have enough to pay for a return trip home to live with my brother and get a job going.

It helps my thinking to be out and about. I spend a lot of time fishing the ponds, crossing blacktop roads where Mexicans and Central Americans toil in the tobacco fields and chicken plants. I wave, they wave back.

I know a few. Lila is friends with their Anglo wives and they sometimes come over for dinner. Bending with short hoes, they pause, in a friendly way kid me to join them, to do some real work. I smile back, hold my rod up and vanish into the forest in search of another pond.

Depending on the harvest time, there's maybe a dozen or so; heads, necks, the entire face veiled in grimy cloth to protect against the sweltering heat, toxic pesticides and insects. No matter how hard they work, you can see the Mexicans were not getting rich; their battered trucks, rusting cars filling the parking lots at pig farms, meat packing warehouses, dairies, slaughter houses, chicken, egg farms, all types of construction industries. . . . Not only men. I see the blood-smudged faces of children coming out of warehouses where they slaughter pigs. Women arrive at dawn, truckloads of them, to work at dairy farms. In the fields, I see scores of laborers—children, women, men—stooping over plants, trimming, hoeing, cutting and picking. It's modern slavery.

I feel bad for them, starting with my very first ride from the airport when I arrived in North Carolina. The brown people were blurry in the distance, hunched over in the shimmering heat, shrouded figures wearing cloth headbands, masks, sombreros and baseball caps, carrying baskets of fruit, berries, carrots, beets or onions to flatbeds to be weighed-in.

All of their used cars are parked parallel to the rows. Coming back from a day of fishing, I see them sitting in tents in camps that lack sanitary facilities. They have no clean water and little of anything else. At least at DYA we had water and lunch breaks.

Imagine cooking every day on a portable butane stove. Imagine water for all your needs poured out of jugs filled at a nearby field faucet. Imagine living on a bare diet of tortillas, beans and rice. Imagine the heat. If you get hurt or bit by scorpions or cottonmouths, there is no medical recourse; you just keep working through the illness. You cannot afford to stop. You work until you drop or die, through the unbearable heat, inhuman conditions and miserable wages. Kids miss school, adults hide from La Migra like escapees and white bosses exploit them in as many ways as their limited imaginations can scheme up.

I know all this about them but don't talk about it. In fact, I try not to think about it, force it out of mind, but I know if I want to get real with myself, I have to admit that these people are prisoners. In concentration camps, white bosses get wealthy off their slave labor. More than once, Lila goes out to read paperwork for them, advise them of their rights. She drives them to the emergency room, brings them towels, diapers, sanitary napkins—the basics for a meager life. She translates for them, speaks on their behalf in court, helps register the kids for home tutoring programs at night, drives them to Walgreens to get them medicine, sets up appointments with the immigration service, finds civil rights lawyers for them and fills police-abuse claims for them against whites who routinely rape the women or embezzle their pay.

If I could help I would, but I don't know how. Then, my plan starts to materialize with an opportunity that drops into my lap the day after my meeting with Frog King. Two guys pull up in two pick-ups and drop off five grand in a paper lunch sack. One of the pick-ups is the same one with a camper shell that Frog King had brought over before, when he wanted me to leave town. Now, he wants two hundred pounds of weed.

After the rain, it smells so good Rodrigo and I, a field-worker friend of ours, sit under a huge magnolia tree, having a beer. Later, we walk over to the pump house to hang out as we do once or twice a week, drinking and talking about Mexico. When I mention my problem, he says he knows where to pick up marijuana.

He seems honest enough, I know he won't run off with the truck and the money. He just had a baby, his wife is still in the hospital. They need the extra income. So I ask him to make the run to the border and back. I pay him enough to cover their hospital bills. He has contacts, he promises the weed is good. I give him the five grand and the truck and wave goodbye. He tells me he'll see me in about a week.

∽ ∽ ∽

October weather is bizarre. The news keeps warning of hurricanes in the Atlantic that can hit North Carolina. Rain. Sleet. Snow. One evening, the trees collude in the illusion of creating a gothic castle, where a menacing spirit abides in the pendulum blades of icicled branches. Light drips. The woods turn black. Trees crack in deep throes of agony, and the earth turns from autumn, readying for the coming winter.

Summer returns for two days. I pass the General, a massive bass, suspended in water just under the surface. He floats around the spill-over pipe. Brandon has staked his claim on the leviathan bass and has warned me never to catch him myself. But that bass is always there, gloomily brooding with those epic, bulbous eyes, just below the surface, staring up at me. On that clear morning, I see all the hooks and spinners flashing from its lips and mouth, evidence of its dismissive arrogance to Brandon's repeated attempts to snag him.

I read *Black Elk Speaks,* Peltier's prose and Trudell's poetry to find some wisdom to extricate me from this quandary. Lila and I find ourselves at home. I expect Peter to come through the door at any moment. I repeat a prayer in my head over and over, a prayer asking Black Elk for blessings.

Soon, Peter and I walk to the pond behind his grandpa's. It is quiet, tranquil. We fish. Fat insects buzz in the air. We kick back behind the cattails on the bank, I tell him about circling a pond last evening and running into my first cottonmouth, coiled up in an exposed tree root by the bank.

The weight of the green- and yellow-leaf world weighs heavy on the air. A cauldron of green trees, green expanses all drip, spring, climb, fan, wave, crowd, push and claw forth like hordes of starving prisoners abandoned by their keepers. As if commemorating the change of seasons, the damp, green world explodes from its pressured confines and foams from the dirt, erupts into the air, careens everywhere; dense, pressed, packed. One second it riots wildly; another instant it bellies underground only to come crawling feverishly up to the raw concessions of lofty trees in the next moment, creating walls of lush green blossoms, leaves and branches in every direction.

I see something stir on the far side of the bank and pucker the surface. The water ripples, bubbles appear next to a big log, half in the water. A white crane floats in above the treetops, perches on the log for a minute or two, then flies off. I reel in, toss, aiming for the log. I feel a soft nibble. Peter sees the whole thing happen. He drops his rod, comes up beside me, instructs me to yank my rod back, reel in, snap the rod back . . . but the line is limp. I reel in the loose line. I've lost whatever it was.

Then I feel the slightest tremor coming through the slack line into the rod. I keep reeling. Then I see it. I toss the rod back, wade in, grab the line, start pulling as fast as my hands can move. Peter is behind me. He picks up my rod, reels the slack line in as fast as the spool can spin. I reach both my hands into the water, grab the hooked line just above its mouth. I drag the fish to the bank. It does not put up a fight. Not one flap in defiance, as if trained to come to me calmly, recline in my hands and surrendering peacefully.

Yes, it is Brandon's. The General. What's done is done.

From tail to head it is at least a foot longer than Peter, who is tall for his eight years. I take my belt off, pull it through its gill and give it to Peter to carry home. He slings it over his shoulder, tail brushing the ground. Back home we put it in the tub. We fillet it in the pump house, and then I cook it in the oven. I'll never forget Peter and me at the table, along with a few other Mexicans from down the road. They keep repeating that I should have weighed it at the store, because it probably was a new North Carolina record for the biggest bigmouth bass caught in a pond.

When Brandon comes through the door, his face has an expression of disbelief. All he can say is, "No, you didn't, you didn't. . . ." And then, "Fuck it."

He takes his soiled baseball cap off, runs his hand over his balding head. His blue eyes behind his spectacles stare at the culets on the table a while before he joins us. As he gets drunk, he talks about everything from good weed to girl-friends and, of course, to fishing. He has me retell the story a hundred times of how the fish put up no fight, no fight at all.

I say, "Well, Brandon, you know, I saw the General almost every day. He likes to swim around the overspill pipe and catch bugs that drift toward him. I've watched water spiders gliding on the water, and the General gulp them in with his huge lips. He resembled one of those brawny, muscled dock workers in black and white movies. No, he looks more like a saber-tooth tiger with fins. He was huge, with all kinds of broken lines, hooks, metal reflectors stuck on his lips. I tell you what, though, he had to be one smart fish to break that many fish lines . . . also, he seemed to know I was standing up on the bank looking down at it.

"Standing there by the overspill pipe, its big eyes would ogle me . . . big bulbous marbles that lazily protruded from its head. They stared at me with a smile in them. Brandon, buddy, I didn't mean to catch him."

∾ ∾ ∾

It is a good break from the crap Lila and I were suffering. Despite the seasonal changes, nothing changes much between her and me. I don't ask her why this is happening or to try to comfort her. I close the door to our bedroom, turn on the bedside radio, listen to AM hate: white guys ranting about how America is theirs. "Blacks and Browns" are destroying it, even as whites murder and ravage communities of color. I can only tolerate it for a minute or two, then I change the channel to the liberals on NPR spouting their wisdom from high above the people of color. They don't see their own biases or entitlement. Both White Hate Radio and NPR carry the same thrill for me I experience at a carnival when I peek into the freak tent.

The October days come and go with dungeon-door finality. I slowly admit I am in debt to Frog King even more. I decide to drive down to break the news. I borrow Lila's car, go by myself. I tell him straight out I got ripped off. I don't know what to expect, but it's certainly not the response I get.

He whales out his barrel-chested, heave-ho guffaw, growls, "I'll be damned." Then he says, "Well, what the hell, here's another five grand. I'll see you when you get back."

At the house, I go through my papers in my boxes, search for the slip of napkin where I had written the numbers of my friends when I got out of DYA. I find it and call.

"Who is this?"

"Who's *this?*"

"You think this is a TV game show? Who's calling?"

"Is Chuy there?"

"Maybe . . ."

"Orlando!"

"*Ese güey!* I didn't recognize your voice. How the hell you been, *vato?*"

I feel an old excitement in my chest like a tornado's just touched down, blowing away everything that isn't rooted by God.

∾ ∾ ∾

Chuy is at the airport in Dallas to pick me up. Despite all his former tall tales of money and nice cars, he has neither. He drives a '63 Impala with no brakes. Chuy is short, maybe five-feet-two; the huge car dwarfs him so much that when he drives, it seems like a child is sitting on a milk crate in the driver's seat, clutching the steering wheel, just barely able to peer over the dashboard.

"*Pinche, ¿qué chingao está haciendo, vato?*" He has a single front gold tooth that shines when he smiles.

"What have you been doing?" I ask.

"Hustling, selling a little heroin and weed for pocket change. Keeps my habit fed, my girlfriend happy. And you?"

"Not much, just gotta clear up a mess I made."

"With that chick? I thought for sure you'd never get back in the game." He slaps my arm. "*¡Pinche vato!*" He teases me with a little half-grin, shaking his head.

"Not with her, Chuy."

"Same old ups and downs."

Small he might be, but no one to mess with. He wears blue oval shades, has a line of blue, tattooed tear drops going from the corner of his left eye down his cheek. He's got nicks and scars, a head full of black thick hair that he constantly combs—in the car, in a café or standing outside on the side-walk. His hands are always busy smoothing his hair. He is meticulous in his mannerisms, impeccable in his dress. A Chicano *locote* to the *huesotes* (bones), he's done serious time. He looks small on the streets, but behind the walls and in the know he is feared. And pity anyone about to step on his spit-shined shoes.

Added to this list of congenial attributes, he is a heroin addict—*un tecato*. He has the suave look of an Arab Prince assassin; he just doesn't have the money or power. He's as ruthless as a banker when it comes to slapping interest on a loan, cunning as a Wall Street broker when it comes to de-ception, evil as an insurance CEO—all the characteristics that give him longevity and success in the criminal world.

As remarkable as his looks are, they are the least of his charisma. It is his walk, talk and facial expressions. Hard to explain. His walk is the Constitution with all the Bill of Rights; it's a kind of rooster's cocky swagger but in a side-ways statement. He throws his weight to his left foot, swings his right leg and hip around. Neither Benjamin Franklin nor Thomas Jefferson could exert more authority in their walk than Chuy. Hamilton might, being a street urchin himself— both had it down.

I'm saying his bearing was brazen defiance; it took years in reformatory to learn how to strut like that—a warship emerging from the mist, everyone in its radar radius a rowboat. He has that kind of samurai-sword confidence. Chuy is flypaper to women. White, Ivy League, black, fish-stockinged ones stick to him.

And the way he speaks, with the provocative cajoling of a mentor to his student, with the edgy humor of a pimp, plying out the approval or agreement under duress. Nothing, I mean nothing, is ever anything to him. "Ain't nothing but a meatball," he says, whether it's robbing Fort Knox or invading a country like Mexico to hijack the cartel's load of cocaine or money—*ni madre, me lo pelan*, nothing but a meatball.

He doesn't put much importance on any crisis, everything is insignificant. He can glide himself through any catastrophe, ain't nothing but a meatball. He usually doesn't deal with weed, only the hard stuff, but there's someone he knows, *El Tote* (pronounced toe-tay), and we're going to see that guy. As we drive through Dallas, I reflect on the last time I cruised in a low-rider to pick up a load of weed in a Dallas barrio, when I was festering with poverty, had no money, food or lodging. I had promised myself then it was the last time.

"*Pendejo*, glad you're here."

I look out the window at the worn clapboards and stuccos, and think, *God only knows what I'm getting myself into again.* Unsupervised snot-nosed kids playing in the dirt, drop-dead gorgeous girls swinging on porches or hanging out on steps or on the hoods of cars while baby crew-cut thugs drink forties, pose in khakis and wife-beater shirts, religious medals hanging from chains around tattooed necks. There is a pervasive stink of oil—oily smells, oily ground, oily gravel driveways, oily sidewalks and oily pavement. Even the elm leaves have an oily residue, the grass blades an oily film.

No matter what my dilemma is, I know Chuy's response will be, "Ain't nothing but a meatball, *ese*." I know in his heart, it saddens him that I'm back in the game. I disappoint.

When we arrive at the gas station, Tote is leaning against a Coca-Cola machine while he wipes his axel-greased hands on a mechanic's rag. I notice three young wanna-be gangsters around him, whispering, looking spooked. They turn to Tote, who shakes his head. Looks like they're trying to convince him of something, but he's against it. One guy walks off, the other two reluctantly follow, then all look back at Tote. He shrugs as if to say *No-can-do*.

Tote is huge, a giant bowl of menudo. I figure, four hundred and fifty pounds. His hair is cropped close to the scalp above his toast-complexion skin. Everything about him is round, if he tipped either way, he'd roll and keep rolling. His eyelids are layered skin; when he opens his eyes on you, it seems like a long time until they actually fully open to shroud you with their lazy but shrewd suspicion.

We park, walk up to him. Chuy gets right into it.

"Yeah, *vato*," Tote says, "I can get all the weed you want. And no, I don't have any on hand."

Yes, he'll give us a great price, but he has to call his brother M on the border in McAllen, Texas. M will drive it up. Maybe a week, maybe two, depends on what's going down at the border.

Chuy says he'll drive down to get it, so I give him the money. He agrees to drive it all the way up to Green Mill. He's excited to go into business with me. We have history, backed each other up in fights inside. You get to know a kid when you see him stripped of his dignity, stomped, kicked and in the face of it all, he pulls the old mule-teeth hee-haw on his tormentors, pisses them off enough to make them swear they'll kill him.

∾ ∾ ∾

On the flight back to North Carolina, I consider how the world is below me, an earth, round and filled with billions of people, all are striving to make a life for themselves. Some make it, others don't. Here I am, twenty-two-years old, trying to put together a lousy deal that will pay off Frog King and make a little cash on the side for me to get something going with my brother.

I don't know whether to clap with optimism or sit down, lay my head on my knees and cry. No matter what, I have to go on with it. I've committed myself. I fell into the trap of owing Frog King. He knew exactly how to play a desperate man.

Lila picks me up at the Durham airport that evening. The first thing I do when I get home is wrestle on the floor with Griselda, take her for a walk, nap with her in my arms on my bed. The unintended consequence of my absence is a widening gulf of silence between Lila and me, but having Griselda to dote on eases my distress.

A few days later, I'm standing at the screen door when Chuy drives into the yard. He gets out of his car with all the pomp and triumph of a returning champion entering an arena in front of thousands of adoring fans applauding his victory and streaming confetti. We drive the weed to Frog King's. I figure once we deliver the load, I'm free of the debt I owe. I not only plan to give him the weed, but also use my portion of the profits to pay for the truck Rodrigo stole. The biggest reward for me is getting free of the debt to a backwoods mafia don.

I carry the two hundred pounds into Frog King's bunker, stack the bricks four high and take a seat on the couch. I stare at the columns of two-pound bricks wrapped in brown butcher paper, wonder how weed has become so valuable. So many people smoke it I guess. On top of the TV sits a rattlesnake ashtray filled with bullets. It seems like wherever there is space—couch, side tables, desk, dinner table—there are pistols and bullets. I sit facing his big La-Z-Boy chair, once again note the elegant, burnished, cherry-wood grand-father clock—time stopped at 12:45 pm. Must have been the time he leaned too far back.

I can hear farm commotion outside: tractors crossing the compound, trucks going by, farmhands yelling, dogs barking. The door swings open, the foreman, wearing a red feed-store cap, plaid shirt and jeans, asks, "He around?"

I shake my head no.

Mexicans are not expected to talk. To redneck tobacco farmers, pig and chicken farmers—all of them wearing American flag patches—Mexicans are beasts of burden, not human enough to have the capacity to think and speak. We do the work, disappear at night, show up at dawn, do the work and vanish into the night again. It's the way of things in a regime run by white racists whose ancestors were slave hunters and plantation bosses.

He looks at the bricks, smiles and walks out.

I sit until Frog King's figure shadows the doorway, huge in his denim overalls and plaid shirt, filling up the doorframe.

"That your buddy?" he says, pointing over his shoulder at Chuy in the car.

His slip-on boots are enormous ship hulls, discolored at the toe humps and molded out to bear the weight of his giant frame leaning forward; his immense foot-pads flatten out and strain the round edges of the soles with constant pressure. He trundles forward, with a sigh plunges down like a huge wave into his La-Z-Boy. He dusts off his cap, slaps it against his thigh and grins large.

"Whatcha got there?"

"Two hundred pounds of Mexican weed. I have to take off now, my friend's anxious to get back. Oh, keep my end of the money for your truck." It's that quick.

"Wanna drink of white lightning?"

I lift my right hand. "Gotta pass."

In a second, I'm in Chuy's passenger seat, speeding past fields and trees, hugging the blacktop, going back to my red-brick house. No sooner are we in the yard than the phone rings. Frog King tells me to come back.

Ten minutes later, when we drive into his yard, in front of us there are a dozen goats chewing the butcher paper the marijuana was wrapped in, green gobs of marijuana stalks sticking out of their jaws. Bricks are scattered on the ground.

"*Pinches locos*," Chuy curses, unable to contain his smirk that these rednecks are completely nuts. He gives a smug chuckle. "Who in the hell would feed *mota* to their goats!"

I go inside to see Frog King in his chair munching on a sandwich.

"Damn goats won't even eat that scrap. You brought me scrap!" His voice splits open like an ax cracking hardwood. "I'll be damned!"

His whole face, gouged dark with menace, suddenly opens with enormous delight, as if the whole episode is genuinely humorous. He roars with laughter.

The weed was no good. Should I go outside, collect it from the goats, take back what isn't eaten, demand a new load, tell them I won't pay one red cent more? They screwed me with this trash. I don't know what to do or say.

"Ain't nobody buying that." He pauses, chews, continues. "I'd say, run on back, get some weed we can sell." He gives me a momentary chilling stare, then covers it with a smile. "What d'ya think?"

His foreman walks in. "What do we do?"

"Get it the hell out, put it back there with the hay, maybe them damn cows'll eat it."

When I get back home, Chuy and I call M and tell him the situation. He surprises us by offering to come up with three hundred pounds, adding that we have to have just half the money ready.

"The weed better be good," I emphasize.

"Tops," he says, adds they are taking off tonight. Expect him late tomorrow. They're going to drive sixteen hours straight.

I know that M knows this can turn out to be one lucrative connection, but he has to deliver the goods. He isn't going to let this connection go, so he's going to work it for every penny. Even if it means replacing every pound of trashy Mexican weed for high grade.

Chuy takes off back to Texas after I assure him that we're going to make some money, I'll call him soon. That's when M and I go into business. I first meet the driver, Centavo (Spanish for penny), called so because his belt, his bowie knife, its sheaf and his boots are all decorated with rows of Indian head pennies—collector's items. He's thin, angular-boned with sharp facial features, a menacing figure with a trimmed beard, black uncombed hair, very dark eyes and a complexion the color of brown leather.

Centavo shows up in a truck stashed with weed, with M following behind in a car. The same day he arrives, Frog King has it sold. The deal goes down right, and Frog King orders more. M wants me to come down, drive it back with him for a considerable discount, I agree. I like him, see the opportunity to make some money. It affords me some respite from the painful silence I'm experiencing with Lila.

I borrow a truck from Frog King, soon I'm making a trip a week to McAllen, Texas, driving the lead vehicle with the weed, M following behind. I plan on saving money to buy some fixer-uppers, tools, work trucks for Camilo and me. I want to pay for his rehab. When the time is right, I'll head west to start our business. Since the money keeps rolling in, I keep smuggling in order to make my plans a reality.

∾ ∾ ∾

October in Texas and up past New Orleans is nice and balmy, but once you hit Tennessee, the cold grinds down, makes the landscape rainy and muddy. Highway wrecks litter the roadside with cars sliding on black ice—I have to be careful.

When I get in, no one is home. I cross the road, ask Peter where they are, he says they went to Frog King's for some kind of election celebration. A party for Frog King's brother, who was reelected senator.

"Frog King's mother's house?"

"Yeah, that's it." Peter smiles.

When I get there, there are so many people arriving that I have to get in line, wait behind others to enter the mansion his mother lives in. A folding table is set up under a magnolia tree, flood lights bathe the green lawns and rose garden.

When I get to the entrance, I have to stop at the table before I can enter. I think they're going to give me a pass or something, but these two women and a man seated on folding chairs ask me for a donation. I tell them I have no money.

"Credit card will do. We accept that too," she pushes.

I shake my head to indicate I don't have credit cards and walk past them. Inside, balloons float overhead tied to congratulatory post cards. Politicians in tuxedos laugh and toast each other. Senator Booker's face smiles from wall posters, placards that kids race past, soaking them with squirt guns.

Black porters roam. Valets hurry back and forth parking luxury sedans. Twang-talking gentry in expensive suits shake hands, slap backs.

I walk over to the foreman, he points me in the direction of the back patio. Large stadium lights beam up the gardens in back, Chinese paper lanterns float around a swimming pool, cast iron Civil War heroes on horses carrying a Dixie flag scan the wide expanse of shrubs and hedges, laughter and delighted shrieks bubble around the looming white pillars of the porch decked out like massive candy canes.

I follow a flagstone walkway to another building, Lila notices me the second I step inside the auditorium–sized room, where dozens of people cluster amid waiters carrying silver trays with finger food. She sees me, then turns as if she doesn't want to talk to me and continues her conversation with several women in elegant gowns. I go through the throng.

I scan the crowd until I see a man who looks like Camilo. He grabs several glasses of champagne from a waiter's tray and gulps them down. As I go up to him, he sways off balance. I catch him. Thinking me a stranger, he turns aggressively, then recognizes me and hugs me.

He and a woman close by him look like tweaked-out grunges in rain slickers with hoodies tied tight under their chins, grinning as they grab finger food and snatch more drinks. They're blitzed, grated by drugs, shredded by too many meth-charged weeks, but that doesn't seem to faze the joy on Camilo's face at seeing me.

"Where you been, little brother!"

I don't say, "Down in Texas, in Robstown, waiting for another load to cross."

"Well, what the hell?" he exclaims.

I don't tell him I was planning to study tonight to take a test to get into night school, get my GED. I hear the wind outside, know winter will soon be pounding Green Mill. He shakes his head and smiles.

"Yo, happy early Xmas, brother. I'm here."

"What?" I'm confused.

"With my fiancée. We drove my little Fiat all the way out here from New Mexico, even though the top ain't got no top. Balls to the walls, little brother. Hell, most of the time it was snowing, raining and hailing. Hell yeah!

"That's right, little brother. I'm here," Camilo repeats, "Here . . . Green Mill, North Carolina. Sis gave me your address. Where the hell you at?" He snaps his fingers in my face. "Come back, little brother. Nothing stops me when I want to see you. And we're getting married."

"Married?" I say, still bewildered.

"Sheryl, the woman I'm with? She won't have sex with me unless we get married."

"What are you talking about? Who . . . ?"

I'm still thinking about what he said when he introduces me to Sheryl. Her shelf-life expired long ago. Her bearing says titty-bar lap-dancer. Of course later, I eventually learn that's exactly where they met. Their courtship consisted of several hours, during which she was giving my brother gold-star privileges upstairs, where customers paid for extra pleasantries— probably with the money I send him monthly. He confirms they plan to get hitched this week.

I ask about our sister Karina. We talk. Then he looks to the main entrance. Something catches his attention, and he says he'll be right back. Sheryl and I small-talk: "Really? You and Camilo drove out in his convertible sports car with a torn rag-top? Wow. Are you really going to get married on such short notice? I mean, you hardly know each other. . . ."

But oh no, it was love at first puff on the meth pipe, love with the first line of coke, love with the rolled joint, love with the first bottle of whiskey. . . . She was sure he was Mr. Right. She'd been married before, she should know the real thing, experience and all. She says she can't believe they drove all the way across the country in bad weather, because when they left the house it was to go to the store for beer. Romantic. Plans changed after they bought the beer, yahooing, hollering with excitement as they accelerated onto the ramp and sped onto Interstate 40 heading east. "Oh, life is so exciting with him."

Flashes of red lights sweep across the ballroom ceiling, people turn to the commotion outside. Perhaps it's an official escort bringing in an important dignitary, like the governor.

Frog King stares at Lila, she comes over and tells me, "Get out there quick before these boys decide to take him out in the field. I mean it. *Now.*"

"What?" I ask perplexed.

"Not you! Him. Your brother's stealing ashtrays off the tables in the patio."

"Ashtrays?"

I hurry past the people, go outside. The cops have Camilo in handcuffs, are trying to put him in the back seat of their cruiser. I run up, beg them to uncuff him.

"Please. My brother, he's visiting. I work for Frog King. Please, let him go, I promise you, you'll never see him again."

Mentioning Frog King makes them pause, look at someone in the crowd behind us, then seconds later resume shoving my brother.

I pull him back, plead with them. "Don't, please! Don't take him."

One of the cops turns in frustration. "You want to take his place?"

Minutes later, I sit handcuffed in the back seat looking out the window. I'm scared, tired, disappointed in myself. My brain is burning up with images of me in DYA. Seeing all those people having a good time with me being driven away like I have some kind of disease. I feel nothing but alone in the world at that moment.

I have so much going for me, and like *that,* it's gone. Everyone goes into hiding. No one wants to meet your eyes, except the cop who's driving: his eyes in the rearview mirror dart at me.

With every mile, my anxiety increases, the sound of the wheels on pavement, the stench of other arrested prisoners' snot, sweat, blood, puke, feces, urine and tears engrained in the upholstery and floor mats, mixing with the air I breathe in in the back seat. The call-box staccatos with sniper-shots of coded information: "10-20 B, 1377, 3030, officer . . . 10-4 . . ." It blurts all the way to the station.

I imagine myself with a razorblade, slashing my wrists. I picture myself bleeding all over, draining every last drop from my body until I collapse and never have to wake up to my life again. *All of this can end,* I think. *I was fooling myself that I could make it.*

I'm numb. The tobacco fields, the plowed fields, the night sky with stars, the country road—all of it is nameless. None of it has purpose or substance for me. At that moment, there is no Lord, no decent people, no goodness in the world. No hope.

We arrive. I get out, go inside and what is supposed to be routine for any other prisoner becomes a recurrent nightmare for me. It feels like I've been pushed out of a ten-story window, I'm hurtling through space, expecting to hit the pavement, shatter into fragments I can never put back together.

When the guard asks for my hand to fingerprint me, tears fill my eyes.

He notices, surprised. "Hey, it's not that bad, just an overnighter for disorderly conduct."

I'm placed in a cell with another guy in the booking area so they can keep an eye on us. I rest my head in my hands, and against all effort not to, I weep. It's too much. My fatigue. My worry. The end is coming, but I don't how the end will come. My survival instincts kick in. I have to prepare to defend myself. Automatically, from a lifetime of being institutionalized, I lock the attitude and load the mannerisms of a juvenile who knows this world. I state loud and clear to myself: BRING IT ON.

At some point, a guard passes, says Lila put up the bail. "No worries," he says, offering a thumbs-up gesture.

The same guard comes by, wakes up the kid across from me and tells him the company is bailing him out, get ready to leave.

The jail noise is familiar: voices yell in the hallways, cell doors clang, constant footsteps drone. . . . The harsh, grim life of being locked up weighs on the air with a toxicity that makes it hard to breathe. The pollution of thousands of imprisoned people's sorrow before me is caked on the walls, bars and concrete floors. The dried blood, hopelessness and hate, violence almost make me gag.

Every minute that passes feels like a year. Ten years. Twenty years. Thirty . . .

I start pacing back and forth, counting, reminding myself of that night not so long ago when I dreamed a judge was telling me I would never get out—maybe the dream was right. I feel so exhausted that I curl up on the concrete floor and sleep. At some point during the night, I'm awakened to go leave.

Just as I'm about to walk out, the new shift captain says, "Not so fast, little buddy. This is from Frog King." Three goons armored in riot gear—helmets, shields, batons and mace—storm in and bum-rush me. They lift me off the ground, hold me as each takes a turn punching me.

Before I pass out, the only thought that runs through my mind is the phrase, "Look at me now," addressed to the whole world out there, to all the people in America: "Look at me now." America: this is what you made of me, this is how your care ended, this is the result of your religious teachings, me obeying you, me trying to do what was right. Look at me now. It seems, for a second before my mind goes blank, that I'm a boy in the orphanage again, so long ago, the boy. . . . Before America demanded blood from me, America slammed me down, rearranged my face, broke my teeth. That boy begged for an outlet, for mercy, escape. . . .

I regain consciousness again. Someone has thrown water on my face.

The guard tells me, "I hear you like whipping women, you piece of shit!"

I crumple in a corner with my back turned to them, as they swing at me, curse. I crouch in fear from so many yelling at me in America, "If you ever come around here again, we'll kill you."

I can't walk. The next thing I remember is being laid on a gurney, wheeled out to a county van and driven to Durham hospital. I've spent the next week convalescing when Lila comes, gets me and tells me someone stole my truck. She says the guards accused me of fighting them, that I was causing trouble for other inmates. Frog King's guys were also looking to beat my brother's ass but he left.

∾ ∾ ∾

It's always been smooth sailing for a while, then catastrophe. Open road, then closed. Possibilities, then absence of

130

hope. Freedom, then crushing captivity. I learned early to expect disaster, learned the three most precious words in the
English language: get back up.

I call my brother and say, "You promised you'd stop the
drinking and drugs."

"Why do you bring that up?"

"Oh shit, I wonder. The fact that I just went to jail for
you."

Silence.

"It's time," I say.

"Yeah, when I visited you at DYA, afterwards I got drunk,
tore up the motel room."

"And another of your fiancées left you," I say.

". . . Long list of fiancées," he adds.

"How can any woman leave a man so handsome?" I say,
to lighten the sadness in his voice. "Sooner or later, addicts
and drunks vanish too."

Another silence.

"You know, if you haven't figured it out, your true enemy
doesn't come as a knife-wielding thug. The worst sneak up on
you in nickel and dime bags of heroin and meth. They don't
come at you with a pistol in your ribs asking for your money.
It's your life, not your money, it wants."

"When you coming back?" he asks.

"Don't know."

"Don't know?"

"I'm trying to figure out how to do it."

"I need you here."

"I just can't go back and do robberies with you. You gotta
stop the meth and drinking."

"And you can't keep living off that woman."

"Yeah. I need to make some money so we can get a business, like we planned. . . . Get some money, buy fixer-uppers

we'll renovate, make a ton of money reselling them. But you have to get off drugs and booze. It won't work otherwise. I don't know how many times I have to tell you, man, that little bit of powder in that little paper may not have a face or body, it's not someone who breathes and has eyes and hands and lives somewhere, but it'll destroy your ass."

"Orlando. . . ."

"I don't want you to die."

"All right already. Takes money for rehab."

"You spent the money I already sent for rehab. And the money you were supposed to be saving for our business."

"I promise, if you send more, I'll use it for rehab. Besides, I have to get serious. I got this disease."

"Going off with a chick, getting high, screwing-our-whole-savings-away kind of disease. Married and-divorced-a-day-later disease."

"No, really . . ."

"What? Cirrhosis of the liver? Hepatitis? Cirrhosis is a bad, bad way to go, you gotta stop the drinking and shooting up. . . ."

"AIDS."

"What the hell?"

"I have sores on my back. Like scabs. From sharing needles. There's medicine."

"How much?"

"I don't know . . . maybe five hundred a month. But I think its curable."

"I'll see what I can do. But Camilo, you have to promise me you'll start rehab."

Later, still sitting on the porch step watching the sky and trees, I hear Lila come out of her office and go into the kitchen. I call her over.

She stands behind the screen door. "What?"

"Can you borrow money from Frog King?"

"Bad idea."

"Can you at least ask?"

She dials and speaks to Frog King, then hands me the phone.

"Listen, you and your brother were lucky to get out alive. He owes, or you do—one of you owes—for my goddamn truck. He dented the front fender."

"I'll cover everything."

"Well, your word ain't shit far as I can tell. I'm doing this for *her.* I'm glad that crazy son of a bitch is outta here before someone kills his raunchy ass. You better keep him out. Send Lila down."

∞ ∞ ∞

The last days of October. I've lost five pounds worrying about my debt. I'm still driving weed, trying not to get caught. I'm so stressed by the smuggling that I grind my molars when sleeping. By my reasoning, the shame of always being dependent on Lila for everything is also too much to bear. In my mind, that kind of justifies my smuggling. I'm tired of being tied to her in every way. No matter how anxious I am, smuggling is what I have to do for now . . . and do it hard.

October is harsh with cold, but I hardly even notice since I'm going back and reloading, sometimes with back-to-back runs to the Valley of Texas, or, as the natives call it, *El Valle.*

I stay at Centavo's house, wait for the phone call to come load up. The weed is packed into a false bottom of a tow truck. They unbolt the top part of the tow truck bed with the winch on it, drop the bricks in, then re-bolt the top on and hitch a wrecked car to it with an American plate. At the border, they say they're towing it back stateside to the owner, from where it was stolen. The guards wave them through, get paid a bonus for every car.

There are other ways they cross the weed: with ropes attached to inner tubes across the Rio Grande or ambulances carrying dead bodies freshly dug up from a cemetery. Crossings always include a payoff to the border guards on both sides.

Centavo is ruthless. On one occasion, waiting for a load to come in, Centavo and I go to Padre Island to kill some time at the beach. Whenever I'm waiting for a load, the anticipation builds to the point of exploding, but being on the beach listening to the tide calms my nerves. The tide whispers an easy rhythm of baby-lullabies, shushing, shushing. My eyes skim the gray water with a melancholy regret that I'm not back at Green Mill looking for a job or applying for night school. I tell myself the time will come.

Black folks down the beach barbecue. I recall with a tenderness the black folks seen that day in Green Mill enjoying themselves. Time seems to have whizzed by. I yearn to be doing what they're doing.

Centavo gets up from the sand where we sit, walks to the outside bathrooms. A tanned man in Bermuda shorts and sandals enters right behind him. A few minutes later, Centavo appears; arms low at his side, face flushed. He sits down next to me, curses under his breath. I ask what happened. He says the man came on to him, says he cut him. His arm comes up. He shows me his knife, throws it into the sand to clean the blood off.

"Cut the punk's neck," he ends.

What's wrong with you? I think.

The tranquil beach, soft waves vanish. Anger rises in me. For a moment I want to drag him into the water and drown him. I loathe people like him; can't talk to express their feelings or what's on their minds, so they operate on one mode: ignorant aggression.

I know he's not just a driver. I'm certain he works for M as an enforcer, debt collector or assassin. He raises his bowie knife to the sky, stares at a blood streak he missed. Throws the knife again between his black boots, stabs the sand repeatedly until the blade is gleaming clean.

I know if I continue to smuggle weed, one day he and I will have a showdown. I also foresee that in time I'll witness an even darker side of him. It's not lost on me that he's driven the weed up with me and M enough to know where I live if ever a misunderstanding comes between M and me.

∾ ∾ ∾

Early November. On the phone Lila tells me Green Mill is quiet, in hibernation. I tell her it couldn't be more different down in El Valle. Warm weather, clear blue skies. I sleep in a small room at Chuy's mother's house. The aromas of morning bring back childhood memories. I feel the way I did when I was with my grandma. I can recall how, when I was four years old, Camilo wrapped some presents for me and celebrated my birthday. Wrapped in toilet paper were rocks, which I licked, pretending they were candy. Then I folded and pocketed the cartoon newspaper clippings with pretty pictures. The last package was a scoop of special dirt. He said all three items came from a magic land and they'd give me the power to fly. I believed him. Since then, I've never had another birthday party.

I mention this memory to Chuy, and he declares, "No, no, you deserve a *real* birthday party!"

To celebrate my birthday, Chuy suggests we get something to eat. His favorite is *barbacoa de chivo*, or barbecued goat.

"But it's not my birthday," I insist.

"It is now," he says. "You have two birthdays, the one when you were born, and the one we just give you."

And so a few of his cousins and I pile into his low-rider and drive off—not to a barbecue joint, as I assumed, but way out of town along an isolated country road, where we pull up alongside a fence with a sign: KING RANCH, NO TRESS-PASSING.

Chuy points to a trailer set off in the field. "That's the guard." He presses his index finger to his lips. "We have to do it quick and quiet. No noise. Let's go."

I climb out of the car with the others, Chuy pops the trunk. Each of his cousins grabs a small bat, we all creep toward the field, climb over the fence.

"Follow me," Chuy instructs.

I'm not quite sure what he has in mind, but I'm definitely not going to beat some guard over the head with a bat. I'm relieved when we sneak past the trailer. The guard is occupied watching an NFL game. The door is open, the game on loud. I can see him in a hard-backed chair, drinking a beer and eating Cheetos.

We crawl past on our bellies until we come to a herd of goats. At the same time as I realize what this is all about, Chuy's cousins spring out of the sage brush and creosote bushes, and in one smooth swing crushes the skulls of a few goats. Immediately, they drag them through the brush and carry them over the fence.

Chuy and I are the last to get ours, and as we're stuffing it into the trunk, shots ring out. I turn, see the watchman standing outside his door with his rifle aimed at us. He shoots again as we drive off.

"Nothin' but a meatball, *carnalito.*"

We get the goats safely to Chuy's and barbecue them. The whole barrio turns up to enjoy the fiesta, eating goat tacos and drinking cold beer as the story is told and retold with more and more invention. It's here at the barbecue that I meet Beto, a squat, thick-shouldered, middle-aged fieldworker from Mercedes, Texas.

∞ ∞ ∞

Beto and I start driving one round-trip a week. Bigger loads. More money. He suffers from breathing problems, his lungs damaged from work in the pesticide-sprayed fields. With a wife and two lovely daughters in middle school, he has to keep the bills paid and life going. Meanwhile, Chuy's life unravels. He is doing a lot of heroin. He goes his way, I continue on mine; it's an old story—you'd think it wouldn't surprise me by now.

To hide the loads, we buy wrought-iron lawn furniture, Mexican clay pots, rugs, wall decorations, pre-Colombian figurines—all cheap stuff to conceal what we're really carrying. Once we arrive in North Carolina we unload the weed at Frog King's as quickly as possible. On weekends we go up to the big flea market in Leesburg, Virginia, sell our lawn furniture and Mexican curios within a few hours. Southern folk have a fascination with Mexican goods; seems they're decorative, inexpensive and broaden their cultural appreciation.

Anyway, the money is pouring in, and when money pours in, it's awfully hard to go back to thinking about making a legitimate reentry. There is always something else I need to buy to set up the future, and although money isn't something I measure my life by nor does it give me any special esteem or make me feel better than others, I blow through it as easily as it comes. I give it away to the Mexicans working in the fields,

throw big *pachangas* and *barbacoas* at parks, send thousands
for my brother's rehab and for our future, and buy two almost-
new trucks for me and Beto and a new car for my sister.

I no longer am a disappointment.

∾ ∾ ∾

I outfit my truck with dual gas tanks, even install a gen-
erator alongside the motor so that in case I break down on
the road, I can crank it up and plug in, have lights, heat and
radio. Frog King is happier than an anteater with six tongues.
Every time I deliver a load, he gives me a bonus of a thousand
dollars, offers me anything I need, from whores to drugs. I
can't believe a man his age, late sixties, can party as hard as
he does, can drink white lightning from a mason jar every
day, wheels and deals with cracker-scum and Nazi-scammers
selling stolen guns and heavy construction machinery, ex-
changing one hundred thousand dollars printed in prison for
five thousand in real money.

I'm also off running more errands, more favors for Frog
King. When I'm home, if he needs something, he calls me. It's
pretty clear I'm his go-to man. I keep it low key. Whenever I
can, I'm off by myself, reading a book of poetry or a novel.

∾ ∾ ∾

Lila suffers more bouts of brooding. I'm seldom around.
It's has been quite a while since we even sat at the same table
and shared a meal. We hardly talk. I feel a pressing urgency
to get out of her house. I can't take the arrangement much
longer, although it's good to see her busy translating Spanish
poetry and writing letters to her colleagues. At heart, she's an
intellectual—forget the other side of her persona. For days,

she works translating Nahuatl poetry, working in a silent co-
coon all by herself. We live together but have separate lives.

When I'm home, I select books from her library in the
main room, read about Mesoamerican culture, how indigenous peoples view the world, as well as about new break-
throughs in the interpretation of Mayan hieroglyphics,
Mechican poetic structures, Incan metaphors, Aztec religious
beliefs, cultural principles of poetic deities, etc. Despite the
obvious gnawing away of both of our souls, of being inhib-
ited strangers in each other's presence, the perplexing anxiety of living together permeates the air. Face-to-face, we are
aloof, maintain a cool demeanor. We don't have sex.

∽ ∽ ∽

One day I open the carton of my personal belongings my
sister sent what feels like forever ago to sort out my papers
and notebooks and store them in an out of the way place. I
open one of the drawers in the steel filing cabinet in my
(Griselda's) office. A picture falls out from a folder. It is the
photo of me taken at DYA, wearing institutional denims.
There are strands of Lila's red hair mixed in black wax, hand-
written notes with moon chants on them. When Lila gets home
from work, I ask her about it. She says she went through my
box, looking for our letters to each other. She admits the hair
and wax are a ceremony meant to insure my safety while I
was on the road doing the smuggling. I think it's her voodoo
ritual to capture my soul to remain hers forever.

I also find a pile of burned letters, ash, hair and chants. I
ask her to burn them all, dump them in the field behind the
house. Scatter them. No more voodoo stuff.

She does as I ask with solemn decorum, no expression of
shame, fury or argument. I put it behind me, resume straight-

ening my office, enjoy Griselda purring at my feet, nibbling my toes, licking my heels with her harsh, abrasive tongue.

Then I am gone again, on the way to south Texas in the big truck. While Beto drives, I open some of the books I borrowed from Lila's library. I find notes among the pages Lila had written during her college days. One says:

Never trivialize the journey with quaint whiny quips. The journey is a hallowed one, not about grandstanding for sex or fame or money, it's a spiritual quest to unfold your soul like a star just discovered in the universe, one that can sustain a worthy human life; it connects you to the Great Mystery, quit pretending. Be worthy to call yourself a human, it's a calling, a mission, a rare gift from the Creator of all life, do not mock it, do not be a charlatan.

After we pass through Baton Rouge, Louisiana, I read Eliot's *The Wasteland*, and the words grab me with such force, I turn to Beto and announce, "That's it, done. I quit hauling weed."

Beto frowns. "Not a good idea, amigo." He thinks a little and says, "I can give you a list of reasons why that is not wise. The money we're making is a blessing from God." He makes the sign of the cross. "Even the lawn furniture and Mexican textiles, the shirts, sandals, sombreros . . . the gringos can't get enough. We don't want to disrespect God's wishes."

He flashes me an expression of incredulity. For a moment, the God-thing almost validates our criminal activity. I look at him, agree in silence that the money is good, God is very good.

He insists, "Happens once a lifetime, *carnal*. You don't know how I've lived in poverty for so long . . . this is as close to heaven as I imagine heaven could be."

Austerity, hard, lean days are written all over his brown face.

"But I need to stop."

With every trip, a bone-handled dagger slowly makes its way deeper into my heart. The longer I spend my days and nights driving the highway, smuggling dope, the harder it is to fit back into a normal life. It is impossible to reconcile my smuggling with my desire for that normal life. But a voice in my head repeats, "Gotta raise enough money for my brother's rehab and our business before I leave." Is it my excuse or my justification? I am not sure anymore.

Smuggling masks my inefficiencies, balances the playing field between me having and not having something, conceals my inadequacies and reveals my skill, because, to tell the truth, although I am not really able to face the lousy mess my life is, I am, I hope, slowly repairing it. It doesn't matter that the means in question are illegal. It is what I have. I am not sure whether I am making more garbage or cleaning up the wreckage. I am certain of one thing, though: I instinctively know, if I ever open those old doors of my past, to the shack hidden in the woods, the scream that will ensue from that child will leave me a broken man.

This is as good as it gets sometimes. I have to take the good with the bad, live in the gray area. I have to learn to accept it: two Chicanos in a beat-up five-ton truck going down an American highway at three a.m., hauling weed to people who can't live without getting high. I'm helping them get by another miserable, despairing day.

Beto continues encouraging me off and on over the miles. He's adamant about our opportunity. "You have it backwards. Money's everything, happiness is not. Show me how you can use happiness to pay a hospital bill? Or buy school clothes for my girls?"

I have no solution. I keep telling myself all I have to do is make a little more money, then I can stop . . . but I recall that that is the swan song of so many kids in DYA. I half-believe there is no turning back, that it's impossible to change. But I know I am wrong. I can stop right now, get out of the truck, hitchhike to wherever. But I don't. I'm lost, confused and realize that my life means so little that in some ways going back to DYA could be a relief. Maybe it's where I belong. Despite all these doubts, something pushes me to take more risks. I have an attitude, I push the edge, postpone a decision on leaving the lifestyle for a while.

It is the money factor. I need more.

∾ ∾ ∾

To complicate my exit strategy, my ego is gorged like a glutton, thinks I'm indispensable. That I'm needed is a great feeling, takes the place of the self-esteem I don't have. Frog King asks me to be his personal driver; I'm flattered. He says Colombian weed is coming back up, flown into Georgia by a father and son team, from there the boys truck it up to North Carolina. Unless the Mexican weed becomes superb, better than the Colombian, which is not going to happen anytime soon, we should leave the business down in Texas until the Columbian bud dries up.

I start driving for Frog King. No limo or black Caddy SUV. No, it's an old beat-up blue farm truck. I still do a couple more trips down to the Valley with M, take weed to Ronny and his father up in Danville, Virginia, where they run one of Frog King's casinos/cathouses.

On one of those trips south, slowed by traffic accidents, there are check points, police roadblocks and rain. DEA agents are all over the border. I get no sleep for two days. While passing New Orleans late at night, I mention casually to M I'm so tired, I can hardly keep my eyes open. Not even sticking my head out the window to let the full force of the wind hit me wakes me up, coffee isn't doing the trick. So we have to pull over at a rest area.

He produces a small brown vial from his pocket, offers me a hit. I've never done cocaine. As soon as I snort it, my brain inserts itself into a 220 outlet of accelerant bliss that ignites every cell in my bloodstream with crystalline sizzling.

I can drive and drive. . . .

We cover six hundred miles in a snap, get to Green Mill in what seems an hour. After we get there, M asks if I can get him some more coke. I say I don't know, but ask Frog King the next day. He sends me over to see this old man with a glass eye—I nickname him Ciego, the Blind One. Ciego and his son, a big tobacco farmer in his late thirties, control all the weed and coke coming into North Carolina. They bring it in boats through coastal Georgia, using the protective guise of oil company tankers, then truck it up to North Carolina in green-tarp Army trucks.

I drive up to Ciego's red-brick house on a hilltop, sit with him by his swimming pool. It's a sunny day, not a cloud in the sky. Behind us, lining a whole side of the pool, there are dog cages and in each one a blue heeler. They yap at my arrival but instantly hush when Ciego scolds them.

He's like any of the good ol' boys—mean-looking, unkempt, kill-you-in-a-second—except rich from selling marijuana and cocaine to the college kids in Chapel Hill, Charlotte, Greensboro and seemingly everywhere else in the South. It seems like the only thing of value to these men are Catahoula dogs, a jug of lightning and easy money. Ciego has plenty of all that.

Ciego's house is bit smaller than Frog King's mother's mansion. It's showy, with alabaster columns topped with scrolled Roman capitals. Behind the house is a colonnaded swimming pool, parked all around are new trucks and cars, a plane, heavy construction equipment, acres of forest land and pastures with black angus grazing. But to see him, a stranger might take him for an old gum-sucking fool, a dull-witted drunk. He wears a crumpled baseball cap, sooty jeans, a faded, torn khaki shirt and grimy, manure-chunked farmer boots.

We sit down in hickory lawn chairs facing the far side of the pool. He crooks one leg over the other. I notice something peculiar, so I ask, "What's that wire sticking out down by your leg there, under your pants by your ankle?"

"Heart condition."

I imagine doing all that pure cocaine gives even an enraged elephant in full charge a pause.

We talk a little about the weed business. He tells me, "Them dumb feds camp outside my boy's house, still can't do a damn thing."

That would be the son who flies a plane-load of Colombian bud and cocaine each week right under the feds' noses. The son who looks out his window every morning, flips off the feds and is richer than most Wall Street con-artists. He has marshalls, local cops and DEA agents on his payroll.

I tell him what I need. He reaches into his shirt pocket, flips me a bag of jeweled rocks. While we talk, a white four-door Lincoln pulls up in the driveway. Four very tall, black men get out, sleek as panthers in very expensive white-linen tailored suits, all wearing the same sunglasses, all bare foot—yep, all bare foot, with very, very large feet.

They laugh with Ciego, talk basketball, chances for winning the NCAA championship. Then Ciego reaches into the box beside his chair, pulls out a pound of cocaine wrapped in brown, wax-coated paper and hands the bundle to the tallest of the men. He doesn't open the package, just smiles and stuffs it into a gym bag. With all the coolness and toothyclassiness of kids who have just found a golden egg in the grass on Easter morning, they grin at the world and stroll off casually. They get back into the white Lincoln and drive off: four swans in a fairy tale, floating on the sparkling water of the American Dream.

"You know who that is?" Ciego asks.

"No . . ."

"Destiny picked that boy to be the greatest basketballer of all time. Ajon. Remember that name if you ever intend on putting money down on a game. Ajon."

I spent the last seven years in a cell without radio or TV. I never heard of anyone named Ajon. I let it go at that. But over the next decade, I witness Ajon rise to the ethereal chambers of greatness, one of the greatest basketball players the game's ever seen.

I keep a bit of the coke, give the rest to M. When he returns to Texas, I am grateful not to be going with him. Every time I go down and come back, Lila tells me I grind my teeth so loud when I sleep that she has to wake me. My body is conscious of my misgivings, reacts by warning me to stop. After every trip, when I fall asleep, I hear the drill bits of my molars grind into my skull and jawbone and reverberate in my cheekbones, down my spine like a miniature jackhammer that shakes me, trying to tell me, wake up before it's too late!

∽ ∽ ∽

I have an addictive personality. When something is good, I ignore the warnings to be moderate. I go all out. But I feel the end of my smuggling days are near when the night frights start. I have this repetitive dream of walking back into DYA. I wake up sweating, gasping, realize with infinite relief it is only a nightmare.

It is time to plan my departure.

Beto's voice in my head makes me hesitate to make any final decision. Recently freed, making decent money smuggling, what kid wouldn't feel invincible, formidable, indomitable, untouchable? That's me until the day I almost get busted coming through Tennessee. Until then, I've felt immune from capture.

It's late October, the winter is grungy: mud, cold, people's dispositions mean and despondent. I'm heading up a long stretch of the interstate, it's snowing so hard that I see at least a dozen tractor trailers jack-knifed in the median along the way. I've come through several times in the last two weeks, noticed narcs park at the overpass exits and gas stations. I never have to stop, thank God, since I have duel tanks on my pick-up.

The feds still have Ciego's son, and more importantly his weed business, on ice. The showdown Frog King talked about never happens, and I'm just as busy as before.

I've got the weed packed in tall refrigerator boxes, about a hundred pounds per box. I see a narc pulling up beside me. It's over for me, I think. I can imagine myself back in DYA. Shit, yes, I'm frightened. And sad. It proves I can't live in freedom, can't make it straight. I'm also relieved, a sense of *at-last* sweeps over me. No more pretending, no more taking risks or pushing the line.

I have to get rid of the little vial of coke in my shirt pocket. Getting busted with weed might bring a light sentence, but the coke aggravates the situation. I figure I don't have much in the vial in my shirt pocket. I could throw it out the window, but that's impossible because the narc is right alongside me. I glance over at him to my left and smile, hoping a goodwill smile will make him leave. It doesn't. I smile again, to make him think it's just an ordinary morning and I'm an ordinary workman. But no, he knows, he is on to me.

I see him make calls on his police radio. I know the truck's paperwork is in order. As luck would have it, the two-lanes narrow to one because of the snow-banks, he has to get behind me. This is my chance. I look straight ahead at the road, reach into my right shirt pocket, pluck the vial out, cup it in my palm, unscrew the cap with my thumb and insert the three-inch straw I have for snorting. I estimate I have only a few hits left, so when I jam the straw into the vial, lift it to my nose, inhale a hit, I realize my estimate is dead wrong.

Tears stream down my face, my brain burns. My cheeks are on fire. My eyes blink like I've been hit by a baseball, my face grimaces into a mask cringing with pain. I have just taken the biggest hit of cocaine in my life, I feel a huge tiger paw slap me across my head. I wince from the pain of its claws burning in my nasal passages.

Just then, the two lanes open again. When I look to my left at the narc driving next to me, he is shocked to see me crying, my face wrinkled up like a wadded up piece of paper. Then, something unexpected happens. I don't know why, but he takes the next highway exit and is gone. It must have given him quite a shock—me crying, my face a crushed piece of paper between a writer's two hands who can't get it right. My face feels like its smoking, tiny nerve ends convulse, twitch, my lungs groan, landmines erupt in my brain.

For the next twenty miles I see blurry, double, sometimes triple phantoms, ghosts leaping out from the roadside, mashing their faces against the windshield; other spectral visitors crowd the shoulder of the highway, waving me down, but I refuse to stop for fear of being taken to the underworld. I know the devil is on my track as sure as a flame on a fuse. I pray aloud, plead with God to intervene, save my miserable, coke-overdosed ass.

He does, but only for another showdown.

∾ ∾ ∾

What is it about this habit of proving to people I am worthy by subjecting myself to danger?

I was only four years old when my cousins at the ranch in Willard had me hold Black Cat firecrackers while they lit them. I couldn't feel my fingers for a week. They were delighted with my pain. Around the same time, another cousin put me barefoot on the back of his dirt bike, drove as fast as he could to purposely throw me off, zig-zagging recklessly through the prairie scrub brush. I lost my balance, the wheel spokes caught my foot, tore through my tendon. It made him laugh. He liked me after that.

I was their freak show. It excited them to see how far I would endanger myself. When bigger boys were around, I'd rush them, barrel into them, hug their legs so they couldn't ever leave me. They'd push me off, but I'd rush back at them, block their way to the door, box them—a five-year-old against a teenager. They'd slap me, I'd swing back. It was play to them, but I was serious in my fear of being left behind, alone. I'd make them drag me away.

I was always the one at the orphanage to take the dare, the one-more-step kid who incited an emergency, who ran away even as the consequences grew in severity. I always disregarded the threats from older boys that if I didn't stop doing something that bugged them, they'd beat me up. I wouldn't stop and they'd bang me to the ground. I didn't carc.

I'd steal the purses of the college girls who came to visit us at the orphanage on holidays. At day's end, I'd climb up to the bell tower, crouch in the dusty space, scaring away dozens of pigeons. I'd sit, the dust and feathers everywhere, peer through the slats at the kids, the nuns, the visitors below and wonder why I couldn't have what they had, why was I so lonely and they weren't, why was I so different. I wondered how to remake myself more like them, to make people feel I wasn't a disappointment. . . .

I'm in the truck with Beto, driving down the highway with two hundred pounds of weed, peering through the windshield at the pigeons on telephone lines. Am I doing this to make people like me? Am I still a disappointment?

∾ ∾ ∾

It was 1966, and I was sitting in the bleachers under the big tent with a hundred other kids bussed to the circus. I kept looking up at Sister Rita next to me. I had a crush on her. Once, out weeding the garden by the dorm, a gust blew the fabric of her brown smock tight against her body and outlined her long legs and breasts. It was instant love. At the circus, a man with a whip was making tigers snarl and leap through a hoop of fire. Pretty girls in tights walked the ropes high up, others in sparkly outfits straddled elephants, did flips on the backs of trotting white horses.

I was wearing a Lone Ranger mask and a Davey Crockett racoon hat. I carried a plastic toy rifle that I'd point at a kid called Big Noodle. I'd fire at him, but he wouldn't die, he'd only act wounded, slash at me with his Zorro sword. My eyes stared up at the lady somersaulting free from her trapeze bar. I gasped, thinking that she'd fall to her death as she sailed in the air with no net below. At the last minute the man on the swing at the opposite pole swung out and caught her. In celebration, clowns spewed confetti from horns, a midget was shot out of a canon.

There's a photo of us the weekend we visited our grandpa in Estancia. I was dressed in freshly laundered jeans two inches too short and a plaid shirt. I even had a little hat on with a plastic propeller, like Spanky on "The Little Rascals." In the afternoon, we stood next to each other for another photo; this time my clothes were dirty, my shirt hung out. I'd lost my little round cap with the twirly. By day's end, my clothes, obtained from Goodwill, already worn and faded, were even more torn and filthy from playing on the prairie.

Back at the orphanage a few days later, I sat with Camilo in a ditch flipping through Spider-Man and Superman comic books, talking about the circus we saw. To prove to him I was a circus boy too, I went over, grabbed a swing, pumped my legs to get as high as I could and I bailed out, flipped in mid-air. For a moment, I flew like the trapeze lady. Then I landed with a thud and broke my arm.

∾ ∾ ∾

A day after returning from another trip to South Texas, I sit on the stoop of Lila's house, can still feel the break at my elbow from that playground fall. I cherish the break; it carries part of the story of my childhood when life was magical, a mystery of benign grace that swept through the day, covering me and everything I touched, saw, heard and tasted with a certain deep knowledge of goodness, living right and living hard. The fields in Green Mill have that same husky bare-chested thrust to the sky.

In Green Mill, the October weather holds steady with cold, a fog covering the fields that doesn't burn off until noon. I like the grayness of it all; it lends a certain intimacy to my melancholy. I grab my rod and head to the woods. By evening, I've caught two nice big mouth bass and a brim. I fillet them at the pumphouse, make a salad for Lila and me. While we eat, she says that she and her sisters are having a birthday party for her father, who'll be 84.

∾ ∾ ∾

Saturday morning guests start to arrive, and with them lilies and poinsettias. The closest thing to a real birthday party I ever had growing up in the orphanage was group outings, the Shriners taking us out to see jugglers or the man who could swallow a sword and spit fire.

Memories of Easter blind me for a minute; I swear that lilies emit light. I remember the lilies were everywhere, including at the chapel's main altar and side altars. I knelt at the marble railing longer than anyone else just to look at lilies set in vases alongside tall, white candles embroidered with gold threads. The chapel was fragrant from the frankincense, myrrh burned in the brass censer. I remember Father Gallagher raising the chalices of wine and sacred communion wafer, intoning the liturgy in somber Latin, wearing a white smock over purple robes. The majesty of the scene lifted me up. I felt as if I was at some king's court among European aristocrats: princes, queens, squires. In this milieu, I was privy to the Lord himself, present in all the votive flames at the side altars flickering in the exhalations of old widows and spinsters praying for the departed souls of husbands and children, or for Jesus, observing us from the twelve stations of the cross that lined the two facing walls of the chapel, His awareness of the pious as powerful as the morning sunlight blazing through the stained-glass windows. I just knew, in this epiphany, that my parents would come back, I'd be home again, that everything would be all right.

I bowed my head in worship to Jesus, pulled a card of Him out of my pants pocket, kissed his wounded heart. I licked the picture to get his bleeding heart's blood onto my tongue, then touched the picture to my forehead in reverence, being anointed, welcomed by Him, blessed with the miracle of my parent's return. I skipped, danced all the way out of the chapel, down the long way hallways to the dining room lined with poinsettias. In the dining room, every table was aflame, lit up with lilies bursting with light. Later, I was under the shed while the nuns played solitaire, kids nearby were playing marbles, others by the sand box playing *piquete*, throwing tops, trying to split the opponent's top with each throw. I got out from under the shed. I hopscotched, even though there were no chalked squares. I jumped rope and recited rhymes, even though I had no rope, because poinsettias and lilies filled the world with the message that all things would be well!

And now, I see Fanny Bell and her husband Big Foot showing up for the birthday party carrying poinsettias. Lila's sisters show up carrying bouquets of lilies, other guests proudly arrive with more and more poinsettias and lilies. I step up, smiling, young again, seven-year-old Orlando hungry for blackberry cobbler, peach pie, butter beans, cornbread, yams, collards, black-eyed peas with red onions and pork. As I step onto the porch and go inside the old clapboard, my mind goes back to the visiting room at the orphanage, the Blue Room, also lined with pots of poinsettias. I was standing in the living room with a crowd of family and friends for the holiday. Even the fog outside snuggled up against the windows to share in this holiday that smelled of rich earth, ponds and green weeds. The room filled with people I hadn't seen in a long time. The Shriners were there, with their tasseled, purple fezzes and purple coats. Someone blew one of those paper roll-out whistles, the kids rushed out for a fire or bomb drill, in twos down the staircases. We packed into the courtyard, looking up at the sky, wondering when the planes might come and drop the bombs. Maybe Santa or an Easter bunny might show.

Standing there with Lila and her sisters, for one divine moment, it all comes together. As I walk from my house across the blacktop to Mr. Chamber's house, I decide these beautiful people are not the folks who shame a kid who carries the mark of trauma, whose eyes reveal him as too willing to please, too wild and crazy to prove his worthiness. He is a kid not usually invited to birthdays.

∽ ∽ ∽

People from all over Green Mill come kicking and stomping their big boots and high heels on the porch planks to pay their respects to their father, our neighbor across the country road. His birthday comes as an accidental redemption for me, affording me the opportunity to reassess what I'm doing with my life. I realize I cannot split myself in two. If Mr. Chambers has taught me anything, it is that good intentions evaporate, what's left are the calluses and scars on a heart.

This day, I see and feel the sweet cumulative abundance of a lifetime of hard work in these folks. These people respect Chambers's honesty and integrity, how this skinny old shred of a man has given off ample grace from having certain principals he would never bend, much less betray. I so appreciate those bony hands almost made claws by age and weather. I appreciate that wrinkled grin of his, those corny jokes, his simple life steeped with field truths, seasonal despairs and harvest hopes. He is rich soil, and from that soil he loved a woman, grew a family, built a house, endured the cold and looked himself in the eyes each morning, never wavering in his gaze because of the foolishness he'd done dreaming the possible. He is not a man to commit the crime of deception against himself. He is as straight-forward and lackluster as that damn beat-up tractor of his. He got the job done; there is honor in that, even love at day's end and grace in the way he walks to the woodstove at dawn to serve himself up a cup of coffee. His life is as simple as a nail in a board, and the board never comes loose. It's held its purpose against the mightiest forces seeking to pull it apart.

The family gathering resets my sights on the possibility of my own honest living, of being someone folks respect. I can possibly have a family, too, return to my life of honest work. I have made a whole lot of mistakes, taken a whole bunch of bad turns, gotten an awful lot of shit wrong, but I can still make a go of it.

It seems everyone has come from everywhere for the party. The day eventually warms up, the fog burns away. People are outside drinking, eating, talking, laughing, and then Nancy and Kimberly call everyone inside to the sitting room to sing "Happy Birthday." After we sing, Chambers sits in his old armchair, surrounded by family and friends. He thanks us, announces he has a surprise. He starts right off without any explanation, reciting from memory the beginning of the epic saga of Paul Bunyan, which, in his opinion, is the greatest book ever written. I've never heard of Paul Bunyan, think he might be a relative of his from colonial days.

After five minutes, I'm impressed that a man his age, as weathered as medieval parchment, can remember that much. After fifteen minutes of his recital, I'm flat-out amazed. After thirty minutes, stunned. I have no doubt he can recite the entire Paul Bunyan book by heart, but one of his daughters stops him after forty-five minutes. The whole time he's offering his rendition of the book from memory, his grey, glacial eyes are looking straight through us as if looking at an angel in the crowd, conveying a message so badly needed about living free.

∽ ∽ ∽

That evening, the scientist who lent us Griselda calls to inform us that it's time to bring her back. They're going to fly her out to the rainforest in Central America. It's time to say our goodbyes, take our last walks.

For many days, I have brushed Griselda's coat, taken her on walks, fed her steak, purred to tell her how much I love her. She is large and will do fine in the wild. I need to let go of my heart-mate, who is growing stronger and bigger every day. She is the closest thing I ever had when it comes to unconditional love and friendship.

That same night, Lila and I sleep in her parents' house, upstairs in her old bedroom. We have lent our house to the kids and friends. I'm resting in bed. I can hear them yelling and having a good time. I'm happy for them. The night is cool, an edge of bone-chill creeping in under the doors and open windows. It gets so cold that I can feel drafts coming from everywhere, and I snuggle deep under the blankets.

I'm fast asleep when I feel a shiver run up my spine. It wakes me. With my eyes still closed, I feel the weight of Lila on me, her knees and thighs against my hips. She is whisper-chanting a witch's rhyme. I feel a strong wind come through the window. I open my eyes to find her naked, pinching a corner of the sheet in her right hand, holding it across my bare chest and draped over her thighs. Her head is craned back in a trance. She is murmuring something.

"Stop!" I say.

She gets up, puts on her nightgown. The moonlight shows her breasts and legs through the fabric. She leaves the room. A minute later, I hear Griselda growling outside. I get up, look out the window as Lila leads Griselda on a leash into the forest behind the house. The wind picks up, the moon is strong. I fear that so many earthly powers combined will make Griselda forget she is our friend and attack Lila. I want to warn

Lila to come back as I watch them vanish into the woods, the strong wind shaking the branches. An hour or so later, they return, and instead of putting Griselda in her cage, Lila brings Griselda into our room, she falls asleep between us in our bed.

∾ ∾ ∾

It's early November and the winter decides to quit playing around. It comes down hard with ice, wind and snow, and through the fierce assault a call from my friend and mentor Denise manages to connect before the lines go down and branches break half the utility poles in the county. I mark it in my notebook: November 12th.

Denise is coming to read at the university at Chapel Hill. She gives me the date, time, tells me to be sure to go. I'm speechless. She's in a hurry, but takes time to ask how my reentry is going. After I hang up, I rummage through the cardboard box beneath my desk, find a bundle of her letters and postcards. I wish I could be more of the poet she thinks I am. A disappointment.

I spend most of the day reading her letters, fascinated how her poignant words cut through the bars like an acetylene torch. I have a flashback to the cellblock silence and the sun rays shining into the dark cell that enclosed me. Back then, her words called out to us lonely, orphaned exiles by our names, like our imagined mothers calling us in from the dark. I remember how her words shielded me in some way from the night screams, the guards' flashlights in my face on their nightly rounds, the gang warfare, the terror and tension and suspicions rampant in the eyes of kids. Her letters allowed me to transcend DYA life and materialize in her poems in the desert, opening my mouth to the rain, my arms to the wind, my toes clenching the dirt.

The day finally arrives when I get in Lila's Volkswagen and drive to Chapel Hill to meet Denise. I notice a photograph wedged behind the sun visor and pull it out. It's one Lila took of me standing on the Outer Banks beach staring out at the sea. The sky dark, the waves gray. Me standing square-shouldered, head turned to the left when Lila snapped the picture. I was wearing Brandon's sheepskin coat. No longer a clean-faced prisoner in denims with a number patch, I looked like Che with a mustache and goatee and thick, black, tousled hair. It was the first time I had seen the ocean. Like a child mesmerized, the shimmering waves seemed to flow into me and lap at my heart, so that it made me certain this other me, this one standing on the Outer Banks beach, yearning for an otherness, was the me I wanted to be.

What did the ocean washing ashore on that late afternoon mean to a recently released young adult? The movement of water deepened my sense of sorrow for the way my life had developed, made me feel tender toward myself, which was rare, sensitive as I was to the injustices of my past. It filled me with wonder for the possible: possible happiness, possible woman, possible self-realization, possible expression of my deepest yearnings. It could happen . . . it could.

Not long ago, this beach was a battlefield, soaked with the blood of Confederate and Union soldiers. Blacks were slaves, whites were masters; a terrible legacy for whites to live with, never to be erased from the history books, a mark of shame that would stain American history and our democracy forever.

I often felt I heard the spirits of slaves breathing in the forest when I walk. I knew slave life infused every leaf of this land, haunting the dreams of the land. And now, now the change was all about—down the beach, Black and White porters pushed baggage carts, checked Black and White tourists into the hotel. Black and White baggage carriers and van drivers arrived with Black and White business passengers, and cars were jammed with Black and White families delivering Black and White college kids.

In the photograph, I notice something for the first time. At my foot, a small crab flails in the seaweed. The ebb and flow no doubt slapped it around. It reached out blindly for some cress to grip, but the waves tossed it back. It tried to cling to the seaweed. The waves pushed it, slapped it sideways as it scuttled on, receding, then moving forward in the flow again.

The crab is me. I smile at that thought as I park the car in the campus parking lot and head for the performance center where Denise is reading.

From the moment I walk into the auditorium, sit in the shadows at the back, I am in awe. Denise is reading a poem. It is my first time hearing her. No fiery rhetoric, no sloganeering clichés, no grandstanding on the stage, no jokes, no bullshit. No sense that all her literary awards have made her pompous and inflated with her own self-importance. She reads slow, soft, the words fit her tongue the way an Indio chisels an arrowhead, each word clean, carved for the soul's hunt for truth and beauty.

I won't lie: seeing her for the first time, even though she is more than twice my age, I feel such an overwhelming urge to make love to her, to belong to her, to have a life with her. I would do anything for her.

I know that it's silly for many reasons, but most of all because she is refined, cultured, famous and I'm nobody. I am appallingly insignificant in her life, but seeing her down there on the stage . . . this close . . . is enough to keep me happy for life. She has more poise than the Mona Lisa, there on the stage, sitting on a piano bench in a black skirt that conceals her knees but reveals her calves. I want to genuflect, kiss her hands, massage her ankles, her bare calves, her legs slightly curled one under the other, left arm leaning on the piano.

She reads with a lisp, her Welsh face framed by brown, wavy hair. *I love her.* Yes, sitting in the last row, in the seat against the wall, high up in the dark part of the theater. From up there, I sense something so raw, knowable, skin-familiar. It takes me back to the loneliness I knew so well while roaming the high desert plains in New Mexico as a child, whirling with arms out in the blowing wind, scenting the high-peak snow in my blood, my bones howling. There has been a reckoning brewing all the way down in my bones; the biscuit batter was ready for the fire, the tortilla for the *comal.* I want to cast aside my fears and doubts, rev up the dervish cyclones where language meets experience. My heart is pounding: *Yes, this is the life I wanted.*

After her reading, I stay distant from the students crowding around her, wait until she has signed her new book of poems for the last student in line. Then, I present myself.

"Hel-hel-lo," I stammer.

"Orlando. Of course."

She gets up, walks around her table, hugs me, then pulls back, holds me at arm's length and smiles. Her brown eyes cast a spell on me; they are a medieval cathedral on a rainy night, its interior lighted by a thousand candles.

I don't know what to do. Soon, we're walking out of the building in silence to the parking lot. I open the door to the Volkswagen, drive her to her hotel. It's a strange moment, one that I have waited for but never thought would happen. We don't speak. I think I should show her the photo, but no— maybe not. I gaze out the windshield, nervous and expectant, anticipating something more, but nothing happens. We're old-mule soul mates, turning over boulders in our separate fields. I drive sharing the same air with her in the car, our silence underscored by the car's humming motor and the bumps in the road. I feel like apologizing. I am not enough.

She turns to me. "Do you think kids belong in prison?"

"No. Most are sent in for minor drug offenses, then criminalized. Many are not criminals when they arrive, just young—they made a mistake. They're not dangerous when they come in, but they are when they leave."

"I see." She purses her lips slightly. She has a tiny gap between her two front teeth, her breath escapes from the aperture.

She turns again, looks at me. "Orlando, how have you been?"

I feel like I'm breathing under water, can't speak. I can't inhale enough air. I want to be the swordfish at the Outer Banks, launch myself up, twist in exuberant joy, but I lull into what seems the longest silence I have ever endured.

"I'm writing . . . trying to. It's different out here. I can't put my finger on it, but I'm having trouble getting grounded. The money thing, you know? I don't have a job, Lila supports me, pays the bills, and that bothers me."

"Give yourself time. And read, Orlando, read. It's a long life, you'll get it down. Don't worry, you were born a poet—you can't escape that." She pauses. Her breath fogs the windshield on her side. "Are you happy with Lila?"

I wait a long time to answer. When I do, it's a strange answer. "Freedom is not what I expected. I had this naïve idea that society would welcome me, that I'd keep my commitment, work at a simple job, then after work climb the stairs to my loft to read. It would be a monk's life—simple, clean, ascetic, devoted, routine. But it hasn't turned out that way."

"I'm not sure what you mean," she says. "You're not doing drugs are you?"

At that precise moment, I have a spectral experience: I'm running in the mountains on a trail that goes past a waterfall and a cave. I can't understand it. It just comes to me out of nowhere.

I glance at her. "No, nothing like that. Freedom is filled with hazards, lots of sharp edges, they cut me at every turn, force me to behave in ways that are against my own choosing."

She smiles as she looks out the passenger window, says, "Yes, yes, you'll be just fine. Freedom is supposed to be a struggle for you. It's supposed to leave you feeling inadequate. Your problems with Lila, your relationship going through changes, not knowing how to deal with the changes . . . that's the way it's supposed to be. I'm proud of you, Orlando. You're actually stepping out of your prison-thinking, stepping into social thinking. Wheels up, my friend. You will never be a green-light crosswalk poet. You were born to cross borders, break boundaries others fear and make your own trail."

"But don't worry about me, Denise."

"I'm not, Orlando. The ones I worry about are the liberal white poets who claim to be the oppressed, the black poets who scream injustice but earn six figures, live in gated communities, the white feminists who live in privilege boo-hooing the establishment but are the very definition of mainstream."

I look at her. She is drawn, exhausted.

"I guess I should ask, are you okay? Is there anything I can do for you? I'll do anything—rob a bank, hijack a plane . . ." I joke.

She smiles and pats my arm. "I'm just tired," she sighs. "I'm volunteering for this Solidarity Movement in Poland; joining in the protest against the El Mozote massacre in El Salvador . . . we have another big march coming up on December eleventh, against US government forces supporting dictatorships. I can't believe it will soon be 1981; our troops are still massacring innocent citizens in foreign countries, all for their oil. When will it end, Orlando . . . when?"

Her expressive face lightens, she feigns a happy interest. "Well, from what you've told me about you and Lila, as intimate as your letters were—now, face to face—it's supposed to be an entirely different scene. It is, right? You were a prisoner writing to her from far away, behind bars; now, face to face, it's supposed to be hard. After all, you've never been trained to be a social creature, you should be uncomfortable sharing your insecurities."

"I can't believe you know me this well," I say, surprised.

"It's what you wrote in your letters. You don't remember or don't believe it now? You wrote in your letters that you could not remember the last time you allowed yourself to cry. You're scared out here. You're incapable of sharing your feelings. That makes me happy because this is your time to change that, and you can with Lila.

"I'm happy for you, Orlando. Remember, you must write about other things besides being locked up . . . a relationship is a good thing to write about. The danger of being a poet in prison is that some poets never can write in freedom. They can only write in prison about prison. You are a poet of the world, Orlando."

I pull in under the hotel marquee, we hug. I promise to go to Somerville someday soon to visit her. Then, I watch her go into the hotel.

At the entrance to the lobby, she stops, turns and walks back to me.

"I chair a committee at PEN in New York; we help poets down on their luck or, in your case, just starting out, with emergency funds. Here, use it wisely."

She hands me a large manila envelope and is suddenly gone. Along with the money, there's a chapbook and note;

"Dear Orlando, I took the liberty of having a friend of mine publish some of your poems. I hope you don't mind. I think they're beautiful. Denise."

I open the envelope, count the money. One thousand dollars. My stomach flutters, I want to cry. For the first time I can remember, I let myself. I sniffle, my face cringing as the tears pour down.

This emotional crap is just too damned hard to deal with. Through bleary eyes, I stare at the oily, leaf-littered driveway under the hotel marquee and wonder at her kindness. It's like I'm leaning over something high; it's dark, I yearn to jump into Denise, never come out, be part of her body. I recall her short-cropped brown hair, her fast walk leaning forward a little, her long neck, her furtive eyes, her small nose, wide cheeks, formidable brow . . . I love her. I can do nothing but stand there feeling my world has changed. Back in the car, I sit for a long time looking out the window.

I turn the radio dial for a talk-show to distract me. Beethoven's "Moonlight Sonata" comes on. I try to collect my thoughts, wiping my eyes, but the tears keep coming. I'm really a baby in a crib, just crying alone. I study the beads of rain on the windshield, blow my breath on the glass. I wipe my eyes with the back of my hand.

∽ ∽ ∽

I was able to convince the scientist to let us keep Griselda a little longer. I pass whatever free time I have with Griselda, mostly taking her, this large jaguar, on walks across the fields behind Lila's house. She has unbelievable strength, unbridled curiosity. From the first day we had her, every whiff of wind, each leaf that floats, every grasshopper that leaps . . . her little ears are sensitive enough to even hear the sun warming the seeds. Her presence is like sunlight, everywhere at once, warm to the touch.

Mornings, I am awakened by Griselda growling, pawing at the office door to get out. Back inside, I let her run wild in the house while I write and read. More than ever now, I'm interested in what jaguars represent culturally to the Mayans and Aztecs, who held them in high esteem. They even had warrior jaguar clans who were the highest class in the hierarchy of indigenous societies.

I move my work space to the kitchen table again, give Griselda the office. I spend more time daydreaming than reading, gazing out the big window that overlooks the forest and dormant fields. Sometimes I see deer, hawks, wild dogs or feral cats, then leave the house to see if I can track them in the forest. Other times I simply walk in any random direction in the forest, wherever the spirit moves me.

When I drive anywhere, I am amazed all over again.

The fact that Denise has just sat here with me, right here in this car . . . the seats, the handle above the glove box that she clutched, the air in the car . . . all of it scented with the fragrance of her skin, hair and clothing. The car interior is filled with her aura, strong, poignant, primordial. To pick up any of her energy still lingering in the car, I run my palm over the seat fabric, touch the door handle, anything she has had contact with, trying to absorb the slightest vestige of her presence.

She has left behind a spirit-print I cannot touch. It is imbued with a wild confluence of emotion and intellect that breaks down the common comfort and creates vulnerable ways of looking at the world . . . conviction that is unwavering. The waterfall gush is her determinism, her compassion is the mist that blooms from that waterfall. Her heart is the place where bears come to drink and snatch salmon. Her spirit-print is that upstream birthing place I find myself in. On the drive home, it grows in me, and again, the butterfly shatters the paperweight, flutters against the windshield. I roll my window down and free it.

God is kind in fashioning my life on what she inspires in me, what wells up in me says that from my suffering and joy may come a sort of grace that allows me to live in a manner I yearn for but have not touched yet. My mind keeps circling around the hopeful idea that if I can make enough to get my brother into rehab, everything will be okay, life will be great. I'm filled with a newfound hope of getting things back on track. I find myself looping back toward the cycle of a celebratory life. I want my brother to be part of it. I've been spat into existence by a questionable accident in which all assembled angles were wrong. I was brought into the world to live with the mark of shame and corruption; it permeates every gesture and step.

Denise cupped the embers of my just-born self, blew them hot, revealing in the glowing embers my bill of rights to live as a human being with dignity. Now as I drive, there is no road, no night, no stars, no cold, no trees or fields— nothing. For an instant, just myself, a swirling orb of illuminated molecules merging with the universe and feeling something wonderful is going to happen to me.

∾ ∾ ∾

It's late November. On my drives I note people are preparing for Christmas. Decorated trees flash in living rooms, fairy lights in shrubs, colored lights in windows, snowmen in yards and Santa Clauses flying with reindeer on rooftops. My Christmas will come when I leave Green Mill, return home with enough money to get things off the ground.

When I get back that evening, Lila says she signed for a letter for me.

"What kind of letter?"

"Some legal form," she says.

I immediately go into a paranoid state. Anything legal—courts, letters, authority—sends me off a cliff. Every time my life got screwed up, it followed one of these.

I stare at the letter with my name on it waiting for me on the table. I pick it up, throw it in the kitchen trash can.

"Your sister forwarded it. She thought it was important. The least you can do is open it."

I refuse.

Lila fishes it out of the trash, opens it, reads it. She looks at me and says, "It's nothing. . . . They just want some information on the time you were in the orphanage."

"How did they know I was in the orphanage?"

"They keep records, Orlando, especially with someone like you who was the ward of the state for so long."

"That's my point: I don't want anything to do with them or that letter."

I retreat to my office, sit down, start reading *Leaves of Grass*. After a couple of hours, Lila comes in, offers me a glass of white wine. She asks if I want to go outside, sit and talk. So, I take a break with her.

"How long were you in the orphanage?"

"Long enough. Maybe seven years, maybe longer."

"You never talked about it in your letters."

"No need to."

"What happened?"

"Why should something have happened?"

"You told me how you react to legal stuff, how you hate priests, did they do something?"

"I don't want to talk about it."

"You know, I was raped by a lot of these boys growing up. They took it all from me. I got real wild after that. Where you'd get your wildness?"

"Said I don't want to talk about it. I'm afraid to look at that letter. I don't care what it's asking . . . and besides, it ain't asking about my orphanage. It's got an official legal stamp from the State of New Mexico. If they're looking for me, I'm not turning myself in. I didn't do anything."

"No, it's not that. They just want to know if anything happened at the orphanage."

"Lots of stuff happened."

"I mean about the priest doing stuff to you."

As night comes on deep and late, I somehow find the courage to share with Lila some of what occurred at the orphanage. It takes three or four hours to tell her about all the horrible things. She gets angry, so angry in fact, she finishes the wine and slugs down half a bottle of gin and hurls the bottle against the red brick front wall of the house—she wants to kill them. She says she wants to respond to the letter, that the priest and nuns had no right doing those things to me.

She goes inside. I sit in the dark, staring up at the stars. I cry. I'm feeling ill, almost as if I'm breathing noxious fumes. Maybe I'm picking up spiritual static. I wonder if my brother is dead. My sister? I feel my skin crawl remembering the things I told Lila.

Then, staring out into the pitch-black darkness of the woods, I hear a voice as close to me as if the person was bent over next to my ear: "Time, Orlando, time."

I turn, I look around, stand up, surveying with squinted eyes every inch of field and forest darkness for some person. I'm ready to fuck him up. I hear a noise coming from my office, turn, see Griselda gazing at me from the window. Her protective eyes are golden and fierce. Her paws are huge

167

cushions on the windowsill, the golden orbs of her eyes on fire with primal instincts, carrying the source of and proof of God's existence.

I smile at her, think the worst: They found an old charge against me, have a warrant for my arrest. Someone died. I didn't complete my full time at DYA.

Lila comes out, "Why don't you come inside now?"

"I don't want to yet."

She turns on the porch light, comes back out, hands me a bunch of papers. "Do you recognize these?"

"I told you, I don't want anything to do with that. Makes me scared . . . I get terrified and don't know why."

"You have every right to be traumatized. *Every* right. Bastards."

I study the papers, see that they're a bunch of old newspaper clippings from my orphanage days. Nuns. Boys. Dorms. Building.

"I recognize them, but what are they doing here? What's this letter? Is my sister acting weird again? Is she on one of her zany treks linking unrelated events together? Coming up with a theory we're all walking dead, or aliens are everywhere . . . or . . ."

"No, Orlando, it's about what they did to you."

"They didn't do anything. I mean, they didn't do anything I can talk about. Just stop this, okay? Stop this. I'm losing my shit here. . . . Please," I beg.

I break down again. Every fortification, every brick in the wall, every formidable, impenetrable obstacle suddenly gives way and collapses.

I spend the next hour answering her questions, catching my breath in shock, other times in sporadic fits of rage and uncontrollable crying. Sometimes I gasp. I put my clenched fist to my teeth, bite down so I don't scream. I pause, I breathe. I lay my palms flat on my chest to get my breath, to feel me to make sure I am still here. I throw the chair beside the door across the lawn. I squeeze my fingers against my face until I make blood appear from my pores. Lila tries to grab me; I throw her to the ground. I almost black out from pain, then I lean over, puke my guts out, gag, let everything pour out of my body. I feel like killing myself. At that moment, if I had a gun, I would blow my brains out and with it the memories flashing through my mind that minute.

I take off. I walk all night. When I return, it's almost dawn. I see the light on in Lila's office. I can see her working away in there.

When I go in and pour myself a cup of coffee, she says, "You don't have to worry about the letter. I answered it for you."

"They're not looking for me, are they?"

"Not in the way you think. It's a lawsuit against the priest . . . but don't worry, I took care of it. It had nothing to do with anything you did. It had to do with them committing a crime against you and other kids."

She asks if I want to read what she wrote. I decline. I want to nothing to do with it.

That night, when I was out walking, Lila filled in their questions based on what I told her:

JIMMY SANTIAGO BACA

UNITED STATES BANKRUPTCY COURT
FOR THE DISTRICT OF NEW MEXICO

In re: Chapter 11
ROMAN CATHOLIC CHURCH   Case No. 18-13027-t11
OF THE ARCHDIOCESE OF
SANTA FE, a New Mexico
corporation sole

CORRECTED SEXUAL ABUSE PROOF OF CLAIM
This form has been corrected solely with respect to the address for hand delivery.
IMPORTANT:
THIS FORM MUST BE *RECEIVED* NO LATER THAN
FEB. 17 , 1979 AT 5:00 P.M. (PREVAILING MOUNTAIN TIME)

Carefully read Notice and Instructions that are included with this **CONFIDENTIAL PROOF OF CLAIM** and complete all applicable questions. Send together with one copy to: Clerk of the United States Bankruptcy Court, District of New Mexico at the following address: Office of the Clerk of Court- ATTN SEALED DOCUMENTS, U.S. Bankruptcy Court, District of New Mexico, Pete V. Domenici U.S. Courthouse, 333 Lomas Blvd. NW, Suite 360 Albuquerque, NM 87102. If you prefer to hand deliver the completed Confidential Proof of Claim form to the Clerk, the physical address for hand delivery is Clerk of the United States Bankruptcy Court, District of New Mexico, 333 Lomas Blvd. NW, Suite 360 Albuquerque, NM.

If you mail or deliver the Confidential Proof of Claim form it must be received by the Clerk no later than 5:00 p.m. (prevailing Mountain Time) on Feb. 17, 1979.

YOU MAY WISH TO CONSULT AN ATTORNEY REGARDING THIS MATTER.

AND YOU MAY ALSO OBTAIN INFORMATION FROM THE OFFICIAL COMMITTEE OF UNSECURED CREDITORS BY CALLING TOLL FREE AT 888-570-6217.

FAILURE TO COMPLETE AND RETURN THIS FORM MAY RESULT IN YOUR INABILITY TO VOTE ON A PLAN OF RE-ORGANIZATION AND RECEIVE A DISTRIBUTION FROM THE ROMAN CATHOLIC CHURCH OF THE ARCHDIOCESE OF SANTA FE, COMMONLY KNOWN AS THE ARCHDIO-CESE OF SANTA FE (THE "ARCHDIOCESE").

UNLESS YOU INDICATE OTHERWISE IN PART 1 BELOW, YOUR IDENTITY WILL BE KEPT STRICTLY CONFIDEN-TIAL, UNDER SEAL, AND OUTSIDE THE PUBLIC RECORD OF THE BANKRUPTCY COURT. HOWEVER, THIS PROOF OF CLAIM AND THE INFORMATION IN THIS PROOF OF CLAIM WILL BE PROVIDED PURSUANT TO COURT-APPROVED CONFIDENTIALITY GUIDELINES TO THE ARCHDIOCESE, THE OFFICIAL COMMITTEE OF UNSE-CURED CREDITORS AND TO SUCH OTHER PERSONS AS THE BANKRUPTCY COURT DETERMINES NEED THE IN-FORMATION IN ORDER TO EVALUATE THE CLAIM.

THIS PROOF OF CLAIM IS FOR SEXUAL ABUSE CLAIMANTS ONLY.

For the purposes of this Proof of Claim, a **Sexual Abuse Claim** is defined as any Claim (as defined in section 101(5) of the Bankruptcy Code) against the Archdiocese resulting or arising in whole or in part, directly or indirectly from any actual or alleged sexual conduct or misconduct, sexual abuse or molestation, indecent assault and/or battery, rape, pe-dophilia, ephebophilia, or sexually-related physical, psycho-logical, or emotional harm, or contacts, or interactions of a sexual nature between a child and an adult, or a nonconsenting adult and another adult, sexual assault, sexual battery, sexual psychological or emotional abuse, humiliation, or intimidation, or any other sexual misconduct, and seeking monetary damages or any other relief, under any theory of liability, including vicarious liability, any negligence-based theory, contribution, indemnity, or any other theory based on any acts or failures to act by the Archdiocese or any other person or entity for whose acts or failures to act the Archdiocese is or was allegedly responsible.

For Purposes of this Proof of Claim, a **Sexual Abuse Claimant** is defined as the person asserting a Sexual Abuse Claim against the Archdiocese, or if a minor, then his parent or legal guardian.

TO BE VALID, THIS PROOF OF CLAIM MUST BE SIGNED BY YOU OR YOUR ATTORNEY. IF THE SEXUAL ABUSE CLAIMANT IS DECEASED OR INCAPACITATED, THE FORM MAY BE SIGNED BY THE SEXUAL ABUSE CLAIMANT'S REPRESENTATIVE, EXECUTOR OF THE ESTATE OR THE ATTORNEY FOR THE ESTATE. IF THE SEXUAL ABUSE CLAIMANT IS A MINOR, THE FORM MAY BE SIGNED BY THE SEXUAL ABUSE CLAIMANT'S PARENT OR LEGAL GUARDIAN, OR THE SEXUAL ABUSE CLAIMANT'S ATTORNEY.

Penalty for presenting fraudulent claim: Fine of up to $500,000 or imprisonment for up to 5 years, or both. 18 U.S.C. §§ 152 and 3571.

PART 1: CONFIDENTIALITY

THIS SEXUAL ABUSE PROOF OF CLAIM (ALONG WITH ANY ACCOMPANYING EXHIBITS AND ATTACHMENTS) WILL BE MAINTAINED AS CONFIDENTIAL PURSUANT TO COURT-APPROVED GUIDELINES UNLESS YOU EX-PRESSLY REQUEST THAT IT BE PUBLICLY AVAILABLE BY CHECKING THE BOX AND SIGNING BELOW. ONLY THE SEXUAL ABUSE CLAIMANT MAY WAIVE CONFI-DENTIALITY IN THIS PART 1.

☐ I do not want this Proof of Claim (along with any accompanying exhibits and attachments) to be kept confidential. Please verify this election by signing directly below.

Signature: _____

Print Name: _____

PART 2: IDENTIFYING INFORMATION

A. Sexual Abuse Claimant

Orlando	S	Lucero
First Name	Middle Initial	Last Name

1114 Tivoli
_____

Mailing Address (If party is incapacitated, is a minor or is deceased, please provide the address of the individual submitting the claim. If you are in jail or prison, your current address).

Albuquerque	NM	87100
City	State	Zip Code

Telephone No(s): Home: _____ Work: _____

Email address: _____

Social Security Number: 575-48-3276

If you are in jail or prison, your identification number:

_____

May we leave voicemails for you regarding your claim?
□Yes   **X** No (please contact my attorneys)

May we send confidential information to your email:
□Yes   **X** No (please contact my attorneys)

Birth Date: 011/01/1952   **X** Male □ Female
              Month Day Year

Any other name, or names, by which the Sexual Abuse Claimant has been known:

_____

B. Sexual Abuse Claimant's Attorney (if any):

Baell, LLC
_____
Law Firm Name

Baell   Duran
_____
Attorney's First Name   Middle Initial   Last Name

320 Gold Ave SW #1218
_____
Street Address

Albuquerque   NM   87102
_____
City   State   Zip Code

(505) 255-6000   (505) 234-6222
_____
Telephone No.   Fax No.

PART 3: NATURE OF COMPLAINT
(Attach additional separate sheets if necessary)

NOTE: IF YOU HAVE PREVIOUSLY FILED A LAWSUIT AGAINST THE ARCHDIOCESE IN STATE OR FEDERAL COURT, YOU MAY ATTACH THE COMPLAINT. IF YOU DID NOT FILE A LAWSUIT, OR IF THE COMPLAINT DOES NOT CONTAIN ALL OF THE INFORMATION REQUESTED BELOW, YOU MUST PROVIDE THE INFORMATION BELOW.

a. Who committed the acts of sexual abuse or other wrongful conduct?

I was sexually abused and repeatedly sexually assaulted by Fr. Edward Gallagher, and also by three unidentified priests who I believed worked at the Servants of the Paraclete Facilities in Jemez Springs or Albuquerque, or were "in transit" within the Paraclete Order, or were Benedictines, or were Franciscans. Regardless, these pedophile priests were serving as agents for, or were empowered and protected by, the Archdiocese of Santa Fe, and whatever religious orders they came from. Fr. Gallagher was the main guy and primary predator at the Orphanage from when I got there until I left in May 1965. Paraclete priests or priests from religious orders were passing through, or visiting, or stayed for awhile, in rooms provided to them on the third floor. Some of the nuns from the Poor Sisters of St. Francis Seraph of the Perpetual Adoration were directly involved, escorting me to the chapel/rectory for abuse by Fr. Gallagher when he called for me to be brought to him, or to one of the sleeping quarters upstairs reserved for visiting priests, under the guise that I needed "guidance and counseling" (because at a certain age, I was constantly a runaway), whereupon they sexually abused me.

b. What is the position, title or relationship to you (if known) of the abuser or individual who committed these acts?

The orphanage in Albuquerque was called St. Anthony's Orphanage, run and administered by Franciscan nuns under the direction, supervision, blessing and control of the Archdiocese, (who for many decades were co-administrators), and I was an orphan boy there when dropped off August 31, 1958, at the age of 6, and was officially there until May 28, 1965, leaving at the age of 13. See attached photocopies of orphanage records for both me and my brother Camilo, showing my date of arrival and the date my aunt took me and my brother to her home. My life during those years was completely under the control of Fr. Gallagher and these nuns, where I was repeatedly beat (with boards—often my entire backside was bruised and welted), and sexually abused. I was virtually powerless until I successfully ran away a few times, choosing to live on the streets at age 13 until finally the police and social services persuaded my aunt DeMacia to take me and my brother in.

c. Where did the sexual abuse or other wrongful conduct take place? Please be specific and complete all relevant information that you know, including the City and State, name of the School (if applicable) and/or the name of any other location.

The Orphanage was at 1500 Indian School Road NW, Albuquerque, New Mexico, and the abuse occurred in a number of places on the premises, including: in one of the offices of the 3-story administration building (pants down, over a desk, while he/they penetrated me); frequently in one of the dorms where I was assigned cleaning duties, (Gallagher would enter while I was dust mopping, scrubbing toilets, cleaning sinks, etc.); in the small living area between the rectory and the altar area (commonly called the sacristy); or in one of the sleeping quarters upstairs reserved for visiting priests in transit, who I believed were from the Servants of the Paraclete, or were Benedictines, or were Franciscans, as their uniforms were each slightly different.

Attached are some photos from the Library of Congress including some sketches of the layout well before I got there, and a newspaper story from the *Albuquerque Journal* dated April 12, 1963, that has a few pictures.

d. When did the sexual abuse or other wrongful conduct take place?

1. If the sexual abuse or other wrongful conduct took place over a period of time (months or years), please state when it started, when it stopped and how many times it occurred.

   Fr. Gallagher began abusing me before and after I was trained as an altar boy, in 1959. He sexually abused me until my attempts at running away in 1965 were getting more and more successful as I got older, and he left at the end of 1965 anyway. I was raped and abused at least 30 times, conservatively speaking, by Fr. Gallagher. I was also "given" to visiting priests or brothers or superiors from the Servants of the Paraclete, the Benedictines, or the Franciscans, on occasion over the 1960s, who would also sexually abuse me. Nuns would come and get me, and take me to them at the temporary quarters on the 3rd floor, or sometimes in one of the empty classrooms on the 2nd floor, or in the auditorium behind the stage where they stated they were going to give me lessons in acting for the plays we often performed. Also, I was abused by visiting clergy in the band section of the auditorium, where they pretended to teach me to play a trumpet or drum and instead raped me, and when I was collecting the sheets on laundry day from the 3rd floor, they'd trap me in one of the upstairs dorms and rape me. (I recall two younger boys whose names I do not know or recall, accidentally walked in one time and caught them in the act). This happened many times, over a dozen, but I don't know the exact number nor the names of visiting clergy. I can name some of the nuns, and there is a photo in the 1992 Calendar of the nuns that look like from my era, for sure. So the answer to the question of "how many times this occurred" is: over 30 by Gallagher, and over 12 by visiting priests.

2. Please also state your age(s) and your grade(s) in school (if applicable) at the time the abuse or other wrongful conduct took place.

I was dropped off August 31, 1958, at the age of 6, and was officially there until May 28, 1965, leaving at the age of 13. See attached photocopy of orphanage records, showing my date of arrival and the date my aunt took me and my brother to her home. See also a picture of my brother and a nun, and a class photo type picture of me in those years.

e. What happened (describe what happened):
Attached is a photo from my first communion classes at the orphanage. I was 6 and they graduated me to altar boy status and choir boy. Trained to believe the priest was God's earthly representative, I trusted him and my innocent trust unwittingly invited the most ghastly nightmare period of my life; when I was assigned duties in the Chapel, (buffing tiles, feather dusting saints, cleaning pews,) filling cruets with wine, folding Fr. Gallagher's

priestly garments—what I assumed a privilege, turned out to be a ploy to make me easily available to increasing sexual abuse. I worked in the Catholic Chapel and here is where I was first offered wine by Fr. Gallagher. After he got me intoxicated, he led me into his sacristy and sat my on his lap and pulled my pants down. He masturbated me, inserted his fingers in my anus, sucked on me, the whole time masturbating himself. And then he penetrated me. I was lost, traumatized, in shock, stunned into paralysis and could do nothing but tremble and shriek inside my head at what was happening to me. Is this what God wanted of me? Is this the way it was done, is this how we socialized, how we learned to be good altar boys, how we worship the priest, is this God's plan? Will I be okay with Him now, will He bring my parents back, will He care for my brother and I, will this make my mother come back? The whole time I was being touched and molested and finally raped, Fr. Gallagher promised me my mother would return, assured me this is what God wanted, explained how I was lucky to be chosen, said I was doing good in God's eyes, that I would be rewarded with a home and family if I continued to let him do the nasty things he was doing. He made me drink more alcohol, ordered me to obey him and commanded I please him by allowing him to kiss my penis, suck on it, run his tongue into my anus to lubricate it, he said, so it wouldn't hurt, (it makes me puke now thinking of it), and then finally after what seemed an hour or two but clearly wasn't, he would come, grunting like a pig and shake all over and then ask me to get dressed and instruct me to never tell anyone, telling me that it was a mortal sin to do so, it has to remain between us and God. God hears and sees all things, so our secret must be ours alone, and if I said anything, I'd be severely punished and my soul condemned to hell forever. It was part of being an altar boy. After I got dressed he would fill my pockets with lemon drop hard candy, gave me a special scapular and a rosary. He said I could never repeat what we did, not even in confession with him. Over the weeks and months and years I would witness what seemed like an army of boys go in and come out, some crying, others dazed and in shock by Fr. Gallagher's sexual perversion, his obscene appetite to lick our genitals, lick our anuses, suck on us and finally rape us. I even saw two boys with blood on the butt side of their pants. I'm also aware that a number of them committed suicide along the way, and that almost all of them became addicts and alcoholics who eventually succumbed to horrible deaths from drugs.

What Father Gallagher and the visiting religious order predators did to us (they wore black and white gowns, sometimes gray, and looked Godly in their robes and hefty rosaries dangling from their waists and sandals), many of the boys copied and were doing to each other at night when the nuns in the dorms turned the lights off, many of the boys scooted under the bunks and had sexual inter-course, fellatio and sometimes committed rape on younger kids who couldn't defend themselves. Strange to see a Calendar of the dorm room from the first year I was there, attached. Over time, I soon found myself aroused by other boy's naked bodies in the shower room, found myself imagining having sex with other boys. Just as Fr. Gallagher did to me, I fantasized doing to them. Many boys did. I grew out of that sort of imagery, upon escaping this place and this Church by age 14.

Unconsciously or not, one is forced to adopt coping mech-anisms to survive the rape sessions, and I soon learned to fight, to hate myself by doing harmful things to myself— becoming a risk-taker, taking chances diving off the pump house where many boys cracked their skulls, smoking dry elm leaves wrapped in comic book paper, volunteering to be the one to leap from the swing even if I risked breaking my bones, running off at midday to Wells supermarket on the corner of Indian School Road and Rio Grande Boulevard and stealing candy; breaking into the shoe-room, burglarizing the bakery and stealing the money from the nun from her day's earnings selling bread, fighting other boys, dry-humping other boys by the slides, hating myself and cutting my arms with glass, refusing directions, running away dozens of times, increasingly until, at 13, I was roaming the city and breaking into stores, disobeying the nuns and my aunt, talking back, etc.,etc.,etc. Such was my childhood and youth.

As I've grown older, the horrific memories grow stronger and more invasive, and I often am reminded of that nightmare period when I run into other orphanage kids—all of them, it seems, druggies, meth-heads, tweakers, cokeheads, drunks, in prison, ex-cons. It's a sad situation and we know, among ourselves, why we've become the worthless trash of society many of us have become—we were treated by the pedophiles as trash, we were exploited as children, our innocence ripped from us, our bodies abused by these evil-doers, with secret designs so diabolical we can never forgive them, we live with the horror every second, and know what they did to us is a terrible, terrible crime. No needle in the arm, no amount of heroin or Oxy or cocaine or weed or whiskey can numb the pain that endures and darkens our every day, our sleep and our waking. We hear the voices of those pedophiles, we're haunted by Father Gallagher's soft voice telling us to pull our pants down and we see his ugly face over and over for decades, and we relive the horror without exit nor mercy. I've used every drug trying to erase the nightmare, every narcotic trying to numb the pain. I've wrecked every relationship I've had. I have tried to commit suicide countless times, I've de-

stroyed marriages, abandoned myself to years of addiction and alcoholism, been to prison, jails, gladiator schools,
juvenile detention centers, foster homes—all to no avail.
All these attempts at forgetting the excruciating torture I
had to submit to by the priests and nuns, which has only
magnified the penance over time. I don't sleep. I've never
held a job for more than a few months. I've used drugs all
my life. I'm anti-social and somehow after all these years,
I've never been able to forgive myself.

I still think it was my fault, so much so in the past in fact,
that I felt I was so evil I needed to go to prison, be removed
from society, and in my teens in D-homes or foster care,
or in my early teens doing hard time in Denver, to feed my
addiction and self-worthlessness, I sold drugs and was
subsequently sentenced to a super-max YA prison where
after a few years in, I learned to read and write.

f. Did you tell anyone about the sexual abuse or other wrongful conduct and, if so, who did you tell and when (this would
include parents; relatives; friends; the Archdiocese; attorneys; counselors; and law enforcement authorities)?

Maybe in bar drinking whiskey or hanging out in a motel
room doing cocaine, maybe in the backyard drinking beer
late into the night, I hinted at it but never elaborated to
whichever friend I was with, as it was too painful, and to
offer details might lead to an outburst of uncontrollable violence, some criminal act, which was always imminent
and often happened when the subject came up with an
alumni—we did crazy things trying to forget what we
knew, but spent a lifetime attempting to conceal and act
like we didn't know it happened.

g. Identify any church or religious organization you have belonged to or have been affiliated with.

Escaping the Catholic orphanage was the equivalent of escaping the Catholic religion, and surviving my childhood and my youth drove me forward. I no longer believe in anything that my senses cannot ascertain. None. I can never bring myself to step into a church again, never allow myself to get close, or in any proximity, time or distance, to a priest or any person or place, secular or otherwise, remotely connected to any religion—in fact, when we moved in with our aunt, the first thing we did and got punished severely for, was to carry all the plaster saints out of my aunt's house when she died, took all the pictures and crosses off the walls, and threw them all down a well. I could never place myself in jeopardy emotionally by affiliating in any manner with any religious organization. That option was nuclearized to ash remains, forever, by the criminal violation of half a dozen priests—monsters—who sexually abused me as a child.

h. State whether there were any witnesses to the abuse. If there were any witnesses, please list their name(s) and any contact information you have.

There were many. Kids who saw what was happening by accident, others who shared with close confidants, some were told after each incident, some knew by word of mouth. I personally saw a dozen or so exiting Father Gallagher's living quarters, some weeping, sometimes even bloody around the crotch area, as stated, but almost all of them too ashamed and terrified to look me in the eye. Witnesses? Yes, but so wounded and damaged as to become mute and deaf for fear of eternal damnation in hell, and if not that, then by the warning of the rapists, who vowed if we ever told anyone, that we would die, we would feel the wrath of God and be visited by Satan himself. A little boy hearing this will take the crime he witnessed and was victim of, to the grave, as many have. We were so scared to say anything, we would have preferred our tongues be cut out, acid thrown in our eyes, for to tempt a priest's vengeance was perhaps the greatest curse of all. Kids saw me taken by the nuns and escorted out of class-rooms, they saw me pulled by the ears until my lobes bled, they saw Sister Anna Louise slap me until I passed out, they saw me come out of Father Gallagher's living quar-ters crying, they heard me screaming at the nuns, they stopped me from beating other boys on the playground. In one form or another, they were witnesses to the crime of sexual abuse by witnessing my steadily violent and disin-tegrating behavior. The abuse was prevalent, that some-times they'd attack me in the dorm, sometimes on the 3rd floor, on the 2nd, in a different dorm, in one of the offices, in the auditorium, etc. That entire place was marked with a toxic haze of criminal residue. Keep in mind, we are talk-ing about a child of 6, 7, 8, 9, 10, 11, 12, 13, and lest we forget, there were many like me. Witnesses? Many of us don't cry anymore.

PART 4: IMPACT OF COMPLAINT
(Attach additional separate sheets if necessary)

(If you are uncertain how to respond to this Part 4, you may leave this Part 4 blank, but you will be required to complete this Part 4 within thirty (30) days after a written request is made for the information requested in this Part 4)

1. What injuries (including physical, mental and/or emotional) have occurred to you because of the act or acts of sexual abuse or other wrongful conduct that resulted in the claim (for example, the effect on your education, employment, personal relationships, health, and any physical injuries)?

First, please review the "what happened" section above, as much of my response there merges into the response to this question. What happened and its impact are not much different. So to my answers above, I continue:

Kept hostage in an environment where you are a play-toy for the sexually crazed, imprisoned with no escape, no access to help, you live and breathe under the duress of sexual predators permitting you to, you're encumbered with a dreadful finality that you need them, that they design your days and control your life, that you are interred in an above-ground tomb and sentenced to walk and play and eat and sleep in predator-made hell forever, that the sequence of time and days are only broken by periodic calls to the bedrooms of predators who rape and consume you. Your life has nothing to do with an ordinary clock or routine time and academic studies or parks and happy holidays. No, your life is broken into rape scenes, and in these scenes you are allowed to be treated like a human being your predator hungers for, craves, desires, and they strip your soul from you, force you to do unimaginable horrors with them, and these scenes mark your growing up. My normal 'school time', is my 'normal', but not normal, because I left the place essentially illiterate. The actual rape, the act of it by a priest, becomes the epicenter of your existence and defines your life, imbues your fear, invades your diction, cauterizes your heart with a numbness so you live as a Nothing, and you are Nothing thereafter, for the rest of your Nothing life. With my peers, we found drugs worked better than the alcohol the priest gave you.

So what injuries? Being fucked by a priest merely fractures your soul and you bleed from your rectum, it's the aftermath—the nightmares, the sweats, the fright, the terror that constantly accosts you and abides in every cell and nerve. I've tried suicide so many times, was addicted for years, spent

185

time in YA. Like the San Andreas fault, the repeated rapes caused grave breakage in my soul and mind, caused me to destroy myself, to squander my time and finances on alcohol and drugs, created crevices and cracks and avalanches in my heart that poured out earthquakes of sorrow for what had happened to me that only drugs could remedy, partially, and violence. I went on violent sprees, against guards, inmates, bystanders, everyone anywhere, without concern for their welfare or who they were, all leading to me being institutionalized for so many years because I was incapable of living in society after what had happened to me. Because of those rapes, I was sequestered in a dark pit called isolation in a max prison and forgotten for three years, because I couldn't live with human beings, because I couldn't trust them. They had done something to me, demons wearing costumes and robes to trick me, came with folded hands reciting prayers and blessings, only to rape me and beat me and destroy me.

Finally, after much self-hatred, self-loathing and self-mutilation, I was able to find solace and reprieve in my poetry and surrender to the hopeful and compensatory passion of writing, which has become my mission in life. I want to be a voice. I got kicked out of middle school when my aunt took us in after the orphanage. I didn't really know how to read and write much.

My current girlfriend has saved me from an early death. Writing is my only personal solace in this world; the damage done by the priests and their associates can never be healed or resolved. Ever. Especially since the brother I love with all my heart was raped at the orphanage by the same perverts and predators many times too, and the pain, in its searing burn, is so deep and incalculable, that even to this day he cannot talk about it.

Being raped murdered his soul and killed a part of me. Psychological reverberations ripple through all aspects of life, even in the prison system. Violence against other inmates in prison is, by extension, violence against other kids in the orphanage, all as perpetrated by the priests. But the government does not pretend to be the Spokesman for God. The Church does.

I don't ever really talk about all this stuff, but it happened.

2. Have you sought counseling or other treatment for your injuries? If so, with whom and when?

No. I've had some counseling for substance abuse issues, but I have not sought counseling for childhood sexual abuse, nor discussed it with counselors in or out of prison. I am mulling over maybe some therapy, to look for connections between the abuse as a child by clergy and my current moment of talking about all this, really for the first time.

PART 5: ADDITIONAL INFORMATION

1. Prior Claims: Have you filed any claims in any other bankruptcy case relating to the sexual abuse described in this claim.
   □ Yes X No (If "Yes," you are required to attach a copy of any completed claim form.)

   If "Yes," which case(s):

2. Settlements: Regardless of whether a complaint was ever filed against any party because of the sexual abuse or other wrongful conduct, have you settled any claim relating to the sexual abuse or other wrongful conduct described in this claim?
   □ Yes X No (If "Yes," please describe, including parties to the settlement. You are required to attach a copy of any settlement agreement.)

3. Bankruptcy. Have you ever filed bankruptcy? □ Yes **X** No
   (If "Yes," please provide the following information)

   Name of Case: _____ Court: _____

   Date filed: _____ Case No. _____

   Chapter: □ 7   □ 11   □ 12   □ 13

   Name of Trustee: _____

4. State whether you have previously commenced any lawsuit seeking damages for the identified sexual abuse. If
   yes, please state: <u>NO</u>

∿ ∿ ∿

The dawn light has turned my office room walls and window a pale rose color. Griselda is at my feet, snoring.

I kind of understand now, after sharing with Lila my orphanage experience—the first person I ever talked to about
why the whipping upset me so much, why I had to convince
her to do it, why I wanted her to go through with all my fantasies.

I now know why I had to write those letters, include all
the sex, why I couldn't accept her as a friend or even a human
being but a woman I created in my mind, in the imagination
born and created in Father Gallagher's living quarters. I had
fantasized grotesque scenes with sex toys and sexual acts that
later made me ashamed. I had even denied writing it. Admitting it was too much.

But I had written it. I know why now.

I rise, stretch and walk into the forest. I cry every tear I
never did, I feel all the pain I buried. I stare at the water, so
brilliant, flashing with sunlight. I see Ghost Boy sitting in a

room, bleeding from his anus. He looks at me with hatred in his eyes, with vengeance. I see him slowly rise, turn the door-knob and walk around the pond toward me. He sits down next to me on the pond bank, a lock of thick black hair waving over his forehead and cheek. He is ten, never smiles; at fifteen he smiles a lot, sneaks under bunks at night to stick his pecker into a kid's butthole. His black hair is now slicked back. Copper complexion, thick eye lashes, his dark eyes linger on me with a deep compassion in them.

"It's time to let me go, Orlando," he says.

I know it too. I raise my hand at him, he nods, jutting his chin up like a macho, knowing that without him I would be dead, that I wouldn't have had the courage to stand up for myself and fight the predators. He knows he taught me the meaning of self-sacrifice, integrity, courage. Our goodbye is quiet, modest, filled with an ominous sense, as if the morning air is the interior of a cathedral, like somewhere up high an organ plays our goodbye music.

He leaps up off the bank, wearing jeans, a T-shirt and black and white Converse high-top lace-ups. He walks on water across the pond, showing off like he likes to do. When he gets to the other side, he turns and waves, a big smile creasing his face, eyes shining with the rising sun.

I watch Ghost Boy vanish into the mist hovering over the forest, into the fog that clings to the pine trees. I watch him disappear as snow from a pine branch above him sprinkles the air with flake-shards that burn a diamond blue and glitter in the air.

When I get back to the house I see Lila has placed the letter in the mailbox by the road.

∾ ∾ ∾

A day later snow blankets the land. It is beautiful and the sky is blue. My sister calls to tell me they have a job for me. I think about it for a while, then decide to take it. It snows lightly the day I take my last walk, following the banks above the pond, my head clears from all the misgivings and doubts I've had recently. I enjoy stumbling through snow drifts, feeling my leg muscles contract to balance me, I go on breaking off icicles with a stick I carry.

I end my walk with a visit to Mr. Chambers. I thank him for his generosity, wish him a Merry Christmas. In the afternoon, I drive up to the cabin, find Frog King there with a bunch of boozy, drugged, tobacco-chewing cowboys in a high-stakes poker game with their dogs lounging around their feet: pit bulls, blue heelers, corsos and catahoulas. There are young, naked college women lounging about. They all drink white lightning from mason jars and plastic milk jugs. Piles of money crowd the tabletop.

Frog King and I go into the bedroom, sit and talk a bit. He begrudges me nothing, compliments my loyalty, says if I ever need him, he'll be there for me.

The next day, after my first cup of coffee, I call Beto and Chuy and tell them I'm out of the game. I call and give my goodbyes to Brandon, Nancy and Kimberly, then I go look for Lila. I find her wrapped in a heavy coat and fur cap sitting on a log by the pond behind her father's house. I sit down beside her.

"Love this pond, fished it a lot," I say. I look up at the blue sky and sigh.

"I was just thinking how you caught the old General here." She takes a hit on her joint, flicks it into the water where I watch it float. "You're leaving." She lets out a stream of smoke and looks at me. "Won't cry, won't criticize, won't stop you. You were right, you know."

"About?"

"Our letters. They created a world you could never live up to."

"I'm sorry."

"I wanted you to be everything you said in your letters you wanted to be . . . but you were a disappointment. It was all about sex, crazy sex you learned from that goddamn priest, and I was willing to do it with you. All those beautiful words on wanting to be the poet, the college student, but you went right back to your old ways. I was sad to see that happen."

"Criminal habits are hard to break, Lila."

The sun breaks through the clouds, I look at her long red hair, admire how the sun makes it shimmer. I want to kiss her, want to walk right out on the half-frozen pond, prove my love for her will keep me from falling in.

She shoves her hands into her coat pockets. "Men and their damn problems with their mothers, or lack thereof . . . either way, you all have obsessions of the heart, and that's what our letters were: your obsessions. Sex. Porn. Crazy stuff you dreamed of doing with a woman because of all that shit you went through. This way, that way, spanking, whipping, slapping. When it comes to obsessions of the heart, there's no room for two."

She looks up at me. I expect her to smile, but she doesn't. I am afraid of what she is going to say next.

"Jeezuz, just my luck to land right in the middle of love with a man who never had a healthy relationship with a woman."

I don't know what to say.

"The women in your life were authorities," she says, ". . . nuns, grandmas, aunts, strict ladies who thought the flesh was a sin, sex was bad, something that would send you to hell for even thinking about it. They made a tangled mess of you when it comes to sex." She lights another cigarette, drags long and exhales. "But all is not lost . . . you've shown yourself to be noble, Orlando—that you have."

"Anything but," I say and mean it.

I feel like I made this whole affair a disaster. I look across the pond, remembering the day I saw a white heron land on a log. I wonder if it was Ghost Boy turned into a white bird.

"I got a question."

"Yeah?"

"What happened that night at the cabin? What made you freak and run?"

"I lost it, don't know why."

"I couldn't understand that, especially with how excited you were in your letters . . . how you rehearsed it so many times, what you would do to me. I did it to make you happy. No matter the content, to me they were the most beautiful words I ever read. You and your letters . . . so, so different once you got out here."

"Yeah," I say, getting up and walking to the edge of the water to look at my reflection in the ice. Lost for words, all I can come up with is, "I'm going."

"You try to compensate for a lifetime of deprivation. Try to free yourself from all that childhood hurt."

"I don't want to talk about it."

"You turn and flip and maneuver into a dozen positions to love, hoping it might free you. . . . I went along with you, searching for a way to help you out of yourself, using all the magic I had to break through that blockage and pour out a lifetime of rejection and arouse in you a feeling of love.

"There were times when reading your letters I thought for sure you'd elevated me to a place where I dissolved and merged with something higher. Your words had that way of replacing reality with your fantasy, hoping your obsession with wild sex would solve your problems."

I can see fish under the ice. I remember the countless times Peter and I tramped through the woods, day after day, for weeks.

"By conjuring my sexual ceremonies with you in letters, I hoped to exorcise the shame I'd been subjected to."

She crushes her cigarette in the dirt with her hand and lights another. "Boy . . . I'll tell you this: you got a beautiful way of talking. It's like someone else is talking."

"I know, I don't know how or why, but I use words, sentences that don't belong to me. Maybe I'm channeling something."

"Wouldn't doubt it . . . I've often thought about that possibility."

We stare across the pond at nothing.

"For days after that happened at the cabin, the word 'trauma' kept clinging to my brain. Clung to my brain like a tick I couldn't pull off, sucking the blood from me. 'Trauma,' 'trauma,' 'trauma,' the word repeated itself like some signal received by a satellite dish from space."

Why'd I freak? Why'd I go along? Why couldn't I stop? Why'd I increase the pain? My counselors at DYA always used the word "trauma" to describe my anger, my temper. When I got into trouble. I mocked them, bragged that nothing could hurt me. No matter what anyone did to me, it didn't hurt.

"But it wasn't true," Lila says. "I could see how much you hurt when you saw your brother. I could see how scared you were when you flew out here. You were a scared little boy."

"I was afraid the counselor would send me away to the nut house. I wanted nothing to do with that word, 'trauma.'

So, I played it off and always put on a show, denying anything could get to me."

"Trauma," she says, "is a bone-marrow stillness and a frightening loss of emotional control. It happens where one's emotions twist up and choke you."

"I always saw it like a rag a killer wipes his bloody hands on after a crime. . . . Yes, I am traumatized. I am a problem. So what? I'm not the only one. I can't change that."

"Just 'cause you string sweet words together doesn't mean you get a free pass from life's problems."

"Means I have to use it . . ."

"And that's the very thing you didn't do, Orlando. You don't even respect your gift."

"It's 'cuz when I write, sometimes I get this feeling I'm cracking up. I don't trust no doctor or shrink messing around with me. I seen what they do to kids they diagnose as sick. They end up zombies."

She stands up, looks down at her boots and says, "Strange."

"What?"

"That after all this time, you talk about it now. After there isn't a thing we can do about it." She shakes her head sadly. "Isn't that life?!"

"Yeah," I agree.

She hugs me and whispers, "Don't be afraid."

I try to keep my voice from breaking, "Okay, okay."

She rocks me in her arms. "Orlando. You want to go back to sleep and be tucked in and kissed by a mother, but you can't. You're all grown up." She pulls away, takes my hands in hers. "One way or another, we each get to where we need to get. When it comes to women, your journey has just started. You belong to the world now."

I push against her.

She pushes back, holds me at arm's length. "I have a favor to ask. . . . Will you grant me one request?"

"Anything."

"Read one."

She reaches into the canvas satchel on the ground beside her, pulls out some letters rolled into a baton, held with rubber bands. "Read what's highlighted in yellow. Just one. I want to remember your voice."

I take a page, read half-way down, hand it back.

"Your voice. Yes, you have it, Orlando. Use it."

A breeze flutters over the pond. A bigmouth bass or a catfish nibbles the water surface.

"I better get back to the house."

"Can we write?" I ask.

"Oh, Orlando . . . sometimes you have to learn to live with that hole in your heart, fill it with purpose, which is as close to love as we ever get."

A white egret flies in on the opposite bank, perches on log branches half in the water. She squeezes my hand, looks at me. "I think you better go talk to Peter."

I find Peter in the forest, watch him stop to look at rocks and study them. He picks up a branch, feels the bark, smells it, licks it, shakes it, snatches twigs off the ground, swats his Levis and walks on.

I have a primitive loyalty to him. "Hey you, what you doing?" I say, huffing as I approach him.

His eyes are ahead on the pond. "What'd you go to prison for?"

"What brought that up? . . . Smuggling weed. Never made any money, just a bunch of wild kids working for the bosses, loading up trucks, making enough to buy sneakers, clothes, food."

"Mom says you're leaving, I thought maybe they're after you. Kill anyone in there?"

"Cockroaches."

"Where you going?"

"New Mexico."

"You scared?"

"Kinda. New beginnings always make me nervous."

"I'll miss you."

"Me too."

"You should believe in God. He helps."

"I went to mass with my grandma. I used to hold her hand 'cuz she was blind, some bomb test at White Sands made her eyes go white as egg shells. Not really religious, though."

We walked. It felt good to walk with him.

"I like the smell," Peter says staring at the water, ". . . the candles, incense, the sound of rosary beads and people praying. You think if we pray . . . me here, you there . . . we could talk through God, use him like a telephone wire?"

"I think he'd be cool with that."

"Then we can talk in our prayers to each other, and God will carry mine to you, yours to me."

"I think so."

"Me too."

"I love you, Peter."

"Me too."

6

I WAS ONE OF those homeless guys you sometimes see during Christmas at truck stops hitching a ride, or rest areas, or climbing some mountain trail by themselves. You'd see me in a bus seat, at a bus window, looking out at all the lit up Christmas trees, families together driving by, holiday bunting, sparkling bulbs and Santas along the way. For me it was my heart, lit up with bulbs and gifts you could not unwrap: gifts of understanding, a sense of peacefulness I had never experienced before.

It's the end of January 1981, when I arrive in Albuquerque by bus. You could not dream of a more beautiful blue sky, cleaner air than what greets me. My sister picks me up, gives me a room. After a meal of blue corn enchiladas, I sleep the sleep of a pine cone in its pine branch.

The next day, I ride in with my sister and her husband to a big construction project. I am assigned to Mr. Martínez, an iron worker. I am to be his helper. I do the grunt work, physical labor. I carry lengths of rebar to him, lay them out, hold them while Mr. Martínez ties them with baling wire. When the work slows we wait for a truck to arrive with a new shipment of rebar. I sit down in the scoop of a front-end loader, read a postcard from Denise. She advises me that when I write her back, to take care with the use of commas, to choose words carefully. (I used to be dreadful when it came to commas and spelling.)

After work I shower, put on some new jeans, a nice plaid shirt. I borrow my sister's car and drive down to the Turquoise Lodge, the rehab in the South Valley where my brother is. I ask for him, but they say they've never heard of him. I explain his drug problem, his AIDS . . . they don't know. I have them double-check to make sure. I even walk to the back of the large communal room where an AA meeting is in session.

I leave pissed. I swing by his pad. It looks abandoned. For the next two weeks, I keep going by his place, but there's no sign of him. Despite feeling plagued with worry about his whereabouts, I decide that's it: Whenever he decides to get real, he knows where to find me.

The next day, still feeling irritated as hell, I stay ahead of my boss laying the rebar in as he comes behind me to tie it. We have our system down. I stop to take a breather, get a drink from the water bucket and look around. Hundreds of workers are busy erecting bomb shelters for the military. It's a big union job. Cement trucks roar in hourly, the mason boys with their big rubber boots slosh in, trowel the slab and foundation in the laid forms. After them come carpenters to lay more forms, then iron workers to lay the rebar. Next are the electricians and so forth. Foremen come and go, yelling orders and commands. Whistles blow, tractor-trailers drop and load supplies, iron workers scale thirty-foot scaffolds to tie the iron, engineers pace around with plans spread out on truck hoods, study them with the foremen.

One afternoon, Mr. Martínez is behind me, off to my right, I see him slow down, clutch his chest. He says something about pain. I shoulder him to the shade, sit him down on the dirt and tell him to rest.

"Don't worry, I'll take over."

"No, you can't, you'll get in trouble."

It makes no sense to me. I attribute his warning to his dizziness, some kind of spell that brings him in and out of consciousness. But as soon as I put on his belt, which has tools for tying wire, some jerk on the crew—must have been about forty of us on this platform all working this wide expanse of wire and rebar—orders me to take the belt off. I guess he's a kind of boss over his crew, but not my boss. So I ignore him. He keeps hassling me, so I finally tell him to take the belt off me himself or shut up. I pull out a hammer from Mr. Martínez's belt—one end pick-sharp, the other flat like a pry-bar. I stare at the guy, he turns away.

I go back to tying rebar. It's wasn't good enough for that guy, he walks off the platform, then another foreman approaches me. Now, that guy orders me to take off the belt.

"No, man, just leave me alone."

He leaves.

I keep working until a white pick-up pulls up. It turns out to be the project manager. He strides over to me with a kind of John Wayne arrogance, looms over me and says, "Think of Karina and Leo and the opportunity you're getting."

I am too deep to back off, so I tell him leave me alone. He walks back to his truck, sits in the cab with the door open, holding a walkie-talkie and speaking into it.

MPs ride up, four in military uniforms and white hard hats, two armed with M-16s. They escort me to their open-air canvas truck, order me to sit on a plank bench in the back. Still wearing Mr. Martínez's belt and my hard hat, I'm driven off base and ordered not to return. On the ride out, I worry about Mr. Martínez. I want to say something about giving him his belt back and when I start to, the MP tells me to shut up.

After showering and eating, I decide to hit the pavement the next day and find me another job. Even if it's washing dishes at Kentucky Fried Chicken, I don't care. The phone rings. I expect my sister to cuss me out, tell me what a worthless piece of crap I am. It turns out to be Chuy. He says Lila gave him my number, invites me down to Las Cruces, three hours south of Albuquerque. He misses me, says we should get together in Ciudad Juárez and party.

I'm up for it. Even though I've barely worked, I need a break. His invitation lifts my spirits; I take the bus next day. Chuy meets me at the terminal, takes me to a Motel 6 in El Paso. The next morning, we cross the international bridge into Ciudad Juárez, Mexico.

Party time. We hit La Zona Rosa, the red-light district, lined with brothels. We find La Brisa, a cantina where Chuy promises the best *chicas* are, where we can party on the cheap. After hours of laughter, lines of cocaine, drinking beer and tequila shots, Chuy goes to one of the rooms in the back with a woman. I need to clear my head, so I tell the bartender I'll be back and go out for a stroll.

In the first ten minutes, my nauseous feeling is gone. Besides the benefit of sobering me up, I enjoy walking and decide to explore. I walk for about thirty minutes, during which a light spray of rain douses the streets. I lift my face to the cloudy sky, rub it with my hands to feel the warm rain. It is so good, and it clears my head right up. And then in an instant, the rain comes down hard. I dash up a street for shelter, thinking I'll wait it out under a tree or under a tarp canopy overhanging some shop. I find none, so I turn down a dirt path where the sidewalk ends and runs into wild overgrowth that opens onto a field with a bunch of footpaths zigzagging toward a grove of trees. I run for them.

I come out on the other end, stop and rest. Up ahead, I see a few men standing under a roof spotlight, which is hanging over a warehouse dock. They're military, uniformed, armed. They're loading the truck with bales of weed. The truck has a green tarp, with the military insignia of the Mexican Armed Forces on the door.

Shit, I think, *I've run right into a cartel operation.* I try to conceal myself, immediately turn to walk away, but it's too damn late. They see me. I hear them talking in urgent tones, then two hurry to another pick-up parked alongside the big truck. They roar out of the docking area in my direction.

I run for my life. I flee, fast as I can. I barrel my way through brush and briars, duck into the forest, hide behind a tree, then run like hell. I hear them crashing through the brush and cursing roughly in Spanish to each other about finding me, wondering who I am, asking themselves aloud if I belong to another cartel or some street gang or maybe the American DEA. They have to catch me, they say. I need to be caught.

I run until I can't breathe and pause to catch my breath. I plant my hands on my knees, bend over, panting. Glimmering in the night not too far off, I see the Rio Bravo, the river-border that separates the United States from Mexico. I've got to make it there. I keep moving until I find a cluster of creosote bushes. That's where I hide, crouching down in the bushes, belly against the ground, cheek to the dirt, praying until I am certain they're gone.

Finally, I get up, walk to the river's edge. The current is strong, the water deep. I check both banks to determine the best place to cross. I can't swim it, I don't have the strength. I need to rest before I attempt it.

I sit in the grass, gazing at the flowing water, feeling weak and sad, grief permeating every inch of my body with regret.

Why did I ever agree to come here? I survey the field behind me, stare at the tree line on the opposite bank, try to see if anyone has followed me.

I feel the ground shake. The air rumbles, I crawl on hands and knees to the bushes. I crouch down, peer at a truck's headlights advancing towards me. It stops near enough so I can see it's a military truck carrying soldiers. A wave of engine heat sweeps over me. The soldiers, armed with pistols and rifles, get down, check around. They talk in Spanish and English, saying they need to find me or the boss will certainly kill one of them.

I stay balled up on the ground, in terror, until they get back into the truck, spraying dirt and rocks from their deep-cleated tires, as they roar away.

The land lightens with the coming sunrise. I rise to my knees, sit on my haunches, afraid maybe one of the soldiers was left behind to watch for me. I hear a distant but near-enough train whistle. The morning mist clears. I climb a boulder halfway in the water, scan the river. I look upstream, downstream, across—everywhere. I make a run for it, sprinting for my life. I know if they catch me, I'm dead. I splash through the knee-high water, crashing into it in with a frenzy. When I reach the American side, I jog into a railyard, slide up to a train's flat car just starting to creep, grab the side railing and lift myself onto its bed. The train speeds up. I'm freezing, my teeth clatter as I watch the distance between me and Mexico widen. I don't know where the train is going. I don't care. I curl into a tight ball and shiver myself to sleep.

Hours later I awake from my fitful nap as the train slows down. I'm so stiff I can hardly move, numb with cold and exhaustion. I slap my cheeks, rub my face. I can't believe my eyes. I must have slept for a few hours because I see a sign that says Santa Fe, 15 miles.

The train sails past Lamy and starts to gain speed again. I leap off. I put my head down, trudge in the direction of Santa Fe. I come upon a residential community of luxury homes. The nearest one to me has its own gym, helicopter pad and landing airstrip and servants' quarters. I'm so hungry and thirsty, I'm willing to chance going down there to find some water.

Then I decide I better not keep moving over the next hill. I stop. There's a pond below with swans, a mansion lording over the immaculate fields where Arabian horses and Black Angus graze. There is even a teepee—not a real one, a gringo teepee used as landscape decoration.

I sneak alongside a barn-sized studio with massive paintings hanging on the walls. I sprint to the pond, conceal myself in the bulrushes, kneel and drink. I discover by sheer accident a nest of swan eggs by my right knee.

I pull out my pocketknife, grab one, cut a hole in the shell and suck the yolk. A terrible shriek shocks the morning silence, scares me enough to almost topple me. A swan screams out of nowhere, flapping angrily at me from the tall bank grass. It jabs me with her beak, nicking me with each lunge. I try to keep the hen away by jabbing at her with my pocketknife, the blade no more than two inches long, enough to warn it to stop spearing me. Then her mate charges, wings flapping and beak spiking my arms and hands. Both snip me with their beaks and, more to keep them away than hurt them, I sweep my knife across the air every time they lunge. I warn them to stay back, stay back.

My blade gives me time to run. Out of breath, I stop, look back. One of the swans is lying in the grass, white feathers stained red, the other one is making weird honking sounds, moaning like a child in its bedroom, crying for its mother, who arrives and hovers over it.

I hurry in the direction of Santa Fe. It's hot. My throat is parched, my stomach cramping with hunger. After an hour or so I hear something, turn to see behind me a dark silhouette floating on the air, wavering in the heat-distance. As it nears, I can make out a figure on horseback galloping towards me. He wears a cowboy hat, an Ohio football T-shirt and grimy jeans. He has fashion cowboy boots tipped with silver and turquoise thread designs.

It's pointless to run, so I stand and wait until the horseman almost tramples me, his horse's chest shoving me back, its hooves stomping the ground. I think, *What's up with this fake cowboy, is he going to kill me or what?*

He reins in the horse, pulls back its neck that arches as its nostrils spew foam and spit. He glares at me from behind aviator sunglasses and shouts, "You little sonofabitch! Why are you here? You killed my swan!"

He draws a pistol from his hip and aims it at me.

I raise my arms. "Please. I'm sorry. I was thirsty and hungry, that's all. They attacked me. I was trying to protect myself. Please, don't shoot."

"You Mexicans come here, think you can do what you want. You ever hear of private property? This is my castle. You not only trespassed but you killed my swan, and you'll pay for it, all right. Cowboy justice."

He lassos me, pulls the rope tight, turns and half-drags me as I run to keep up. Just like the old cowboy and Indian movies with John Wayne, "Gunsmoke" and "The Rifleman," I follow on foot behind him to the ranch house.

He locks me in the tack-room of the barn. The first night and the next morning, he affixes some kind of dog collar to my ankles, locks it in and tells me, if I try to run, it'll electrocute the hell out of me.

"Don't try," he snorts, "you'll get a nice little jolt. You owe me; it's time to pay back."

In the morning, he lets me wash the blood off at the spigot beside the barn, then he has me undress. He gives me gray overalls to put on, clips another small lock to my ankle band. He then flips a switch on a hand-held remote he carries in his back pocket.

"This here little device carries enough juice to knock you flat outta of your wits if you try to run. I'm warning you, don't test it. Now, you're gonna pay me what my swan was worth in good ol' American hard work."

The next four weeks, he has me dig post holes for a fence, lay irrigation lines and sprinklers for his acre-large garden, re-pair windows in his studio, cut and nail steps to his utility shed, stain wood decks, clean out a tractor trailer, pile all the trash in a truck, run the weed whacker around his mansion, trim back trees and bushes and chain-saw a bunch of logs into cords and stack them.

I tell you, it is a relief, I needed a break from freedom. I feel like I'm back at DYA or the orphanage. I have someone to tell me what to do, to feed me, give me a cot. I don't have to make any decisions, just obey. I'm happy to be of service.

I start on the floors—buff the tiles in rooms, wash win-dows, polish the stainless-steel appliances. His wife, who runs some kind of art gallery in Santa Fe, has me move fur-niture around. I feather-dust the paintings hanging on the walls, mostly cowboys killing buffalos, wagons and home-steaders and pioneers. This guy is way over the top when it comes to wild west scenes. Photographs of Gene Autry, John Wayne, Charlton Heston and the actor Ronald Reagan are displayed prominently. Silver-trimmed saddles and lasso ropes flank the entrance, lucky horseshoes are nailed above the door. Gold-plated spurs hang from a living room *viga*.

Finally, after a month and half of labor, he calls me to the back patio and says my debt is paid. He offers me a chair at the table, where his Mexican maid pours me a glass of sweet tea. He explains the reasoning for the way he thinks of his place in the world:

"There was a time, a long time ago, when these gentlemen got around a table. Back in the days of chivalry. It was King Arthur's table, and these men were brave knights in search of the Holy Grail. Every one of them knights had ponds, lakes and swans at their palaces. They believed their palace was as close to heaven as you could get on earth. When you killed my swan, you weren't just killing my swan, Orlando, you were attacking my idea of heaven on earth, my place as my kingdom, where there is no crime, no poverty and my justice is everywhere. Nothing is out of order. This is my heaven. You see why I got so angry? You'd besmirched the mythical dimension of my life, you corrupted it with your presence, you defiled it. You understand?"

"Yes, sir," I answer.

"Now, come here, let me take that band off. We won't be needing that anymore, will we?"

"Thank you, sir, I appreciate it."

"Oh, I don't think there was any call for the law to get involved. . . . Hell, 'round here, we do it the cowboy way. Listen, Juanita is gone for the day. You Mexicans know how to barbecue—on weekends you all fill the park like cockroaches, all of you around a barbecue grill. You think you might break bread with me in a kind of mutual parting of ways? Can you make us up some of them buffalo burgers in the freezer? I'll get the colas and ice, you go on and get a start. Call me when you're done, I'll be taking a nap."

"Yes, sir," I say.

I get the grill going, put out the mustard and ketchup, cut the lettuce, red onions, tomatoes and cheese and set plates on the table. I can't find the buffalo burgers in the fridge, so I check the freezer in the garage. Right next to the package of buffalo burgers is the frozen corpse of the swan.

During the meal, he compliments me: "These are the best damn burgers, son. You sure know how to cook 'em." He fills his glass for the third time with whiskey.

"The spices, sir."

"Does 'em justice. Yep, sure does."

We finish, and he offers me a ride to the bus station, gives me the fare. "You know, you're always welcome to come back, work for me. I could use a good hand like you."

"Thank you, sir. Goodbye."

As the bus heads out of Santa Fe, south on interstate I-25, I think soon enough he'll realize he was eating his swan. For a second I consider getting a chuck wagon, setting it up at the park on Sundays, serving up swan tacos to all my Chicano brothers and sisters; swan burritos, green-chili swan burgers.

～ ～ ～

I get off in Bernalillo. I want to walk. It's early March and the world is beautiful. I'm so happy to smell the prairie air. I jog along an arroyo toward the four dormant volcanoes on the horizon. The sun warms the earth. It's Sunday morning, lots of folks are in church. I'm just walking. My lungs swell with fragrant sage, the incense-scent of sand and stones. A roadrunner jitters behind a *nopal*, flicks its firm, white-spotted gray tail feathers.

I inhale deep lungfuls of prairie air, the inhalation a divine blessing from the llano. I think back to the weeks spent at the cowboy's kingdom. He was, for all his weird beliefs, a decent man. I can explain such men in a way that I cannot explain Lila. She goes deep. He is shallow water. She's a vast ocean. I walk straight through the prairie grass and weeds. Walking out in the middle of the prairie makes me feel all alone in the world, but the loneliness isn't the kind that hurts.

My mind goes all the way back to my boyhood, before the orphanage, when I used to go with Grandpa to take the sheep to the village pond where they would drink and graze on the lush grass. I'd walk around the pond all day, seeing all kinds of frogs and minnows in the water, hawks in the branches. I'd even see coyotes come up, sniff around. Other times, some of the ranchers would show up with their horses, other kids would play on the swings and slide with me. We would chase each other, play tag, hide-n-seek, sometimes roam the dirt roads around the village. The quiet was so heavy it defined everything one touched, smelled, saw. All the kitchens were filled with silence. The roads brimmed with quiet. The trees slept. The dust slumbered. The air put away its guitar, slept in a corner in a small room. Men and women napped, dreaming of their youth, lost loves, their losses. The spirits of young men and women who had passed on before their time walked arm in arm down the street or sat on porch swings watching us playing at the pond. The silence understood where pain came from, knew the scar that slashed across the face of a marine back from war, knew the young girl's first period, her yearning to sneak away to the pinball arcade to meet her boyfriend from another village, understood why the priest should have never been a priest. The silence kissed the small ears of a newborn in its crib, swaddled in home-sewn baby quilts, the kind of silence that the past, that shimmered in the locket or ring given a young child by grandparents after their passing. The silence unfolded the silk cloth, once again allowed the eye to look and cry, the silence carefully folded itself around each flower and handed it to the heart like a lover's bouquet. Silence floated in the blood of mothers, fathers missing their grown children. It never punished you, you sat and ate with it under a tree as it told you a story of the girl you liked, of the mother gone, of the beautiful morning, the afternoon visit by relatives from the big city. Silence never aged.

With such a silence all around me, I skirt thawing rattlers on the road with a childish, catch-me-if-you-can delight. I dash swiftly up hills and sprint down, distend my chest to its full capacity, breathe in the whole prairie. I count the cedars and junipers, stare as if I will never see them again. Scrub-brush claws my legs, jackrabbits spring across arroyos, the sun sketches light and shadows on the ground. I love my sweat-soaked T-shirt clinging to my chest. My knee aches, the sharp pins of pain stab at my ankles as I kick through the sandy arroyos.

After a while I get back on the interstate, hitchhike a ride into Albuquerque and go to Camilo's. He still isn't home. There is another addict sleeping in his room. When I ask where my brother might be he directs me to a motel on East Central Avenue. I find him there, drinking with a Navajo woman. Both are on a binge. I ask about the money, he says he spent it.

∽ ∽ ∽

Back at the orphanage, I was friendly with some of the nicer nuns. We played cards, strolled, talked, laughed. Among the kids, I had countless friends. I ran away when I wanted to experience the free world. From time to time, I got to see my grandparents. At the orphanage, there was so much joy in the festive holidays. During Thanksgiving, Christmas, Easter, the whole world lit up with laughter, toys, smiles. I shared stories with dozens of kids, felt their kinship, made my first deep bonds with other human beings. I heard some of the greatest stories, too, played basketball and soccer. Nothing was given to me unearned, it felt good to feel freedom pulse in me, to be left to my own instincts, to fill myself with wonder, to go to bed marvelling at life in all its richness and diversity.

And now in late March, I'm back in Burque, whose streets are broad and bustling. I feel a sense of awe as I sign up for school. I rent a room by the university, in an area called the student slums. I share the house with other students while I attend night school to get my GED.

The first week in April I get my acceptance letter. I buy a rusted junkyard scooter I nickname Mosquito and ride up and down Central filling out applications at burger joints. I nail a job at a wood yard stacking and cutting logs. One afternoon, as I am going back home I see this chick strolling casually and I pull up beside her. Over the sniveling staccato of the muffler, I ask as casually as I can, "Need a ride?"

She turns, gives me a long up-and-down appraisal and takes her time articulating every word with cavalier contempt: "I wouldn't ride that if it was the last ride on earth and I was stranded in the middle of the desert."

Genuine disdain. I like that. No pretensions.

I sit, lips clamped tight, not knowing what to say.

"But," she adds, "you can park that loathsome creature and you can walk me to class if you wish."

That evening she comes over to my apartment on Sycamore and Central. She walks in, pushes me back on my couch and has sex with me.

Eva Romero, 5'8", twenty-three-years-old, black hair, caramel complexion, bright brown, intelligent eyes. She has a hiker's body with commanding breasts and a compelling laugh. A warm personality, great talker, she chatters away over a bubbling pot of pasta on the stove, sipping a glass of red wine. I sell my scooter and move in with her.

∾ ∾ ∾

I am back to 1964, to the little boy in the orphanage bell tower with the pigeons, where I dreamt of meeting someone like her. Beyond and below the entrance with the grotto of La Virgen de Guadalupe, I see the gravel circular driveway, cars coming and going, the women dressed in black high heels, tight skirts, blouses that pressed their breast, red lips, long hair, thick eyelashes and painted fingernails. I dreamt of the day when someone might be my wife, lover, girlfriend. No more being different, existing on the outskirts of society. No violent, chaotic environments, no disastrous existence, no more trauma, no more DYA, no escape into what my intuition tells me; no more endless depths of brown, suffering eyes, no more having to be prepared to do whatever is necessary, no more sacrificing youth, no more embracing danger, finding refuge in penance; no more offering of my life to win approval, no more eyes that hold the sadness of deprivation and neglect, no more jail guards I resent.

Now, it's only a child in the cupola, now the bell tolls to awaken the world, to send the pigeons flying, the sun to enter the lair of iron and feather. Now, the little boy sings to the eastern sun rising above the Sandia Mountains.

∾ ∾ ∾

It doesn't matter when she tells me she was married, then divorced her husband a month later, is currently having an affair with two married men, both drug counselors. From the first day we meet, she decides to make me hers.

She needs to control me, benignly. She regards me with rare sincerity and passion. I am a colorful, plumed exotic bird she keeps in her cage. I learn to talk to her. I learn to fly out and return. I learn to take food from her hand. I am a rough gem, someone to shape to her liking, mold to her preference without too much push-back. I rarely argue. I defer to her experience. She has parents, a sister, an older brother—a normal upbringing.

My outlaw past fascinates her, my orphan status evokes compassion. She harbors a misplaced narcissistic duty to "fix" me, to make me social, to make me "normal." She doesn't see what I see: that she needs someone to control, needs to have power over me. I am okay with that. After all, this is my first face-to-face relationship, no letters.

It surprises me that most of her married friends are having sex with someone on the side. Even though she is studying to be a drug and alcohol counselor, she snorts coke, drinks and smokes cigarettes and weed.

I drive her to school, she persuades me to sign up for classes. I lie on my application about not having a criminal record, get a grant and small loans. I find myself strolling the university quad or walking home with a backpack of books, just like a regular student. I excel in my creative writing classes, nearly have a draft done of a new poetry manuscript. I start a long narrative poem, carry it with me everywhere, work on it a little here and little there: Dunkin Donuts, park benches, bar tables.

After I move in with Eva, I sit at her kitchen table, comb through every stanza and line at least a dozen times. I read the work aloud late into the night, turn it in at the end of the semester, simultaneously submit it to a poetry house in New

York. The class scoffs at any chance I have of being published. My professor shakes his bespectacled head and mutters, "Ridiculous," and admits he's been submitting to the same house for years with no success.

"You simply don't understand," he repeats, "how difficult it is to write a good poem. You think you can just flip open Grandma's recipe book and cook one up like you do your tortillas?"

He doesn't know he is dealing with a renaissance Chicano, an outlaw Buddha who has found love, has seen death at a time when others kids were learning the alphabet, who never had anything guaranteed and once had bitterness against the world, struggled to endure his own barbarism, and now knows a woman's love. He has been blessed beyond his capacity to express it.

This May 19, 2019, a wife in the next room practicing yoga, a daughter in her room studying for pre-med, a son in his room studying to be a photographer. I can tell you that beneath the brown parchment of my face that this is what you'll go through to get there: another and another violent subjugation of an American orphan caught in the system who will survive, though many will not.

This is the place I call home now, where I answer to the name Papi. I speak four languages fluently, wherever I go, I carry my notebook, jot down notes of things I see, remember, want to do and dream of one day achieving.

When I married Eva, when our first child was born a year later, no bestial purpose corrupted my courteous demeanor or veiled insidious and selfish motives or lewd cravings. Others envied my humanity, others mocked me, smirked that no matter how much time passed I was still a criminal, an addict, a drunk, a womanizer, a scammer. They rumor-mongered, the one-book sensations who puppet courteous Spanish culture for white approval. Noses lengthened more to snarly hooks with the evil intent of their gossip—I let them be to gnaw on their own witchcraft brew-spoons. No more howling in the deep forests and hills of my heart, despite the lettered brutes spewing venomous banter simply because they could not understand how I could write such lovely poetry and get published. No matter. Eva loves me, my children love me. At dawn, I step out of the shower, see myself in the mirror, love myself; my big ears, my thick lips, my big round head, little pot belly, runner's calves; love the folded-up pieces of paper I find with my scribbled thoughts, pieces of paper that declare me no self-deprecating charlatan, no grant-award-grubber, no. . . .

∾ ∾ ∾

I wait with a sense of dread for grades to be posted on the English department bulletin board. Except for one or two token Chicanos, the professors in the English department are white men and women who hardly understand Chicano culture. They're recruits from the Midwest, infatuated with our indigenous culture.

It's my turn to go the professor's office for consultation on one of my assignments. I've turned in the same manuscript I submitted to the publishers, I'm certain to get an A+. I haven't yet learned the importance of keeping a copy. He has the only copy besides the one with the publisher. I imagine, after gloating during his praise of my brilliance, I'll bring his copy home, congratulate myself with a good dinner and sex with Eva.

I go into the building, climb the steps up to the English department on the 2nd floor. His door is open, so I walk into his office, take a seat. Without wasting any time, he looks at me, says he isn't reading narrative poetry and, besides, that wasn't the assignment.

What?

He continues. "Narrative poetry is dead, Orlando. Now it's Language Poetry, that was the homework assignment: to study and write about the Language poets."

I almost pull an imaginary pistol from my waistband and shoot the bastard.

I picture myself lunging at him, slamming his head against the wall. I bang my fist down on his desk in repentance that I was such a fool. I beg his forgiveness for having the gall to believe I could write. I do none of this. I only sheepishly apologize for having misunderstood the assignment. I walk out of his office, detached from the world of the living.

I don't remember much else about that day, except getting home, drinking some tequila, sitting around and staring out the window until Eva comes home. When I tell her about the professor, she is pissed. I'm telling you, you don't mess with Eva. She goes into a hallelujah rant about how she's going to go over there tomorrow and deal with him.

Later that afternoon, when I'm heading out to apply for a job, Eva runs out to the driveway and asks, "The manuscript? I want to see the comments this jerk wrote."

"Threw it away."

"You did what? Idiot!"

"In the dumpster at the post office."

She opens the door, leaps into the passenger seat. "Drive."

She's still in her work clothes, but that doesn't stop her from jumping into the dumpster at the post office, wading through all the discarded papers. Minutes later, her arm shoots up, shaking my manuscript, her begrimed face appears with an *aha!* smile. "Found it!"

I think she's nuts, and I tell her as much, but she doesn't care what I or other people say, she loves my poetry. That manuscript went on to later win the American Book Award.

∽ ∽ ∽

The second week in April I turn twenty-three, for my birthday Eva gets me a job as a night watchman at the adolescent treatment center she works at. It's weird getting a job for a birthday present, but I like it.

I go in for the interview, get the job. The next day I start work at LoveMore house, situated on the outskirts of Albuquerque. It's as isolated, forgotten a house as any I've ever seen, but perfect in its negligible decrepitude for its teen-aged delinquents and homeless immigrant clientele. It houses court referrals for up to a year. They're mostly kids with emotional problems who have committed minor crimes.

They are me . . . not long ago.

∽ ∽ ∽

The first Saturday in May, Eva and I drive around looking at houses. Buds on the trees are fattening to the edge of unfurling, city workers are out spreading manure over the parks, homeowners rake their garden beds and women exit garden shops with baskets full of flowers and fertilizer. A sense of optimism fills the air.

Real estate agents have advised us on the desirable neighborhoods. We turn our attention to the South Valley, a semi-rural area still unincorporated by the City of Albuquerque. As soon as you turn off Bridge Street and go south to La Vega and Riverside, you can smell dung, earth, water, humidity, the river and the hefty scent of cottonwood leaves. You can hear geese migrating north again, see horses, goats, cows in fields.

I feel at home.

This is where we both agree we want to live. It seems the type of community where you find poets, folks sharing meals, women running life, a bartering system in full operation (goats for wine, veggies for fruits) and a good night's sleep. The Rio Grande runs parallel to La Vega, with a burly forest of giant cottonwoods, cranes, herons and hawks ascending and descending. The land has its own conscious mind, is preparing for a celebration to commemorate ordinary life, welcome all around to its sensory feast.

One of Eva's friends is starting out in the real estate business. He urges us to buy a house. He's certain we can qualify for a small loan for a down payment. He can arrange the sale. We don't have credit or much money, but we rationalize that it can't hurt to look. We have fun riding around. Eva is curious about the South Valley.

As we ride, I show her the place where a family fed me, where I used to sit under a store awning, a road where I had to leap from a school bus to escape a bully, until we come to a FOR SALE sign in front of a rickety shack by the Rio Grande. To say it's in bad shape is to be generous. Six hundred and fifty square feet of boarded up, uninhabitable shack. A first glance evokes my sympathy and pity. No structure should have to stand so wounded by time and negligence. It has taken every abuse, the worst, most vile derelicts can dish out. The shack clings to life only by a few formidable nails that refuse to let go out of sheer stubborn resistance to all who entered intent on destroying it.

We peek inside through the board cracks and are shocked to see piles of booze bottles, junkie needles and discarded clothing and blankets that homeless addicts have left scattered about.

"I can do something with this," I tell Eva. "I can make a home."

I see myself in all the places I slept before, on couches in people's houses who were kind to me, in small, cubby rooms of friends who gave me clothes to wear. In my heart, I always dreamed of one day having a place of my own, but never believed for a second it might be possible. Now, I realize dreams can come true, even dreams that are old, wretched, broken down, smelly, caving in . . . a dream that crawls to me with its last breath, trampled, beaten beyond recognition. I can pick it up and nurture it back to health. It can give me my wish. It whispers, *I am yours. I embrace it.*

I jot down the number on the FOR SALE sign and we have our real estate agent look it up. He says a couple of thousand down will get us in the house, no credit check, just a simple real-estate contract between the owner and us.

Eva and I empty the bank, borrow the rest from friends. We come up with the down payment, and within a week, we are homeowners.

Without a second's hesitation, I get up at 4:30 am and jump into the work with joy. I pull out and strip the interior, clean the boards, cut off the warped ends and use them again. What old stuff I can't scrub new or clean up and use, I replace with donations from neighbors, who are happy to see the old eyesore undergo a facelift. They give me bricks, cement, roof tiles, windows, boards, linoleum, old sinks, a used propane heater, a kitchen table, bed frames and electrical wiring.

Within a few weeks the house transforms into a home. We cook our first meal, sleep in a bed with clean, open windows letting in the Rio Grande river breeze and the sounds of birds. The house makes me someone. I am somebody I always knew I was meant to be but never had the opportunity before to prove it. I am someone who can make a home, offer shelter to loved ones. I understand the damage inflicted on this shack, so I am tender in re-building it, often talking to it, saying, "It's going to be okay, I'll take care of you, treat you good, I promise."

I feel like the house recognizes me, as if it has been waiting. I feel it. Seeing gouge marks in the walls, burn marks on the boards, gashes everywhere. I ask myself the same question many times: How could they do this to me? I was warehoused for smuggling weed at eleven years old, locked up for seven years. Everything about the house, my work on it, has an origin; it goes from an eye to a brain to a tongue and lips and gives purpose and worth for its being: windows, doors, beds, tables, light switches and laughter inside, strung together to implicate me in something bigger than just this day and this body.

One day, Eva comes home and says she asked her boss at Lovelace hospital if I can come in and read poetry to the patients. Her boss invites me with open arms. Most are addicts and alcoholics, my age or younger. Since I've been down that road, I gladly agree.

I'm so busy renovating the house, I put the poetry reading out of mind. A few days later, I'm busy wiring the closet in our bedroom to install an outlet so I can have a desk and lamp and make it my cubby for studying, when Eva rushes in.

"Hurry, hurry . . . we have to get ready! We have to go, we only have half an hour before we're to be there."

So, I just drop everything, throw tools and material on the floor, clean myself up, throw on some washed jeans, a denim shirt, and we head out. Around two in the afternoon, I

follow Eva up to the second floor and enter a large room. She
introduces me as someone who has been where they are now.
Tongue-tied at first, I look out the windows that wrap around
the room, giving a view of Albuquerque. I remember so many
episodes of my life, homeless experiences when I roamed the
streets: places I slept, stores I stole from, highway underpasses
where I hung out, parks where I got into fights. I don't know
why, but standing right there in front of everyone, I lose it. I
see myself bawling like a baby. I see myself cry for my beautiful friends at the orphanage; Tony (the Clubfoot) Baloney,
Coo-Coo Clock, Big Noodle—all huddled on a sunny afternoon on the ditch bank, rolling dried elm leaves into a strip of
comic book paper and trying to smoke it like a cigarette. I cry
for the pigeons in the withering cupola, the bell I longed to
ring, but every time I tried to push it, it wouldn't budge. I
would rap my knuckles against its dark brooding metal and
all I got was sore knuckles. I remember the light that shot
through the slats like golden sabers, cutting at the dust and
feathers and nests and bees, me raising my hands to the light,
picking each length of sunlight from the air to clutch it, wrapping it around me like a golden glove, wrapping the sunlight
around my waist like a sash and around my head like a sweat-
band. There and then, in the small space of the bell tower, I
became a superhero, I became the Sunlight Kid, able to shoot
my light over the world, to fight the darkness, to light the
path of orphans as they walked toward their parents again. I
see myself crying at all these memories flooding through my
mind. . . . No, I don't cry, despite the memories flooding in,
saddening me.

Instead, I breathe in with great effort, stare at my boots,
at the glistening tiles of the hospital floor buffed with wax,
then at the back of the room lined with the hospital staff in

their crisp, white uniforms and smocks, then at the eighty or so people sitting in steel folding chairs staring at me.

I pull out the chapbook Denise published for me. I open it and read my poem, "I Just Want to Communicate."

I can't say it's an Oscar-winning presentation, but at least I haven't passed out like I thought I might. When it's over, to my utter astonishment, I get a standing ovation. It feels so good to be recognized for something I do. I don't know how to take compliments, don't know how to act in the face of approval and am very self-conscious until, thank God, Marium, my wife's boss, comes up to me, places an envelope in my palm. I open it, a hundred-dollar bill.

~ ~ ~

Later, flush with fulfillment, I turn down the street we live on, Vito Romero. I see smoke. It billows out of the roof and windows of our home. There's a crowd of neighbors. A couple of men spray the flames with garden hoses. I pull over, park in a daze.

Everything I own, all my DYA notebooks, all my writings are in the house. Even as onlookers and neighbors try to hold me back, I rush into the smoke-filled, still burning interior and see the flames consuming everything, mostly coming from our bedroom. They spread and the heat is intense. I choke on the smoke, cough, cover my face. I go to grab a stack of my writing and then see our couple photographs, recently taken. I push forward and grab as many pictures as I can from the dresser and walls and bedside table. Then I glance at my boxes of notebooks and manuscripts. I realize I have to leave them all behind as flames ravage them, curling pages into ashes and embers that float red on the air.

I fall from dizziness, I can't get enough air to get myself up. My face is against the floor, already hot enough to scorch my cheek. Lying low on my belly, clutching the family photos, I drag myself forward but lose consciousness. At some point, arms grab, pull and lift me. For a second, I fight to rescue my papers, even as flames reach high all around us. I regret to leave my writing behind. I want to go back and save them . . . but they are gone.

All the people I had written about, all my friends at DYA swallowed up in flames, all the unsent letters I wrote my parents asking them why they left, describing to them who I was, that I miss them and love them, that they should come and get me and my brother and what I think about their abandonment; pages and pages about the kids I knew, the nuns and the director at the DYA and the guys I fought and befriended at gladiator school and those that saved me from getting jumped by opposing gang members, the county jail guards who were kind to me and my brother . . . all my memories of my brother and me sticking together and me running away and the night and days on the streets—all gone up in smoke. The friends, people, places, words the fire touched like red fingers that peeled back the ink from the letters so words became invisible, now merged with air, words without ink, spirit-words, breath-words, ink peeled from them, now rising like feathers of a smoke-bird, freed from the incense censer I swung as an altar boy at Mass . . . I witness them all rise into the air and fade into the sunlight, into the sky and the universe.

Hours later, after the firemen leave, the neighbors return to their homes, look sadly out their windows to make sure I am okay. All that is left is me standing alone with the night coming on with my sorrow. I'm remorseful, thinking I had made the choice: my couple pictures or my writing. I chose Eva, and it feels good to know I made the choice I did.

God burned what I could not. God lightened my burden. In my mind, his low rumbling voice, like that of an avalanche, says, "Why carry this stuff on, why keep it? Take courage to be the new man, Orlando. It's gone, so now you start clean, free. Close your eyes a moment, say goodbye to them all. Clasp your hands in prayer, be thankful for this burning that has cleansed you of your past. No longer the orphan, no longer abandoned, you are a family member, a relative to all my creation, dear Orlando. The world is your mother, the Spring is your mother, the earth, the water and trees your relatives. Now, be the water more than you, be the wind more than you, be the moon and light more than you, and grow as they do, my son. I am your father, the Sun, Quetzalcoatl; I will protect you.

I stand in the embered hush. There is little left of our bedroom—smoke, piles of ashes, charred lumber. I asked the fire chief how it started. He said faulty wiring in the bedroom closet.

I step through the wet, dark world, smoldering mounds of charnel, see the fire has burned my three boxes. Oddly, what the voice said to me is true: I feel lighter. Gone is the weight of carrying my work everywhere, pulling me down. I kneel, pick up burned paper, read hardly—legible, blackened words. The words crumble to ash in my hands.

My eyes don't see the burned rubble, but turn inward on all those memories now disintegrated into blackened trash. I kick the smoking debris, kick the pyre of my past life. Sparks shoot and scatter, burning paper flakes float. Smoke, the dark smell of incinerated wood and paper choke me, force me to cover my face with my forearm. I turn to leave. My boot pushes a heap of still burning papers, scatters them. Something catches me eye. I bend, pick up the picture of me wearing denims at DYA, looking impenetrable. I brush it off.

Burned on the edges, bits of black wax stick to it, strands of red hair, plus shredded paper with some kind of prayer words: "O Goddess Moon. . . . ." Part of Lila's incantation. I place it in my shirt pocket.

Over the next few days, I clean up, cart trash to the dump. Neighbors bring me lumber, nails, concrete and windows. And I start over. We have no money. We sleep at a Mexican neighbor's guest house. One afternoon, I'm on my pitched roof with my carpenter's bag, nailing sheets of plywood across the rafters, when the mailman comes, tells me I have to sign a letter. I climb down the ladder, he hands me a clipboard. I sign for a letter. It's an official letter, probably from the city lawyers telling me I need permits, have to stop building until I get them. I don't even open it. I toss it in the kitchen trash can and go back up on the roof to finish before it rains.

7

September 9, 2019

Someone said our lives can be explained by accidents. One year ago, starting this book was really an accident. I had no intention of writing it until my wife ordered me to get the Christmas tree out of the living room. I have this habit of leaving the Christmas tree up an extra month or two until my wife has enough of it, demands I take it down. She tells me to march my mangy butt into the garage and find boxes. I go to the garage but don't find any empty ones, so I get two half-filled ones, dump the contents of one into the other and, *voila!*, bring the empty one in. I start with Xmas balls that have been with us for decades, some with our names inscribed. Others commemorate our children's births—I have five. They bring back lots of memories, but none so unsettling as the memories that are sparked by what I find at the bottom of the box: a grimy manila envelope with my sixth-grade report card from the orphanage, my birth certificate with an inked impression of my infant foot. Ink and paper, me writing this, it was meant to be.